Murder Under the Midnight Sun

Also by Peter N. Walker

CRIME FICTION
The 'Carnaby' series (1967–84)
Carnaby and the hijackers
Carnaby and the gaolbreakers
Carnaby and the assassins
Carnaby and the conspirators
Carnaby and the saboteurs
Carnaby and the eliminators
Carnaby and the demonstrators
Carnaby and the infiltrators
Carnaby and the kidnappers
Carnaby and the counterfeiters
Carnaby and the campaigners
Fatal accident (1970)
Panda One on duty (1971)
Special duty (1971)
Identification parade (1972)
Panda One investigates (1973)
Major incident (1974)
The Dovingsby death (1975)
Missing from home (1977)
The MacIntyre plot (1977)
Witchcraft for Panda One (1978)
Target criminal (1978)
The Carlton plot (1980)
Siege for Panda One (1981)
Teenage cop (1982)
Robber in a mole trap (1985)
False alibi (1991)
Grave secrets (1992)

Written as Christopher Coram
A call to danger (1968)
A call to die (1969)
Death in Ptarmigan Forest (1970)
Death on the motorway (1973)
Murder by the lake (1975)
Murder beneath the trees (1979)
Prisoner on the dam (1982)
Prisoner on the run (1985)

Written as Tom Ferris
Espionage for a lady (1969)

Written as Andrew Arncliffe
Murder after the holidays (1985)

Written as Nicholas Rhea
Family ties (1994)
Suspect (1995)
Confession (1997)
Death of A Princess (1999)
The Sniper (2001)
Dead Ends (2003)
Sergeant Simpson's Sacrifice (2005)
Prize Murder (2006)

THE 'CONSTABLE' SERIES
Constable on the hill (1979)
Constable on the prowl (1980)
Constable around the village (1981)
Constable across the moors (1982)
Constable in the dale (1983)
Constable by the sea (1985)
Constable along the lane (1986)
Constable through the meadow (1988)

Constable at the double (1988)
Constable in disguise (1989)
Constable through the heather (1990)
Constable beside the stream (1991)
Constable around the green (1993)
Constable beneath the trees (1994)
Constable in the shrubbery (1995)
Constable versus Greengrass (1995)
Constable about the parish (1996)
Constable at the gate (1997)
Constable at the dam (1997)
Constable over the Stile (1998)
Constable under the Gooseberry Bush (1999)
Constable in the Farmyard (1999)
Constable around the Houses (2000)
Constable along the Highway (2001)
Constable over the Bridge (2001)
Constable goes to market (2002)
Constable along the Riverbank (2002)
Constable in the Wilderness (2003)
Constable around the Park (2004)
Constable along the Trail (2005)
Constable in the Country (2005)
Constable on the Coast (2006)
Constable on View (2007)
(*several also appear in paperback*)

THE 'MONTAGUE PLUKE' SERIES
Omens of death (1997)
Superstitious death (1998)
A well-pressed shroud (2000)
Garland for a Dead Maiden (2002)
The Curse of the Golden Trough (2004)

THE 'ASSURED' SERIES
Some Assured (2004)
Rest Assured (2005)
Self Assured (2006)
Life Assured (2007)

Written as James Ferguson
EMMERDALE TITLES
A friend in need (1987)
Divided loyalties (1988)
Wives and lovers (1989)
Book of country lore (1988)
Official companion (1988)
Emmerdale's Yorkshire (1990)

NON-FICTION
The Court of law (1971)
Punishment (1972)
Murders and mysteries from the North York
    Moors (1988)
Murders and mysteries from the Yorkshire
    Dales (1991)
Folk tales from the North York Moors (1990)
Folk stories from the Yorkshire Dales (1991)
Folk tales from York and the Wolds (1992)
Folk stories from the Lake District (1993)
The Story of the Police Mutual Assurance
    Society (1993)
as Nicholas Rhea
Portrait of the North York Moors (1985)
Heartbeat of Yorkshire (1993)
Yorkshire days (1995)

MURDER UNDER THE MIDNIGHT SUN

Nicholas Rhea

Constable • London

Constable & Robinson Ltd
3 The Lanchesters
162 Fulham Palace Road
London W6 9ER
www.constablerobinson.com

First published in the UK by Constable,
an imprint of Constable & Robinson, 2008

A copy of the British Library Cataloguing in Publication
Data is available from the British Library

ISBN: 978-1-84529-695-7

Printed and bound in the UK by
MPG Books Ltd, Bodmin, Cornwall

PEFC

PEFC/16-33-111
CATG-PEFC-052
www.pefc.org

CRUISE SHIP RINGHORN

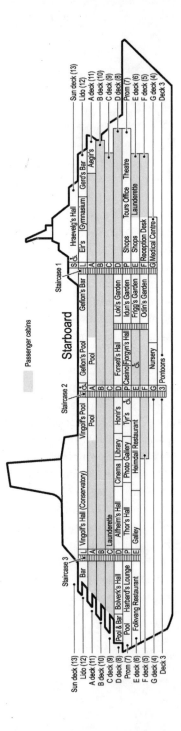

Passenger cabins

Starboard

Sun deck (13)
Lido (12)
A deck (11)
B deck (10)
C deck (9)
D deck (8)
Prom (7)
E deck (6)
F deck (5)
G deck (4)
Deck 3

Chapter One

Clutching their pink boarding cards, each marked with a large letter G, Detective Superintendent Mark Pemberton and Detective Constable Lorraine Cashmore waited to board the cruise ship *Ringhorn*. They were in a large building not unlike an aircraft hangar, part of a cheerful, good-natured queue steadily moving forward. Just ahead, some passengers were assisting an elderly man in a wheelchair. His companion, a man in his fifties, was on hand to guide the chair but one group had managed to create an unwitting obstruction, unaware of the wheelchair's silent presence immediately behind. One or two made noises like car horns going pip-pip but it was all good-humoured; everyone was cheerful because they were looking forward to a relaxed and happy time. Queuing like this was by no means as stressful as boarding an aircraft, one factor being that, on arrival, their luggage had been taken from them by helpful crew members.

When Pemberton and Lorraine arrived at the marquee-like exit, they found it opened into a small adjoining area, a darkened place equipped with lights. It reminded Pemberton of an entrance to Santa's grotto. A camera was flashing at regular intervals – and that was the cause of the queue. All were having their photographs taken for what would be the first of many such souvenirs. Every formal event would be photographed – the cruise operators would do a brisk trade in souvenirs.

As Pemberton and Lorraine awaited their turn, the photographer, an auburn-haired girl in the blue, white and

7

gold uniform of the cruise line, made a slight adjustment to the camera's angle and reduced its height to cater for the man in the wheelchair. Once he had been photographed, the camera was readjusted to its former state to accommodate his companion. They were photographed separately, probably because they occupied separate cabins. The companion, tall, grey-haired and rather distinguished, was wearing a light tan jacket and looked fit and healthy. Pemberton could not see his face, however, nor that of the older man in the wheelchair, although he seemed to be bearded. His companion stood for a second or two, smiled and was photographed, then moved on. Soon, the wheelchair and its steersman disappeared along a wide, well-lit tunnel which led into the departure lounge. The walls were adorned with enlarged photographs of Arctic scenery, glaciers, snow-capped mountains and spectacular fjords, a hint of pleasures to come. Now it was the turn of Pemberton and Lorraine.

'Name, deck and cabin number,' asked a young woman assistant as they reached the camera booth. Like the photographer, she was immaculately dressed in a blue, gold and white uniform.

'Mark Pemberton and Lorraine Cashmore, C203.'

'You're together?'

'Yes, we are.'

'Good, then smile, put your arm around her, look happy – this is a cruise, remember. You're here to enjoy yourselves.'

There was a bright flash. 'There we are . . . a nice one for the album. If you want a copy, you can collect it tomorrow afternoon from the photo gallery.'

Without any bulky luggage to impede their progress – it would be taken direct to their cabin – they strode into a huge room which was almost a replica of an airport departure lounge and settled in some seats to await the call to board. There were toilets and facilities for refreshments. The place was filling rapidly as Pemberton and Lorraine

8

sat in silence, looking around and absorbing the ever-changing scene.

This was a tiny proportion of the entire passenger list for they were to board in manageable groups of about fifty. That helped to disperse the passengers once they were on board and avoided the plague of slow-moving queues. The man in the wheelchair, grey-haired, bearded and rather stooped even when sitting, occupied the end of a row in front with his companion seated nearby. Naturally curious and interested, Pemberton picked out others he had noticed in the preceding minutes. This gathering of excited, chattering holidaymakers was a microcosm of life in the world outside – he'd often thought you could pick, say, fifty or sixty people at random and they would be re-markably representative of society in general with their differing ages, outlooks, problems and professions.

Immediately within his view was a very tall blond man in his forties who looked Nordic or perhaps Dutch; his wife or partner was equally blonde and impressive, a most handsome couple. He could imagine them displaying their perfect bodies beside the liner's swimming pools. The man was using a small hand-held video camera to record the scene prior to departure and was ranging across the whole crowd, observing their behaviour and filming some as they obtained snacks and drinks, then catching others as they merely sat quietly and waited patiently. No one seemed to object to his activities.

Pemberton noticed a pair of short people, probably man and wife, who looked as if they were in their nineties, then he saw a party of four noisy young women clearly head-ing for a good time, none older than twenty-five. He spotted a young couple sitting close and holding hands while gazing adoringly into one another's eyes. They were a complete contrast to the man who sat entirely apart, mak-ing use of a solitary chair against the rear wall rather than one situated among the others. There were groups of twos or fours, men and women, chatting quietly as they waited, not attempting to strike up a conversation with strangers.

He noticed several clearly on their own, men and women, young and old, who might have joined this cruise in the hope of meeting someone – or even romance. These single-tons were sitting among the main assembly, not apart like the man on the lonely chair. One of them was a dark-haired man in his mid-thirties wearing a denim blazer, pink shirt and light trousers. He looked very smart – an official of some kind? Customs perhaps? Keeping observations for someone in particular? Another man, a thick-set character with a balding head of black hair and wearing a bright yellow silk shirt, was also taking photographs; they were stills but Pemberton thought his camera was digital.

He wondered why they took such mundane pictures – people queuing, enjoying their food, chatting, reading or just waiting in silence. Hardly the stuff you'd show your friends back home to highlight memorable aspects of the cruise!

Standing at the back, watching over everyone and occasionally walking around the huge room, was one of the *Ringhorn*'s stewards. He was a tall, slim, dark-haired man in his late twenties immaculately clad in the distinctive uniform bearing his name badge. His job would be to look out for problems and assist anyone who required help or advice; he'd have to ensure they were treated like humans and not a crush of cattle during this busy time. As he strolled past, Pemberton noticed his name badge – it said *Lionel* but there was no surname. Another thing he noticed was that the steward looked surprisingly like the companion of the man in the wheelchair, albeit much younger. It was said everyone had a double somewhere in the world – but it was the sort of thing an observant police officer noticed.

'You're very quiet. What are you thinking?' Lorraine asked.

'Nothing in particular, just watching the world go by.'

'As you always do!'

'I enjoy people-watching. If you really want to know, I was thinking how alike are Wheelchair Man's helper and that steward who keeps patrolling around. People do come in types, you know – they can look alike, walk alike, behave alike. And you realize these people could be from anywhere – ordinary folks, the sort you'd see in any high street. I grew up thinking cruises were for the rich and famous, but look at these folks around us.'

She followed the wave of his hand as he continued. 'They're ordinary people who are prepared to spend a few extra pounds of their hard-earned wages on this kind of undisguised luxury. I bet some have saved up years for this.'

'Like us, you mean?'

'I reckon I'm fairly ordinary. Certainly when I was a young bobby on the beat, I never thought I'd go on a cruise! Cruises were far too expensive, certainly not for folks like me. My parents never went overseas, they were content with a week in Scarborough or a bus trip to see Blackpool Illuminations. They never considered going to foreign parts or flying on a plane.'

'You've worked hard and you've been promoted because of your efforts. Now you can enjoy your money and status. That's the reward for dedication and professionalism, Mark.'

'I intend to!'

'Good. It's right that you should. That's what these people will be doing, spending money on something they're going to enjoy after working hard. I see there's a fair smattering of grey heads among them too! Pensioners enjoying a well-earned fling before they're too old. I think a cruise is a great idea when you're heading for the final decade of your life.'

'I'm still not sure what to expect. It might be like a big village on board where everyone knows everyone else. In no time at all, you make friends, find your way around, get into a routine . . .'

'There are more facilities on this ship than in the villages near where we live! Cinema, theatre, casino, library, lounges, launderettes, umpteen bars, a gym, cyber-study, children's play area, beauty parlour, hairdressers, shops, computer cafés, restaurants, swimming pools . . . Those are the sort of facilities you'd find in a big town, not a village. The villages on the moors around us are lucky if they have one shop, a pub and a community hall.'

'I think I was worried we'd never get away from people. With more than two thousand people on a single ship for two whole weeks, I thought the decks would be always crowded!'

'It won't be as bad or as crowded as Whitby seafront on a bank holiday. One of my friends said it's the most relaxing holiday possible. Bags of space, bags of time to unwind, room to relax without being hassled, top class food and wine – and you can forget work. That's what I expect from a cruise!'

'Well, there's a first time for everything and I am looking forward to this. Honest. Thanks for pushing the idea.'

'You take some shifting at times! There are occasions when I wonder if you really like going on holiday. Now, of course, for the next fortnight the most important thing to remember is you're not at work.'

'I couldn't have got further away if I'd tried.'

'It's one place you can get completely away from police work and police officers. Your colleagues won't come knocking on your door to ask your help, even if you are on holiday, and we're not joining friends and neighbours either. There's just the two of us, Mark, so we can forget all about work!'

'Do I ever talk about work on holiday?'

'It has been known.'

'Well, not this time. If we're in the middle of the North Sea or cruising along the Norwegian coast and fjords, we're nicely out of reach of telephones and heavy, urgent night-time knocks on our door.'

'And I hope you'll keep your mobile switched off!'

'It might not work on the high seas.'

'I don't want you trying to find out, Mark! One thing's for sure, though, out on the ocean waves, you're not going to be called out to investigate a murder. There's no reason for the office to try and contact you.'

'In spite of that, they know where I am, that's one of the drawbacks of my rank – I have to leave my holiday address or a contact number in case I'm needed in some emergency. And we did crack the Stevens case before I left. We've identified him as the killer, thanks to DNA. We've all the evidence we need.'

'He's not been arrested though, has he?'

'Not yet, but it's just a case of finding him and bringing him in. It would have been nice to get that case completely wrapped up before I left, but happily the team can do it without me.'

'Well, whatever happens, they can't get you off this ship unless they send a helicopter and if I know the finances of the force, they'll never agree to that, even for an important detective like you!'

'I'm beginning to think a cruise is a brilliant idea for a detective on holiday.'

'So it is! Why do you think I wanted you to come? Just think, Mark. You've got two whole weeks to unwind. Forget work, forget your worries, forget the staff in your office. Ignore rising crime figures, put the Stevens case to the back of your mind. Just relax. All we have to do is eat, drink and enjoy ourselves among some of the world's finest scenery.'

'So what do I say if anybody asks what I do for a living? We're bound to pal up with somebody on board and people are sure to ask – the English are obsessed with what a person does for a living.'

'I thought you had a stock answer for that sort of question?'

'Usually I say I'm a button salesman. There's not a lot anyone would want ask about that. The trouble is I once met a chap who asked what I thought about a new hi-tech self-adjusting button for gentlemen's overcoats but I wasn't sure whether he was joking. I know nothing about buttons, you see.'

'Don't some policemen say they're ambulance drivers when they're on holiday? And some leave it rather vague by saying they work for local government or the council, without saying exactly what they do.'

'Yes, and others say they're office managers or security guards or lorry drivers ... After my wife's death and before I met you, I had a weekend in the Lake District and made friends with a fellow hiker who was in my digs. I realized he wasn't saying what he did for a living. I didn't either so we two lonely fellers spent a lovely weekend on long walks and visiting little pubs, but always avoiding the question of our jobs until it was time to go home.'

'Didn't you ever tell him?'

'Yes, moments before we parted company for our return trip home. We both knew we'd been avoiding the question, so we agreed to be honest as we were saying goodbye.'

'And?'

'Well, after our farewells, I told him I was a police officer; it turned out he was a bishop. I must admit I wondered what I'd said to him, and how I'd said it!'

'So what are we, then? On this trip? You could be an office manager for the council.'

'OK, I'll say I manage a council transport depot, my job is to make sure the snowploughs get to all parts without complaints from road users, that the bin-lorries are serviced so they never miss a collection and that all other council vehicles are in top class order. That sounds important. And you?'

'Before I joined the force, I worked in a building society, secretarial duties. I'm a bit out of touch now, but I think I could convince someone I'm an office worker for Rainesbury Building Society.'

'Right, so we've both got fascinating new careers! I wonder how many people do this sort of things on cruises, or on holiday? I can imagine doctors not wanting all and sundry to know their profession. They'd be bombarded with stories of people's operations. And if you say you're a lawyer, you'll be expected to give free legal advice. It always happens.'

'People are so predictable, aren't they?'

'They are,' and then the loudspeaker burst into life. 'Listen, we're being called.'

The announcement said that everyone bearing pink boarding cards with the letter G should proceed to Exit B in preparation for boarding. All should have their cruise cards ready for inspection. By this stage, their passports and tickets had already been checked. People with letter H on their boarding cards would be assembled shortly and then called. In response, a group of people with G cards rose to their feet and made for the exit. Pemberton and Lorraine followed and once out of the lounge were guided by stewards, including Lionel, as they crossed the final stretch of dry land before ascending the gangway into the depths of the huge cruise liner. They found themselves in a large and almost circular hall with lifts and spectacular stairways leading to each deck. Everything was well marked with signs and notices; this told them they were in reception on F Deck. There was a long counter at one side staffed by three smartly uniformed young women.

It was deep inside the bowels of the ship and people were milling around looking for their own route to the cabins, some asking advice from the staff. He saw the old man in the wheelchair being propelled to a doorway not far from reception, probably to a cabin on that same deck, but Pemberton was soon heading for the stairs leading up to C Deck.

'Come on, follow me upstairs. It'll be quicker than waiting for the lift.'

It was. With remarkable ease they found themselves stepping on to C Deck and following arrows towards their cabin. In addition to being a means of identification and a sort of credit card for on-board purchases, the computerized cruise card, in its distinctive blue folder, served as a door key. Each had their own card, given to them after their identities had been confirmed when checking in.

Moments later, they were in their cabin. Their luggage hadn't arrived but they explored the lounge-cum-sitting area and the bathroom, plus the comfortable-looking king-sized bed with plenty of room around it. There was ample wardrobe space and sufficient drawers for their belongings while a large square window provided a wonderful view, currently of the quayside and the port buildings beyond. The dressing table and bedside cabinets bore introductory leaflets, notices and the ship's daily newspaper. In addition to a note of welcome there were tickets to say dinner had been booked for this evening, in their case for the second sitting, on Table 36 at 8.30 in the Folkvang Restaurant.

'You'd think we were in a top quality hotel,' said Pemberton, having checked their cabin. 'So this is our home for the next two weeks.'

'Mmmm, it's nice and looks so comfortable,' was all Lorraine could think of saying while secretly hoping everything would be as wonderful as she hoped.

Because their luggage hadn't arrived they couldn't unpack, so Pemberton thought it a good idea to explore. They could find essential places like bars, restaurants, lounges, theatre, cinema, shops, swimming pools, and anywhere else of interest, including the Promenade Deck. That's where they'd go to watch the spectacular departure. He'd already memorized the route from reception because, like a hotel, that was the focal point for so many activities and enquiries. The Purser's offices were immediately behind: the Purser was a cross between a hotel reception-ist, an information centre assistant and a bank manager. The reception desk was under his jurisdiction.

For Pemberton and Lorraine, there was no great urgency to find every location in just one outing and, in any case, departure was not due for another couple of hours. Nonetheless, if they wanted a good vantage point to watch the band playing and the crowds waving as the massive ship inched sideways away from its berth, it made sense to locate the Promenade Deck. It did not bear a prefix letter like the others, but was between D and E Decks. On the way, they would obtain a glass of champagne and establish a good place near the rails ahead of departure.

Their plans to explore were thwarted when a steward knocked on the door, introduced himself as Knut Michelsen and said they should prepare to make their way to Thor's Hall in about an hour's time for a compulsory demonstration of life-saving techniques and practice. The session would be completed before departure. The call to assemble would comprise one long blast on the ship's whistle followed by seven short blasts. Knut added that a map on the dressing table showed the location of Thor's Hall. The ship's newspaper would also provide details of all the day's events. Then, as Knut left, their cases and holdalls arrived.

'It's all go!' muttered Pemberton. 'I thought cruises were supposed to be relaxing and hassle-free. We've never stopped yet, and we haven't really started!'

'Look, after the life-saving demonstration, we can go straight to the Promenade Deck and buy our champagne on the way. We can watch the departure, come back, unpack at leisure and head for a relaxing meal after a nice shower. We've all the time in the world to find our way around the rest of the ship.'

'Let's get unpacked before we do anything else,' he grunted. 'That'll be one important job out of the way, it won't take long.'

And so, with no thoughts of investigating murders or questioning suspects on that fine day in June, they began their cruise from Southampton via the North Sea to the mesmerizing Norwegian fjords, plus a visit to the Arctic Circle and views of the midnight sun.

From the quayside, Richard Mansell had watched the passengers boarding *Ringhorn*. With his binoculars, he had easily identified the companion of the old man in the wheelchair – the years of research and enquiries had been worthwhile. All those years in hospital and all the degradation he had suffered could be avenged. The fact that the fellow was on board was quite wonderful, the icing on the cake as it were. He would be the first and then it would be the turn of Lionel Chadwin. Maybe in his case it would be just a chat because there were other problems to solve in the very near future. But both his target and Chadwin were on board *Ringhorn*. That had to be a bonus.

Once aboard his own cruise ship, which was due to complete boarding very soon, he could put the rest of his plan into action. Mansell moved away through the well-wishers, anonymous and unnoticed but more than a little excited.

Chapter Two

Smartly dressed as advised in their cruise literature, Pemberton and Lorraine easily found the Folkvang Restaurant. It was a spacious and handsome oak-panelled room at the stern of *Ringhorn* with extensive rear-facing views of the ocean and ship's wash. This was one of two huge dining rooms, both on E Deck and each catering for more than 400 persons per sitting. Each had two evening sittings. Their table was large, oval and beautifully set, and for this first night it bore their names at place settings. Here they met their first contacts.

'Hi,' said Mark as he took his place at one end of the table. 'I'm Mark.'

'Lorraine.' She took the seat next to him, on his right.

'Brian,' said a man midway along the table to Mark's left. 'And my wife Sue, her twin sister Josie and at the far end, Josie's husband Russell.' Pemberton noted that this was a family group, the twin sisters being in their early thirties with Brian and Russell probably in their late thirties. Both men were tall, smart and well groomed, noted Pemberton. They looked like businessmen. Or even policemen! The remaining couple were older, probably in their early seventies, and in Pemberton's judgement, not related to the other four. All were pleasant people and friendly; he'd not noticed any of them earlier in the waiting area or reception. They had probably been allocated to different boarding parties, with table seating being one of the ways to ensure a good mix of passengers.

'I'm Rob.' The older man stood up to shake hands. 'My wife Ellen.' Everyone shook hands, some leaving their seats to walk around the table to do so.

All repeated the names of their new friends in an attempt to remember who was who. An Indian waiter introduced himself as Arman and took orders for food and wine, then the chatter began as it did at every other table, growing louder by the minute. From his seat at the end of the table, Pemberton had a wide view of the restaurant – just as he liked. If he had chosen his seat, it could not have pleased him more; whenever he entered a bar, restaurant or café, he always tried to find a seat that provided a view of the whole place. If there was one thing he hated, it was sitting with his back to people in the room. Tonight, therefore, during those inevitable lulls of conversation, he found himself studying the other diners.

Although some people clearly already knew each other, many were just beginning the delicate task of warming to complete strangers. Some would be singletons but he couldn't see anyone eating entirely on his or her own. He thought it might be the ship's policy not to isolate passengers by placing them on tables for one unless specifically requested. If anyone did want to be alone, it could be arranged – and of course, they could always eat in their cabin. For many single people, however, a cruise was the ideal means of meeting others and making friends.

When booking the cruise, and upon the advice of his travel agent, Pemberton had opted to join a table of eight, believing that if he disliked one or two of his enforced and unknown companions, there may be others to whom he was drawn. He and Lorraine could have had a table for two, or shared with another two people. They could even have shared with another four, but a table of eight, with its allowance for any problem relationships, seemed wise. They would now have dinner each evening with these same people, although breakfast and lunch could be taken elsewhere on board, as well as in this restaurant, albeit with no set places. As he continued to look around, he noticed several tables with only two people, one couple using such a table being the man in the wheelchair and his companion. They were close enough for Pemberton to catch snatches of their conversation during quiet moments and it was then he noticed the dog collar and dark suit worn by the bespectacled invalid. Visible beneath the man's bushy grey beard, the dog collar was of the style worn by Catholic priests – it had not been evident earlier. The companion, a serious-looking man in his fifties, looked like the priest's son. But Catholic priests did not have sons – unless they became priests late in life, after marriage and family. The priest, who would be in his late seventies or early eighties, sported heavy dark-rimmed spectacles and a good head of thick grey hair which matched his beard; unlike some clergymen, he clearly had no wish to conceal his real vocation even while on holiday.

As Pemberton was settling down, the waiter asked the priest's companion if they would like to order wine, but he declined, saying neither drank alcohol. A bottle of still water perhaps? The waiter would attend to it. Pemberton noted they spoke in English and the companion later signed the chit for the drinks. The cost would be included on his cruise card account.

Then a smart blonde woman in a grey suit came to chat with the priest and his friend, clearly saying it was nice to see them back again and she was sure they'd later catch up with one another's news. After a brief conversation, she left. Pemberton didn't notice any of the others he'd spotted in the boarding lounge – of course, they could be in the other restaurant or attending different sittings. Realistically, catching sight of them again could not be guaranteed because *Ringhorn* was massive. With 1650 passengers plus a crew of 700 it was almost equal to the capacity of a small market town in Yorkshire, so it was not surprising you might never set eyes upon the same person again. In the short period of only a fortnight, one could hardly become acquainted with everyone on board, whether passengers or crew members.

'Is this your first cruise?' Mark was suddenly aware that Rob was addressing him.

He would later discover this question was asked very frequently as a means of opening a conversation; those who had cruised before loved to tell others about their experiences and offer advice.

'It is,' he responded. 'We've usually gone to one of the sunny countries for our holidays, Spain, Italy, Greece or Ireland. We hire a car but this year we fancied a change. Everyone says how lovely the Arctic is under the midnight sun. We thought this was a fine way of getting there!'

'We've done a few, the Med, Pacific, Indian Ocean, Aegean, Caribbean, Galapagos Islands, you name it, we've done it, even the Scottish Western Isles . . . all wonderful, but yes, the Arctic is very special, unique in fact.'

'Maybe we'll get a taste for it,' smiled Mark. 'Cruising, I mean.'

'I'm sure you will,' and so the conversation continued, with Mark doing his best to involve the group of four, all of whom were experiencing their first cruise. As the food arrived, he noticed his neighbour, Sue, switch the position of her knife and fork, the action of a left-handed person. Josie did not alter hers. It transpired the twins were celebrating their thirty-fifth birthdays in a few days' time. They would be partying on board and their respective husbands had arranged this cruise as a joint surprise. The experienced Rob said he would speak to Arman, their waiter, to make sure the occasion would not pass unnoticed. A cake with candles would appear on the evening of their birthday, along with a free bottle of champagne. He told Mark, out of earshot of the girls, that it was customary, on such occasions, for a team of waiters to arrive at the table to sing Happy Birthday to You as an embarrassing surprise. That small act provided a focus and Mark decided he liked his companions – it was a very good start.

They enjoyed the meal and left the table at 10.30, the entire party of eight deciding to head for Hraevelg's Hall, a large and comfortable bar on the uppermost deck – the

Sun Deck – at the prow. There they could enjoy a nightcap in the brilliant light of the midnight sun before retiring to the privacy of their cabins.

Lionel Cooper was pleased no strangers had approached Brother Luke. There had been some worrying reports of a man persistently calling at his house, asking to speak to him or be put in touch, but his housekeeper had managed to deflect the enquiries, although the man had refused to give his name and address. An unknown man of similar description had also called at Lionel's home in his absence but had refused to give details to his neighbour, saying he would return to speak to Lionel. But so far, he hadn't. With Brother Luke being old and frail, Lionel regarded his role as more than merely complying with the ship's rules – he wanted to ensure the old man was not being targeted by unscrupulous people. But it was hardly likely such people would follow him on board a cruise.

During the following days at sea, sometimes in dense fog, Mark and Lorraine made the most of the opportunity to explore the ship and enjoy its amenities. Soon they began to confidently speak the names of the Norwegian features on board, often sounding surprisingly similar to an English word. Most of the public rooms were called Halls, these being named after Scandinavian gods and goddesses, a strong feature of Norwegian folklore – although there was no Hall of the Mountain King. The name of the ship, *Ringhorn*, was that of a god's great boat with its curved prow – that god was Baldur whose funeral pyre was on that very boat. They noted the range of entertainments, some on deck such as shuffleboard, cricket, swimming and tennis, and others indoors like dancing tuition, plays and entertainments by famous personalities in the theatre and cinema, and talks by experts. There was bridge and other card games, an art auction, an amusement arcade, soft-toy making, children's magic, hairdressers, beauty treatments and a gym. In addition, of course, there were plenty of bars, and food was available in one or other of the restaurants, buffets or bistros literally twenty-four hours a day.

Tours of the galley were also available in organized groups. Everyone who made the visit – such as Rob and Ellen – said how large, clean and efficient it was. They commented upon the utter cleanliness even where the cooking took place; this was amazing in spite of producing some 8000 meals every day, seven days a week – breakfast, lunch, afternoon tea and dinner with snacks in between. Run with military precision, the galley occupied a massive space between the two restaurants on Deck E, and during their tour Ron and Ellen said they had noticed the priest touring the galley in his wheelchair, as usual being guided by his companion.

Each evening there was a recommended dress code for dinner – clearly no one could be compelled to appear in formal evening dress, smart lounge suits or casual clothes, or even something different like a black-and-white evening, or perhaps fancy dress reflecting, say, the 1960s or Edwardian times. Nonetheless, most of the passengers did their best to comply which meant each evening's dinner had an added factor – certainly, when it was formal evening dress, the sense of occasion was delightful.

As the ship, constantly on the move, passed through a bank of fog, its hooter repeatedly warned other vessels of its presence while the wind hissed through the bodywork. The chill fog-bound air of the North Sea caused almost everyone to remain indoors even if it was late June. As those early days passed in a blur of non-stop activity, eating and get-to-know-you parties, including the Captain's Welcome (with photographs), Pemberton began to recognize individuals. He could identify some as they perambulated around the ship. He saw the same few nodding off in the library, others always sitting in chairs in quiet areas with books or magazines, the same young men and women jogging around the Promenade Deck or trying to get a tan by relaxing near one of the swimming pools. Even in these northern waters, there could be warm sunshine in sheltered places.

There were those who sipped cocktails in quiet bars or enjoyed coffee in one of the so-called gardens, and a couple who apparently always wanted to sit in the same chairs each time they patronized a bar or lounge.

It reminded Pemberton of his days as a village constable on the North York moors. One of the facts which emerged through his keen observation of village life was that people tended to do the same thing at the same time. Very easily, they slipped into regular habits, albeit unwittingly. The same people walked to the shop every morning at the same time except Sundays to collect their newspapers; if anyone omitted to make that walk, his or her absence would be noticed. The same men went to the pub every lunchtime for a pint and a sandwich; the same cars came through the village at the same time every workday, en route to their offices or shops. Then they returned each evening. The same mums accompanied their children to school, always at the same time and via the same route. Others behaved likewise. For example, old Mrs Preston always walked to the post office on Thursday mornings at half past nine to collect her pension and so she would be missed if she failed to turn up – people would go and see if she was all right. Mr Prentice always lit his fire at 7.30 every morning and if smoke did not appear from his chimney, someone would check to see if he was all right. Then there were the dog walkers, the younger mums with babies in prams, neighbours popping round for cups of coffee in the morning or tea in the afternoon . . . and all this was known in police circles as local knowledge, just one tool in the everlasting battle against crime.

Pemberton began to realize the same thing was already happening on board *Ringhorn*: people were beginning to adopt a pattern of behaviour, which he found intriguing. For example, although he had noticed three other men in wheelchairs, he had not encountered the priest anywhere on the ship other than during dinner or when entering Forseti's Hall. Classical concerts were held there most days; clearly the old man liked good music. While the priest and his friend occupied their usual table each evening, the blonde lady would sometimes return for a brief chat and it was evident the waiters also recognized them. So where else did the pair go? Pemberton told himself it was nothing to do with him – but he did find such trivia very interesting! At this early stage of the cruise, he was able to recognize people who adjourned regularly to the bars before dinner to sample the cocktail of the day or to meet new friends. One well-dressed woman in her mid-sixties spent much of her time looking around the shop where fashionable clothes were on sale, and some men were regular visitors to the casino on the Prom Deck, even during daytime hours. The predictability of cruise-ship life was already making itself evident.

As passengers and crew settled into their routine, therefore, he and Lorraine quickly became accustomed to the leisurely lifestyle. Using their cruise cards, they bought several souvenirs and some clothes from the shop, not to mention more than a few drinks and bottles of wine for dinner. It was impossible to make a cash purchase on board – everything, even something as small as a stamp, ballpoint pen or postcard, was paid for with the cruise card.

It was a cashless ship, although local currency could be obtained from the Purser if required for shore visits. Just before disembarking on the final day, all passengers would be presented with a bill, to be added to one's credit card whose number had, in the meantime, been recorded and verified by the Purser's office. Pemberton and Lorraine had been advised, by their travel agent, to prepare for that final shock at the end of the trip. With cashless shopping on board, anyone could very easily overspend.

As the ship headed north towards Norway, having passed the Yorkshire coast and Rainesbury en route, all clocks and watches were put forward one hour to cater for

European time. Their first shore visit would be at Bergen. As darkness fell that night, a violent thunderstorm raged at sea, presenting a remarkable picture from the dining tables in the Folkvang Restaurant. Wind-driven heavy seas made the ship rock very slightly as darkness enveloped them but tomorrow, their third day at sea, they would reach dry land by disembarking at Bergen. That Tuesday morning was another misty and dull June day as the giant ship cruised slowly along Hjeltefjorden and Byfjorden into the port, gliding majestically through assorted cruise liners and smaller boats already moored. This was a popular calling place for cruise ships large and small. As Pemberton and Lorraine had booked a morning tour of Bergen and district by coach, they had to assemble in the theatre under the banner of Tour A1. There they would join a group of about fifty who would be taken ashore; shore visits, with their mingling of passengers in groups, were another means of persuading people to get to know one another.

A coach tour of the Fyllingsdalen district, sounding so like Fylingdales near Rainesbury where Pemberton's office was located, with a visit to the Edward Grieg hotel for coffee would begin their tour, followed by lunch back on the ship, then a leisurely return visit on foot to the centre of Bergen for shopping and sightseeing.

Before leaving the ship, all passengers were reminded to keep their cruise cards with them at all times – without them, they could neither leave the ship nor return. Indeed, the card would assume the same status as a passport; it was quite remarkable that, as passengers on this ship, they could go ashore in a foreign country without a passport but not without their cruise card. All passengers' cards were subjected to computerized checks when leaving or returning to the ship. Quite literally, they were counted out and counted back in again.

Among Pemberton's group he spotted Rob and Ellen, their dinner companions, but they were talking to another couple and so, when the call came to leave the theatre and make for the disembarkation exit, Mark and Lorraine went alone, descending the metal gangway which led directly on to the quayside where a guide indicated the waiting coaches, all clearly identified.

Pemberton noticed the priest in his wheelchair, the faithful companion in attendance to negotiate the traffic and help with access to footpaths or road crossings. After the tour and coffee, they were taken back on board for lunch, their handbags, clothing and any shopping bags being searched before boarding.

They had to re-pass through the gates where their cruise cards were zapped to record their return, then those who wished could leave the *Ringhorn* again after lunch for a two-hour visit to Bergen's shops and sights. It was possible to walk into the town centre with its picturesque harbour, pretty wooden cottages and warehouses, all painted in bright colours like dolls' houses. Pemberton and Lorraine decided to take that stroll – among the delights was a wonderful fish market and stalls with Norwegian crafts such as woollens, reindeer skins, seal skins, souvenir trolls, wooden toys and clothing. It was a real town at work but also a honeypot for tourists. Here, of course, they could spend money without relying on their cruise cards and so bought a few mementoes, some with kroner and some by credit card.

As they explored the town on foot, they recognized several of their fellow passengers, some of whom acknowledged them with a smile or even some light banter, while others walked around as if in a dream world without recognizing anyone. Some were in groups of four or six, others in pairs and one or two quite alone. As they had to be back on board before four, in readiness for sailing at six, everyone passed once again through the barriers where bag and body searches were conducted with electronic gadgets, and then through the gates where their cruise cards were zapped to record their return. Pemberton, ever curious, wondered if the ship would wait for anyone who failed to return on time for there were always stragglers on occasions like this, people who had got lost, or who had

28

ignored or forgotten the timetable. He supposed that if someone did get left, they could rejoin the ship at its next shore visit, even if it meant an enforced stay with tricky negotiations to complete.

In this case it seemed everyone had returned because the gangways were raised shortly after four o'clock. There was no reason why *Ringhorn* shouldn't leave Bergen promptly at six. Back in their cabin, it was time to have a relaxing shower and then dress for dinner, this time in evening dress, the meal being preceded by the cocktail of the day in one of the wonderful selection of bars. Over dinner, they would chat with their new friends about their day's activities – and so far, no one had asked Mark Pemberton what he did for a living, neither had he asked anyone. Maybe that was how things were done on cruises?

As they were preparing for the evening, however, their cabin telephone rang. Pemberton answered it. It was one of the girls from reception.

'There is a message for you at reception, Mr Pemberton, an email,' she told him. 'It came this afternoon while you were ashore in Bergen. Perhaps you could collect it when convenient?'

'I'll be there shortly,' he responded.

'What is it?' asked Lorraine when he replaced the phone.

'No idea, there's an email for me at reception.'

'Email? Who on earth knows where you are?'

'My office,' he said. 'It could be important, I'd better collect it.'

'Why has it come to the ship, and not direct to you?'

'Because I haven't brought my laptop, and I'm keeping my mobile switched off so they can't text or ring me. I thought that was the whole idea, leaving the trimmings of modern technology behind and getting away from it all?'

'Well, so long as they don't want you to return for work.'

'I'll have to swim if they do!' he cracked.

When both were ready and dressed, they made their way to reception where Pemberton presented his cruise card to confirm his identity and received a plain white envelope bearing the name 'Detective Superintendent Pemberton'.

'Well, that's blown my cover!' he grumbled to Lorraine.

'Only to the receptionist.' She smiled, even if her face told him she was not too pleased. 'Well, aren't you going to open it?'

They found a seat in Odin's Garden, a quiet sitting area decorated with indoor plants. It was opposite the reception counter. He opened the envelope to find an email which had been redirected to the *Ringhorn* via its office in Southampton. It had come from Pemberton's office in Rainesbury and was very brief. All it said was, 'Thought you'd like to know we've arrested Stevens and he's been charged. So you don't have to worry about him any more. You can relax in the knowledge the job's getting done without you, enjoy your holiday.' It was signed Paul Larkin, Detective Inspector, Rainesbury CID.

'I'll wring his neck, sending this while I'm on holiday!'

'Don't be too hard on him, Mark, he probably thinks he's doing you a favour. You have been wondering if they would find Stevens, so obviously Paul's saying you can forget about work.' She was so pleased it was not a summons to return to duty.

'That might be so, but he's let the ship's admin staff know who I am!'

'They won't publicize it,' she said. 'Why on earth would they do that? What's it got to do with them anyway? It's not as if any of the passengers are going to find out, only a handful of the crew in the office will know. I'll be surprised if they're not under orders to respect the confidentiality of passengers and it's not as if you'd be expected to investigate a crime committed on board, is it? Isn't that the Captain's responsibility? And remember we're not in British waters. I'm not sure you'd have jurisdiction here anyway, so why are you worrying?'

'Me, worrying? I'm not. I'm just pleased I'm away from the office!'

'Me too, so come on, buy me a drink to celebrate Stevens' arrest – after all, it's another major crime detected, a welcome boost for your crime statistics. So that email is good news!'

'You're right,' he said.

He stuffed the envelope into the inside pocket of his jacket, took her hand and led her towards the nearest bar, asking, 'Cocktail of the day, madam?'

'Perhaps two,' was her response.

For their next trip ashore, they had booked a visit to Andalsnes, a lovely small town with wooden houses clustered together on Romsdalsfjord. Viewed from the comfort of the ship, this was a placid mirror-surfaced fjord surrounded by high snow-capped mountains, all afforested. The morning sun was reflecting upon the smooth water and glistening from the polished white of two other liners, while in the mountains the snow never melted and the glaciers remained solid and blue.

On this occasion, their outing was the morning following their visit to Bergen and so, now familiar with the routine of having their cruise cards checked, coping with gangplanks and finding the correct coach, Pemberton and Lorraine settled down for another visit to a stunning part of Norway.

Andalsnes, classed as a city even with a mere 3000 inhabitants, had little to offer other than its magnificent setting and so their coach carried them towards the famous Trollstig Road, opened as recently as 1970 by King Haakon. Trollstig means road of the legendary trolls, small hairy elf-like creatures which were believed to inhabit these wild regions. There is also the stunning Trollwall, an overhanging cliff and, at more than 3000 feet high, the highest vertical cliff in Europe – a challenge to climbers from the world over.

Road signs warned of trolls as they began the awesome ascent of the Trollstigheimen Pass with eleven stupendous hairpin bends and breathtaking views of the Stigfoss waterfall as it tumbled and crashed almost 600 feet down the mountainside. When, with some relief after the hair-raising ascent, their coach halted at the summit, they found themselves at Trollstigheimen Mountain Lodge where food, drinks and souvenirs were available, along with ski lifts and ample time to walk around and admire the incredible landscape – with the sobering thought that in winter, this hotel complex is buried under 25 feet of snow. That fact is more remarkable when one realizes that strawberries and cherries are among the delights which grow in profusion in the valley far below.

As they explored the dramatic landscape surrounding the lodge, they recognized more passengers from *Ringhorn* including the priest, who seemed to be enjoying this outing. He was sitting alone in his wheelchair, overlooking the vast panorama of mountains below while his companion had evidently gone off to do a bit of lone exploration; they had not been aboard the same coach as Pemberton and Lorraine because several vehicles had been needed to transport the *Ringhorn* passengers to this highly popular and very spectacular spot.

There were coachloads from other liners too. Then, after a further coach tour of world-class scenery, it was time to return to the ship. Later, with casual dress suggested for dinner, they took their places at Table 36 and chatted about their day in the mountains. As the conversation intensified, Pemberton sat with his own thoughts, watching the people around him, and it was then he noticed the priest's companion hail a waiter. Even though the companion was in casual clothes, the priest's dress had not changed – he always wore a black suit and dog collar.

'A bottle of wine,' the companion smiled, producing his cruise card. 'Red, one which will complement the steak I've ordered.'

'We have a very good Merlot,' responded the waiter.

'That would be fine, then we can take it with us to celebrate as we watch the midnight sun.'

When the waiter returned, the man signed the necessary chit with his left hand. Pemberton noticed that – it was the sort of thing he tended to notice, something slightly out of the ordinary. He hadn't previously noticed him use that hand when signing chits. The two men sat enjoying their meal with the companion constantly looking around the room, watching the skill of the waiters and clearly showing a keen interest in how the restaurant functioned so efficiently. And then he said, 'Sorry, Brother Luke, I must find a loo! Won't be a moment, it's all that wine,' and he left the priest, returning about fifteen minutes later, saying, 'Sorry about that.'

Meanwhile, the girls and their husbands from Table 36 decided they wanted to dance to live jazz after dinner, but Pemberton felt he simply wanted to savour the atmosphere in Hraevelg's Hall where they could watch the midnight sun. After the meal, therefore, they all hurried to the Hall to find a good table from where there would be a panoramic view of the never-setting sun. In the light of day, and with jazz playing, even Rob and Ellen took to the floor, if only to revive memories from their past. Pemberton, now alone at his table with Lorraine, and taking advantage of the music's noise, leaned over to her and said, 'I think the priest has got a new minder.'

'What makes you think that?'

'The other night in the restaurant, he said they didn't drink, but tonight he ordered a full bottle of wine. Not the sort of thing a non-drinker does! And he looks slightly different – similar but different, in fact you'd almost think they were twins, but this chap's left-handed. The other one wasn't, I'm sure of it, not when I saw them at dinner. Same age, though, same colouring, even a similar style of clothes. You'd be hard pressed to distinguish one from the other on their looks alone. And he's not a priest, he's a brother – Brother Luke. I overheard his name being used.'

'So what are you saying, Mark? You're not playing at being a detective, are you? Doing a Miss Marple or a

Hercule Poirot? Seeing villains lurking behind the curtains or on the Promenade Deck or whatever?'

'No, it's just that I noticed a few differences.'

'It's nothing to do with you, and besides, the ship does put people ashore as it goes along, and takes new passengers on board. There's nothing odd in that priest or brother or whatever having a new companion who might have joined the ship at our last port of call – or, of course, he might have been here all the time. Maybe there's two of them, they might take turns in looking after the old man. You can't expect them to be at work twenty-four hours a day every day.'

'Some carers work like that, all day and all night.'

'I would hope not, not in our modern society. Not even a workaholic like you does that!'

'Sorry. Am I behaving like a copper?'

'Mark, you're not on duty. Relax! I know you soon get bored when you've nothing to do, but that's the whole purpose of a cruise. It's a chance for you to forget you're a detective. Come on, I want to dance!' and with no more ado, she seized him by the hand and dragged him on to the dance floor. Ever alert even while dancing, Pemberton was observing the others in the huge bar with its views over the glistening sea. The place was crowded with both passengers and off-duty crew members coming to see the spectacle; he noticed the steward who had attended them in the boarding lounge and then noticed the brother in his wheelchair. His companion had been able to guide the chair to a viewpoint from where the old man could observe nature and the work of God at its most impressive. The steward, so similar to Brother Luke's companion both facially and in his build, was standing close to the priest but not speaking and no one else seemed acquainted with him.

The blonde woman did not join him here. Neither Pemberton nor Lorraine had spoken to him, so perhaps he did not want the chore of making pleasant conversation? Perhaps he welcomed the break from talking, something

34

which was so much a part of his daily work? Maybe a cruise was a form of enjoyable retreat from the real world?

Lorraine was saying, 'We can dance all night because we've no outings arranged for tomorrow, we can enjoy the midnight sun then sleep in as late as we want.'

'Pardon?'

'You're not listening to a word I've said, are you?'

'Pardon?' he joked.

As they danced, he spotted one man, middle-aged and rather thick-set with dark hair, slightly grey. He was sitting alone with a glass of lager before him but no friend or companion. The man seemed to be taking a keen interest in the clergyman; he was watching him for most of the time, although he did not approach him. Was he seeking an opportunity for a chat? Pemberton thought the man looked lonely. After his own wife had died, Pemberton knew what it was like to be alone and always felt a twinge of regret when he saw anyone in that situation – even if Lorraine had often said he shouldn't concern himself with other people's problems and lifestyle. Having enjoyed the sight of the midnight sun apparently dancing on the horizon and keeping the night as light as day, the brother and his colleague left around half past midnight.

Pemberton and Lorraine continued to enjoy the company of their dining friends until one. Rob and Ellen said they would turn in now but the others wanted to stay a little longer and then perhaps pop into the nightclub for a final dance or two. As Mark and Lorraine left for their cabin the bar remained busy with passengers continuing to watch the spectacle, even if drinks were no longer served. Pemberton reckoned there must be almost fifty remaining in the bar when he and Lorraine left, plus of course those in the other bars, in the casino, in the nightclub, in the quiet rooms and even in the library. They passed through the decks during their long walk back to the cabin, bidding goodnight on occasions as they descended, sometimes in a lift and sometimes by the stairs. Even at this time of morning, the ship was busy – just like any town on a Saturday night, but tonight was different because the sun never set and the ship's newspaper of the day contained no times for sunrise and sunset.

With no more shore visits for three clear days, and with the crossing of the Arctic Circle ahead before reaching Spitzbergen (and another special trip ashore), the ship would continue its smooth way from the greyness of the North Sea into the chilliness of the Norwegian Sea. There would be occasional excitements such as a passing school of whales or porpoises, a soaring albatross or another ship hooting a greeting but apart from that, all the entertainment and socializing would be on board.

Like all the passengers, Pemberton and Lorraine would take pleasure in making use of the extensive facilities, relaxing in the bars, going to the cinema, visiting the theatre, enjoying the sunshine in sheltered places on deck or merely sitting quietly or enjoying the waist-expanding diet. Sometimes during those three days they would be alone, and sometimes they would share experiences or have coffee and drinks with some or all of their new friends from Table 36. Three days without a sign of land was a daunting thought; Pemberton hoped he would not become bored through lack of activity or interest.

Even up to this stage, however, the question of what any of them did for a living had never arisen. That's how it should be, thought Pemberton. As he lay in bed that night, he realized he had no idea what any of his companions did by way of a profession or career, although he had to admit (to himself) that he had tried to work out the answers from clues dropped, albeit unintentionally, during conversations. He thought, for example, that Bob was a retired doctor or surgeon, but he was not sure what the two younger men did. At one stage he would have said they were young businessmen but then he'd heard them talking to one another and using words such as fraud, public relations and unwelcome press interest. Most of their social chatter had been about football or cricket, with their wives admiring the beauty facilities on board, and the hairdressing salon. As he grew to know them better, he decided they were people he could like and trust.

It was midway through the next morning that the ship's tannoy broke its silence. Pemberton with Lorraine at his side had enjoyed a leisurely breakfast after being late to bed following the extraordinary sight of the never-setting sun, and they were enjoying a relaxing coffee in sunny Vingolf's Hall on the aft of the Lido Deck when the male voice on the loudspeaker announced:

'Would Mr Mark Pemberton please contact reception as soon as possible. I repeat, would Mr Mark Pemberton please contact reception as soon as possible.'

'Oh no!' he groaned. 'What now?'

'What's happened, Mark, what do you think it is?'

'Search me.' He shrugged his shoulders. 'Maybe I've lost something and they've found it, or perhaps our cabin's on fire . . . who knows?'

'Don't be so flippant! It might be important. You'd better ring from one of the phones on this deck.'

'I'd rather go down and see for myself,' he said, standing up. 'Are you coming?'

'I don't think so. I'll stay here and guard this table for when you return. You won't be long, will you?'

'I hope not! There's a lift towards the prow, I'll use that.'

Less than ten minutes later he was standing in front of the reception desk, waiting for one of the girls to attend him. All were busy but soon a lovely blonde approached him, smiling.

'Yes, can I help you?' The badge on her uniform said she was Alison and there was no trace of a foreign accent. The crew of this ship seemed to be multinational with Alison being evidently so very English.

'My name is Pemberton, there was a tannoy message for me.'

'Ah, yes, thank you for coming, Mr Pemberton. Captain Hansteen wishes to speak to you. In his office. I'll take you through.'

'What about? Any idea?'

'Sorry, no. Follow me.'

She emerged from the protective shield of the huge curved counter and led him downstairs and along a corridor which was out of bounds to the passengers; on this deck – G Deck – were more offices, adding to the total of the Purser's section on the deck above. They strode past several until they arrived at one marked 'Captain'. She knocked, listened for the call to enter, and then did so, inviting Pemberton to follow.

'It's Mr Pemberton, Captain,' she announced, and then left. Pemberton entered the spacious office with its grandstand view of the prow and ocean ahead.

'Ah, Mr Pemberton. So good of you to come like this. I am most grateful. My name is Hansteen, Jakob Hansteen.'

He rose from his chair and extended his hand for Pemberton to shake. Hansteen was a small neat man with dark and slightly wavy hair carefully trimmed; he was clean shaven and without spectacles. Pemberton reckoned he would be in his late forties, immaculately dressed in his uniform, but without a jacket. He wore a white shirt with epaulettes bearing his insignia and a badge on his breast bearing his name and rank. Pemberton was not sure of his nationality, but he spoke perfect English; from his name, he guessed he was Norwegian.

'Please sit down, Mr Pemberton.' Hansteen indicated a chair before the polished oak desk. 'Can I get you a drink?'

'No thanks, I've just had a coffee,' and he sat on the chair.

'Something stronger?'

'No thanks, it's a bit early in the day for that.'

'You might need it when I explain why I have asked you to come here,' he smiled with an air of seriousness. 'You are wondering, no doubt?'

'Of course I am.'

'First, I need to establish certain things. I hope you don't mind. I understand you are an English detective? Is that correct?'

'Yes, a superintendent.'

38

'Still serving?'

'Yes, I'm on leave at the moment.'

'With your wife?'

'My partner, Lorraine. She's on board, having a coffee right now. Can I ask how you knew my profession?'

'An email arrived recently, unusually coming into the Purser's office via our Head Office instead of to you direct. Clearly, you have not been using our personal on-board computer facilities in the cyber-study, or don't have your laptop with you?'

'No, I'm on holiday. No emails, no computers, no mobile phones!'

'Very wise, I must say. Now, it is evident your office felt it important to contact you but I have to say we vet all emails that come through our official channels, it's done for security purposes as I know you will appreciate. From its contents and place of origin, I came to believe you are a police officer. You have some proof, perhaps?'

'Before I do that, can I ask why you want to know all this?' Pemberton was now feeling at a disadvantage, giving information without knowing the reason.

'I would like you to help me investigate a crime, Mr Pemberton, here on *Ringhorn*. This morning a passenger was found murdered.'

Chapter Three

'Murdered?'

For a split second, Pemberton was unsure how to respond. The Captain continued: 'He was stabbed. He was found about an hour ago although I don't know when the crime was committed. It is my duty as Captain to invest-igate any murder on this ship while at sea – definitely not part of my normal routine! I'm not experienced in this although there are guidelines, but guidelines are no sub-stitute for experience, Mr Pemberton. I am sure you'll agree. We get the occasional theft or fights between drunks or even alleged rapes, things my crew can handle very well, but I've never had anything like this.'

'Surely there are procedures?'

'There are, but I would welcome your assistance and advice. Even though I'm charged with the task of invest-igating the murder, I'm encouraged to co-opt the help of experts where possible. People like you.'

'I have no jurisdiction at sea. Am I right in thinking this is a Norwegian ship?'

'She is registered at Southampton, and if the crime had been committed while we were in a British port, it would be the responsibility of the local shore police. However, we are at sea, beyond the jurisdiction of the British police; nonetheless we are a British ship even though our crew members are from various parts of the world.'

'There's a distinct Norwegian flavour on board!'

'It helps to create the right atmosphere, Mr Pemberton, and it is no coincidence I am Norwegian. Now, the fact that you are on board suggests you are on holiday but I must obtain the best possible advice so the culprit can be identified and detained with the minimum of disruption to our schedules. It is my intention to continue our cruise – there is little else we can do in this part of the world – and we shall put into port as shown in our itinerary. Our next call is Spitzbergen. Normally I would request the attendance of detectives at our next port of call, or even hand over the killer to the authorities, but that will not be possible at Spitzbergen. It is three days away and lacks the usual port facilities. It is a remote island with only a few scientists living in wooden huts, the site of a polar research station and little else. You can see why it is vital to have the crime detected while we are at sea. We are now in the midst of the ocean without helicopter landing facilities, so we cannot import detectives or have the killer removed. And, more important, we do not want a murderer at large on *Ringhorn*, which is why I am seeking your help. The killer must be found before further deaths occur. That is the simple truth. If you have any commitments, then I am sure they can be accommodated.'

'Commitments?' he smiled. 'Yes, we have commitments – your crew keep us very busy enjoying ourselves!'

'So they should! We keep you busy and you keep us busy! But if you have any spare time, however short, then all I ask is that you help by giving me advice with the benefit of your experience. I do not want another murder to occur, Mr Pemberton. It is a worry, knowing we probably have a killer on board.'

'Probably?'

'Almost certainly is perhaps more truthful. No one is missing, according to our records, all those who have gone ashore have returned. And so far as I know, no one has jumped overboard!'

'I can understand your concern but before I commit myself I'd like to speak to my partner.'

'The company will make sure you are well compensated for what you do.'

'I wouldn't want a fee, if that's what you mean.'

'I understand but there is another point to consider. We need to limit any adverse publicity which might damage the company's reputation and it's of paramount importance that we do not alarm the passengers. They will not be happy to know there is a killer among them.'

'You're asking me to investigate it, but at the same time cover it up?'

'All I am saying is that we need to proceed very carefully. Surely there is no need for the passengers to be made aware of this dreadful event?'

'If I am to investigate the murder, Captain, I must do so with complete honesty and with the help of the passengers. I will need their input, we can't conceal a murder. In my force, which covers a large part of Yorkshire, we keep the public informed through television news, radio broadcasts and newspapers, albeit with the various legal and practical restrictions in mind. That is standard procedure.'

'We are not on shore, Mr Pemberton, we are on board a ship.'

'I can't see the difference. If we are to detect crimes of this kind, we need help from the public, we can't shut them out. If you want me to help, you must allow me to interrogate any passenger or member of the crew, at my discretion. We will need their co-operation, they are the ears and eyes of the ship.'

Captain Hansteed paused to consider this, then said, 'Clearly, you are the expert, you must do what is necessary.'

Pemberton continued, 'It's inevitable that news of the violent death will filter through to most passengers as we conduct our enquiries. We needn't announce it as murder at the beginning, indeed it might not be. At the moment we don't know what happened. We could begin by describing the event as a sudden or suspicious death to get everyone used to the idea, only later revealing it as a murder, perhaps after the post-mortem. That would be quite normal.'

'That's a reasonable compromise, Mr Pemberton.'

'I will proceed cautiously, I assure you. Depending upon precisely what has happened, it might not be necessary to question every passenger, we may resolve the matter without that. Whatever happens, though, I can't see our enquiries would generate mass hysteria. Many small on-shore communities have suffered similar crimes without undue alarm or panic being created. Concern perhaps, but not panic.'

'I follow.'

'Good. Now, Captain Hansteen, I must remind you that I cannot and must not be considered an employee of your company, even in the short term. I must remain independent.'

'Of course.'

'It's more than that, Captain. Company policy must not hinder any enquiries I might wish to conduct, or in any way impose conditions upon how I operate.'

'I'm sure your professionalism will accommodate any of our on-board procedures and restrictions. Now, I have made my request and you have expressed your reservations, so would you like time to consider this?'

'It's a considerable undertaking, even in an advisory capacity . . .'

'I know it must be a great shock and do understand you are supposed to be on holiday. I will not hold it against you if you say you cannot help, nor will I exert undue pressure to persuade you to change your mind.'

'Captain, in a case like this, there is no time to waste. As you say, the killer is surely still on board so we must begin immediately. I'm not sure what facilities are at my disposal but the likelihood of a quick detection inevitably dwindles as time passes.'

'I notice you said *we*. Does that mean you will help?'

'Yes,' he said without hesitation. 'I have taken an oath to protect the public and investigate crime so I must consider it my duty. I will conduct enquiries to the best of my ability and trust that any difficulties can be overcome with goodwill and honesty from us all. Now, you asked for proof that I am a police officer.'

He delved into the inside pocket of his blazer and pulled out his wallet.

'This is my warrant card but you should also contact my office in Rainesbury and my Force Headquarters for the necessary confirmation and authorization.'

'Of course.'

'They will also have to be made aware that I am assisting an outside agency and that we might need their help, even from this distance. I will need to contact police agencies such as the criminal record office and even Interpol, Europol and foreign police forces to check the records of the crew and passengers. As you are registered in Southampton, Hampshire police should be told of this incident and of your action, particularly my role.'

'You must be thankful for computers, email and the internet but yes, I will ensure that all the necessary agencies are informed.'

The Captain then recorded details of Pemberton's warrant card, and the addresses and contact numbers of his office and Force Headquarters.

He said, 'I must inform Head Office that you are on board and have agreed to assist, but that is a formality. So shall we start? Like you, I do not want to waste valuable time.'

'Before I do anything else, I would like to contact my partner.'

'Yes, of course. Can I help you do that?'

'Her name is Lorraine, I left her in Vingolf's Hall, having coffee. With your permission, I should like her to assist me – she is a very skilled and experienced detective too – with the added and valuable intuition of a woman, I might add.'

'Then I think the gods have blessed me! A crime-fighting team on board at such a time! Yes, I'll get a steward to bring her to my office then we can commence. So what is your partner's rank and surname?'

'Detective Constable Lorraine Cashmore, stationed at Rainesbury.'

While a steward was dispatched to find Lorraine and invite her to join them, Pemberton asked the Captain if he would provide a full account of the murder when she arrived. The Captain, in return, asked if Pemberton would object if his secretary also joined them to take notes of the meeting. It was necessary for the ship's log. Pemberton had no objections – in fact he felt it was important to produce a record from the very beginning.

He took advantage of this brief lull to request notebooks for himself and Lorraine; they'd need them to record their enquiries. He also asked whether, before the investigation got under way, secretarial and administrative help would be available. He explained that any murder enquiry inevitably generated a mass of paperwork, much of it destined to provide written evidence for any prosecution that might follow. He also asked whether a secure office was available which could serve as an incident room. Captain Hansteen assured him that an office was available immediately with all the necessary facilities. If he required anything which was not there, all he need do was ask. Cabin 11 on G Deck would be theirs for the duration of the investigation, and it would be secure. He was given two computerized key cards for it. They agreed that Captain Hansteen should remain nominally in charge of the investigation, as was the ship's procedure, but that Pemberton, with his valuable experience, should carry out the actual enquiries with constant liaison between the pair.

Pemberton added he might call for additional help if it became necessary, with Hansteen assuring him that all the facilities on board would be at his disposal including the ship's photographer and medical officer. It was rather like the relationship between a chief constable and his detective chief superintendent – the former was ultimately responsible for the actions of the latter. As a prelude to his enquiries, Pemberton said he would need a complete list of passengers with as much detail as possible about each one, including their home addresses, travel agents' names, cabin numbers and passport details, especially their dates of birth. He would also need a similar list of crew members, if possible showing the date of birth and country of origin of each one, pointing out that this was necessary both to check for criminal records, and for the purposes of elimination from this enquiry. Everyone who was interviewed would be asked to account for their movements at the material times – but at the moment, Pemberton had no idea when or where the stabbing had occurred, neither did he know the identity of the victim.

As they awaited Lorraine, Captain Hansteen repeated his offer of a coffee and this time Pemberton accepted. Hansteen pressed a buzzer to summon his secretary, inviting her to join them with her notebook. He also asked her to arrange for a full list of passengers and crew to be prepared. Then Lorraine was shown into the office.

Clearly, the steward had been unable to offer her any explanation for this unexpected summons to the Captain's office. When she entered, her face was a mixture of puzzlement and concern, relieved only slightly at the sight of Mark. Pemberton rose to his feet to greet her, albeit remaining concerned about her reaction once she discovered the reason for this meeting. Would she display despair, anger, disbelief, resentment?

'Lorraine, this is Captain Hansteen. Jakob Hansteen. Captain, my partner Lorraine Cashmore.' And they shook hands.

'Sit down, Miss Cashmore. Coffee is on the way.'

Lorraine settled on the chair next to Pemberton, puzzlement still very much in evidence on her face. Captain Hansteen chatted to her for a few moments, asking whether she was enjoying the cruise and what she thought of the parts of Norway she had seen to date. He was doing his best to put her at ease. His secretary arrived with coffee and biscuits, busying herself pouring it and offering it to the guests before settling on a chair beside the Captain's desk, with her notebook open and ready.

'This is my secretary, Erika Lampes,' the Captain introduced her. 'Before you arrived, Mr Pemberton, I discussed the likelihood of you requiring a secretary, should you decide to join us. Erika readily agreed, she will welcome the challenge. You will have the best while I make do with one of our other very capable secretaries.'

'Oh, good, thank you. Well, hello, Erika, nice to meet you. I am Mark Pemberton, and this is Lorraine. Detective Constable Cashmore to give her full title,' and he went across and very formally shook her hand. She responded warmly, and then went over to Lorraine and greeted her.

'It will be very exciting, I have never done anything like this.' She was in her early thirties, estimated Pemberton, a smartly dressed and very slender young woman with shoulder-length blonde hair and blue eyes. Lorraine had not missed the reference to her rank. Her face showed a mixture of what looked like disbelief and dismay, sensing that somehow this meeting was rather more formal than social and that it involved some kind of police work.

'Miss Cashmore, I have invited you here at the suggestion of Mr Pemberton. Now I have the bad news. Unfortunately, it appears that a murder has been committed on board, the body of a man was found little over an hour ago. He is one of the passengers. Although investigation of a crime on board, while on the high seas, is ultimately my responsibility as Captain, Mr Pemberton has kindly offered his assistance.'

'Mark, you haven't!' He wasn't sure whether she spoke with good humour or anger. Was she putting on a show of anger or was this one her jokes?

He spread his hands in a gesture of helplessness. 'What could I do?'

And then she broke the tension by smiling. 'He was getting rather bored doing nothing, Captain, I could see he was becoming restless. So this will keep him occupied, he gets irritable very quickly with nothing to do. And when he's irritable, he becomes miserable. And if he is miserable, that makes me miserable. We don't want that on a cruise!'

'I was hoping you might help me,' interrupted Mark.

'Many hands make light work, you mean?' and there was a twinkle in her eye. 'Yes, if my presence will help to get this finished in good time, we can enjoy the rest of the cruise!'

'So you'll help?'

'You know I will,' and she leaned across and planted a kiss on his cheek. 'I hope you weren't thinking of leaving me all alone while you conducted your very first murder investigation on the high seas. I'd not see you at all then, would I?'

'There's your answer,' Pemberton smiled at the Captain. 'Two willing volunteers. So, Captain Hansteen, let's get started. Tell us what happened.'

According to the ship's passenger records, the victim was Lionel Cooper, a gentleman of fifty years of age who occupied an outside cabin on F deck; it was number 150 with a single berth and was on the port side. Captain Hansteen added that Mr Cooper was the companion of a wheelchair-bound passenger, explaining that there were eight cabins especially constructed on F deck for such passengers. Some were double occupancy, others single, but all included refinements such as wider doorways and grab rails, and were located conveniently for lifts and wide passageways, and also close to reception. All were currently occupied.

'Mr Cooper was accompanying Brother Luke, a Catholic monk,' the Captain added. 'Brother Luke is a regular on our cruises. You might have seen him around the ship? Many think he is a priest and call him Father, but he has not been ordained.'

'I've noticed him, an elderly man with a beard,' Pemberton nodded. 'And his companion. We followed them on board. I've seen them around the ship and at dinner. In fact I saw them together last night in Hraevelg's Hall, watching the midnight sun. I haven't spoken to them, however. I can't claim to know either.'

'We've only one clergyman in a wheelchair on this cruise,' said Hansteen. 'The old monk is very noticeable, and he is known to others, people who have been on previous cruises at the same time as him. Some of our crew know him too.'

'I need to confirm it was him I saw last night, if only for my own peace of mind. If the victim is the monk's companion, it appears he was alive last night, this morning to be precise, around 12.30; he was with Brother Luke in Hraevelg's Hall, enjoying the midnight sun. I saw him there. That being so, he must have died overnight.'

'Ah, as recently as that?'

'It narrows the likely time of death to a few hours, not days. Of course I will need positive proof of his identity, so the monk might help with that. But if his companion is dead, who has been looking after him this morning?'

'One of our stewards. Brother Luke can get around reasonably well by himself, he doesn't depend totally on help. Having a companion on board for a wheelchair user is one of our rules.'

'And the cabins for wheelchair users are all together?'

'Yes, they're on F Deck, four to port and four to starboard, all very close to reception. The wheelchairs must be stored in those cabins, that's another of our rules. It means the invalid has access to a chair at all times and can manoeuvre himself or herself out of the cabin, and to most areas of the ship. Other people will help him into a lift, for example, or by opening doors, but that is what the companion is for. That's why Mr Cooper was on board.'

'Do you know how closely connected he is – er, was, to Brother Luke?'

'Sorry, no.'

'So is he Luke's only companion on board? I wondered if there were others, sharing the work and perhaps operating in shifts?'

'No. To my knowledge, he's the only one.'

'And his cabin is close to that of Brother Luke?'

'Yes, next door. The monk is in F152 – even numbers are on the port side, odd numbers on starboard. Mr Cooper is in F150.'

'So if it is not known precisely when Mr Cooper died, why did Brother Luke not raise the alarm when Cooper failed to appear for his duties?'

'When Cooper did not appear as expected, Brother Luke rang his cabin. When he got no response, he thought he'd better get assistance for himself from reception. He decided to pay them a visit on his way up for breakfast.'

'Reception is very close to his cabin?'

'Yes, he could easily get there in his chair. When he emerged from his own cabin, he saw a "Do Not Disturb" sign on Cooper's door.'

'He thought his companion was having a lie-in? And didn't wish to disturb him?'

'So it seems, which is why he went to find a steward. Reception provided the necessary help. One of our stewards took him up for breakfast which is how I know this – at that stage, of course, we thought help would be needed on a very temporary basis. Because of the sign on the door, we made no attempt to rouse the occupant of that cabin, so we had no idea he was dead.'

'So if no one entered the cabin, how or why was the body discovered?'

'All our cabins have an automatic heat detector in case of fire. Most of the passengers are unaware of it but in this case, it sounded this morning to alert the crew and, of course, that overrode any "Do Not Disturb" sign.'

'So who went in?'

'A member of my cabin crew went in, we have master keys. He found the body. It was while Brother Luke was having breakfast.'

'But there was no fire?'

'Fortunately, no. The heat had been generated by one of those electrically operated water heaters, the miniature sort you stick in a mug to boil a cupful of hot water to make a drink – this one had been left switched on, it had dried up the water and had grown red hot.'

'Enough to set off the alarm?'

'Yes, a centre of unduly fierce heat is not normal for a cabin, it was enough to trigger the alarm.'

'A very sensitive system?'

'Very, but also very necessary.'

'So what happened next?'

'The steward realized the man was dead, there was spilt blood in evidence, but he switched off the heater, recognizing it as the cause of the alarm and perhaps a source of further danger, then retreated, secured the door and alerted me. I called the ship's doctor and together we entered the cabin. He examined Mr Cooper and pronounced life extinct.'

'I will need to speak to the doctor and the steward. So what did you do next?'

'We secured the cabin and left; we moved nothing. I reported the death to Head Office who instructed me to follow our procedures. Hence my call to you. The body is still there, until all the necessary procedures have been completed.'

'So what are your procedures?'

The Captain picked up a sheet of paper from his desk and passed it to Pemberton, adding, 'There's not a lot, as you can see.'

An extract from Fleet Regulations, it reiterated the rule that action taken by the first responsible crew member at the scene was vital, and that every effort must be made to apprehend the alleged offender or prevent his escape, albeit without other lives being put in danger. The bridge must be informed, and everything possible done to prevent anyone touching or moving any objects and thereby interfering with fingerprints, footmarks, blood, property or other evidence. The scene must be made secure and photographs taken from as many angles as possible. In the case of murder, the body must not be moved until it has been photographed and examined by the ship's doctor who is

51

requested not to disturb the scene more than necessary, other than to confirm death. A decision as to which authority or investigator has to be informed would be taken by Head Office, and if the offence occurs while the ship is in port, then the relevant authorities must be notified.

'All very basic stuff, but complicated by the fact we are at sea. It's not an easy situation but as you said earlier, there is no substitute for experience,' said Pemberton. 'And I would say you have followed this procedure so far.'

'It's easy to follow set procedures. One does not have to exercise one's imagination or initiative.'

'Rules are for the obedience of fools, and the guidance of wise men!' smiled Pemberton. 'Good. Well, from what you tell me, it seems the scene has not been contaminated any more than necessary. Nothing seems to have been touched in the cabin, other than the switch of the water heater?'

'Right, I touched nothing else and neither did the steward. I know to leave things alone. I have watched a lot of crime series on television!'

'I shouldn't really admit this, but they are often very good tutorials! So what about the murder weapon? You said the man had been stabbed.'

'That was the doctor's initial opinion from a visual examination; a chest wound. He has not carried out a post-mortem. I must admit I did not see a murder weapon, although we have not searched the cabin.'

'Good. I mean good that you did not search the cabin, we need to remember it will contain important evidence. Nonetheless, if there has been a stabbing we must find the weapon.'

'Won't it have been thrown overboard?'

'Quite likely, but we must still make a search. Now, Captain, did anyone touch the notice on the door?'

'No, I left that in position, chiefly to prevent other stewards entering.'

'Good, but I need to secure it as evidence,' said Pemberton.

52

'There is such a notice in every cabin, as you know, for use when necessary.'

'Yes, just like hotels. My guess is that it was placed there by the killer, to prevent discovery of the body, perhaps for a considerable time. Whatever his motives, it may bear fingerprints or DNA evidence, we'll need to keep it. I know I can't organize those tests while we're at sea, but they can be done later.'

'My thoughts too.'

'Maybe the killer was hoping the body would not be found before we reach Spitzbergen, then he could leave the ship and disappear before the crime was discovered? Mind you, there are not many places to hide on Spitzbergen! And I would imagine it's very difficult to get off the island. Perhaps the killer was hoping to reach Southampton or a Norwegian port before the body was discovered?'

'All very likely, Mr Pemberton, although I think our stewards would have alerted me if the cabin was out of bounds for an unduly long and unexplained period. We do keep a check on such things – even people who spend days in their cabins need food! However, we can leave it undisturbed until we return to Southampton. If you remove that particular notice, we can substitute another to keep the cabin secure. I can also lock it so that no one else can enter.'

'Good, that will need to be done in due course. Right now it's time to examine the scene. Can you take me to the cabin? I think we should all go, including you, Erika, to take note of all that occurs. And can we arrange for a photographer to attend? Preferably while we are there? I may need to direct him or her towards certain shots.'

'Yes, Erika,' said Captain Hansteen. 'Give the photo gallery a call, get someone there as soon as possible. Tell them to treat it as very urgent.'

'And Erika,' said Pemberton before she departed, 'I shall need some plastic bags to hold items of evidence, such as the door notice. Various sizes. Can you fix that too? A dozen or so to be going on with.'

'Yes, the medical centre will have some.'

As Pemberton began his investigation, he felt the adrenalin begin to flow; the lethargy which had threatened to envelop him had now been replaced with a sense of determination, a challenge of the kind he had never previously encountered. With rather less than three full days before reaching port there was an added sense of urgency.

Captain Hansteen leading the way, Pemberton and Lorraine followed along the corridors and up a staircase until they arrived at reception.

'This is F Deck, as you know,' he said as if giving a guided tour. 'Reception here with Odin's Garden opposite, that's a quiet area with seats as you can see, but running along the outer boundaries are the cabins. Passenger cabins, both inside and outside, fill about two thirds of the length of this deck. The remaining third comprises some crew cabins and the Purser's offices, out of bounds to passengers, of course. Obviously, the cabins do not overlook reception – you'll note it is impossible to see any from here. And, of course, there is no view from any cabin other than the ocean. No cabins have windows looking into the ship – no one can peep into them.'

A door on the port side led into the corridor along which the outer cabins were situated. Captain Hansteen ushered them through and directly opposite was F150, the 'Do Not Disturb' notice still in position.

'This is not very far away from the madding crowd, is it?' said Pemberton, outside the cabin. 'The killer couldn't have picked a cabin or a murder scene much closer to the nerve centre of the ship!'

'As I said earlier, the wheelchair users' cabins are here, they need to be close to reception if they require help – only this door separates them from assistance.'

'A well-planned deck,' smiled Pemberton. 'It will always be busy here with people passing through ... always someone around to give help and with all these people about, I hope someone saw or heard something unusual.'

'Reception is not open all night, but we do have night

duty crew members who patrol the ship and are aided by security cameras.'

'Good, then we might learn something from them. So, Captain, in we go. Remember not to disturb or touch anything.'

Using a master key, Captain Hansteen opened the door and a faint stench of death met them. It was not too overpowering, nothing like it might have been if this victim had been here for days. The cabin had a large window overlooking the sea but it did not open, air-conditioning being used for temperature control and fresh air. The Captain stood back to give Pemberton precedence, but at first he remained on the threshold to observe the scene inside. He kept his hands in his pockets to prevent himself inadvertently touching anything.

From this point, he could see into the shower room because its door was on his left, with the wardrobe on his right. The wardrobe did not have doors, being little more than a rail suspended between two boards. No one could hide in there. The rail bore a few items of male clothing: a lightweight jacket, pair of trousers, a long-sleeved shirt. Ahead to the left was the main area with its single bed, work surface-cum-dressing table, chair and corner cabinet bearing a TV with drawers beneath.

One side of the bed was tight against the cabin wall with the head abutting a wooden partition which separated it from the work surface-cum-dressing table. The body was lying partially on the bed with its upper right side against the wall, trunk on the bed and arms and legs awry, the feet touching the floor. The head was on the pillow. Some small signs of spilt blood were evident on the body and wall – he would take a closer look shortly, but more immediately he was pleased to note there was no one else in the cabin, dead or alive. Pemberton waved the Captain closer, indicating he should obtain a good view of the interior but not touch anything. Erika had arrived complete with some plastic sample bags, her miniature tape recorder, notebook and pencil. She was ready to begin recording. She said a photographer would come soon.

'Listen to what we say and try to get it all down,' Pemberton told her. 'As much as you can, and if in doubt, stop us talking and ask for guidance or whatever. Now, Captain Hansteen, for your future reference, it's a good idea to do this, to stand back and observe the scene before touching anything, then take photographs of all that we see, before anything is moved. We might have to refer to this view later and certainly bear its features in mind when interviewing suspects.'

'I understand.'

'I'll deal with the body shortly but meanwhile we should note the small work surface-cum-dressing table, separated from the bed by a wooden partition which is the same width as the bed. It is therefore concealed from anyone lying or sitting on the bed. The mug with its miniature water heater still in position is on that surface but switched off, an action we know was performed by your steward. I see nothing else in the mug but it will have to be forensically examined to discover what it contained, and to support the steward's account. Who does the mug belong to? Did the killer bring it, or did it belong to Mr Cooper? It is not the ship's issue, is it?'

'No, it's not one of ours, Mr Pemberton.'

'Then perhaps Mr Cooper brought it with him to make himself a drink – medication perhaps? Cup of tea? Clearly, as there is no break-in, Mr Cooper opened the door to admit his killer, so was the drink for him, or for Cooper? Whatever its purpose, it seems that after killing Mr Cooper, he left it switched on. And were the cabin lights on? Did your steward switch them off? They were off when we arrived . . .'

'Yes, they were off when I arrived earlier too. But it was broad daylight.'

'So was Mr Cooper killed with the lights on, and did the killer switch them off before departing? That is very likely – I know the midnight sun was shining and it would be

56

daylight outside, but these cabins are small and dark. If he did switch off the lights, his fingerprints might be on the switch. That has to be borne in mind. Now, the victim is wearing the clothes he wore last night for dinner – remember I saw him there – so I suspect he died sometime after 12.30 a.m. today. How long after, I wonder? The doctor may have an idea of the more precise time. More questions to consider. So what else do we see?'

He paused as Erika turned a page, then began to dictate:

'This is a preliminary examination by Detective Superintendent Mark Pemberton, Captain Jakob Hansteen and DC Lorraine Cashmore. The fully dressed body of a middle-aged man is on the bed of Cabin F150; it is a single-berth cabin containing a narrow bed with its right side abutting the cabin wall. The head of the bed adjoins the dressing-table area and is separated by a wooden partition which is the same width as the bed. The body is lying partially on the bed in a half-prone position with the upper right side of the back against the cabin wall, the lower back on the bed and the feet touching the floor. The head is on the pillow, the arms and legs are spread wide and the body is lying on top of the covers. The bed is made up, it was apparently not slept in last night. There is no sign of a break-in at the cabin, the door was locked with a "Do Not Disturb" sign placed outside, this is retained for evidence. There is blood on the man's clothing in the area of the chest, in the vicinity of the heart. The man is wearing a light tan long-sleeved shirt with buttons at the front, light trousers of similar colour, brown shoes and fawn socks. The shirt is buttoned up, and the trouser zip is also closed. It appears the wound is beneath the shirt front, suggesting the buttons were refastened after the wounding. The fabric would reduce the spurting of the blood – so it appears the man's shirt was open when he was stabbed. I doubt if he was naked when stabbed, as with blood around it would be virtually impossible to dress the body and leave so much of the clothing unstained. A post-mortem will show whether he bled to death or was knifed in the heart. Now, Captain, does the clothing tell you anything?'

'Open-necked shirt, light tan colour, smart with long sleeves, no jacket. Well-pressed brown trousers. Smart but casual brown shoes. You said you'd seen him at dinner, dressed like this? So he may have come to his cabin in the early hours of this morning, but not gone to bed? He is not in his night clothes.'

'Right. Does this suggest he had arranged to meet someone? Or that he was followed to his cabin by the killer, let in and murdered before he got into bed? Maybe the killer was waiting outside and forced his way in when Mr Cooper returned? There are plenty of possibilities. What is not in doubt, however, is that someone else visited this cabin, and was admitted, after he returned around 12.30. We can therefore state, with some certainty, that the time of death was between 12.30 and the time the steward found the body. Which was?'

'9.30 this morning,' said the Captain.

'9.30 it is. However, we know the monk saw the "Do Not Disturb" sign earlier than that. I have to wonder if the assailant was still inside at that time. Probably not, but we must consider the possibility. Now, Captain, take another look at the shirt front. What do you see?'

'It is heavily bloodstained.'

'There is no cut in the fabric,' said Pemberton. 'I want you to see this. It would take a lot of strength to stab a knife through fabric, skin and flesh, so either he was naked from the waist up when the blow was struck, or his shirt buttons were undone and his shirt front wide open. There is a small amount of blood on the wall of the cabin too, close to his bed, but it doesn't appear to have spurted there.'

'How would it get there?'

'From the killer's hands, I think. If he tried to button up that shirt to smother the bleeding, his hands would be stained. I think he must have touched the wall to maintain his balance or even lever himself off the bed after the stabbing. We need to know whether anyone with bloodstained hands, or sleeves or clothes even, was noticed overnight, moving around the ship. Hurrying away from here, even taking clothing to one of the launderettes. A job for your security team? And in the meantime, all I have to do is find out where everyone was between the relevant times! Many would be in bed, but clearly not all. Now, you say reception is not staffed all night?'

'It closes officially at midnight but we do have stewards on duty throughout the night. They patrol all the decks and attend to anything that might be required, always with the proviso that if a problem arises which is beyond their capabilities, they can summon assistance. And, of course, help can be summoned by telephone or panic button from every cabin, and from other points around the ship. There are also security cameras operating round the clock in every part of the ship.'

'Just as I would expect. Now, this is a preliminary examination but at some stage, I will need to search his clothing and cabin for personal documents and positive identification, relatives' addresses and so on, including these drawers and contents of the wardrobe. And we need to find what was in that mug – has he brought teabags with him? Or did the killer use the mug? It might bear fingerprints. As I look around the cabin, I can't see a murder weapon, it is not sticking out of his chest as we often see in cheap films. But before we search for that, or anything else, let us make a mental note and a record of the contents of this cabin. Are you coping with all this, Erika?'

'Yes, no problems.' She sounded both efficient and confident.

'I had no idea you paid such attention to detail,' said the Captain.

'It's vital, we must be extra careful at this critical stage. Once anything is moved or touched, it means the evidence is contaminated or even destroyed for ever. There are no second chances! First, I need to look for the obvious.'

As Pemberton continued to view the contents of the cabin, a young woman arrived and announced she was the photographer. Pemberton asked her to wait a few minutes because he had not completed his appraisal of the scene. Dictating to Erika during his progress, he examined the top of the bedside cabinet, the dressing table and all surfaces in the small shower room. He saw nothing which was out of the ordinary, it was just as a bachelor cabin would or should appear. It was functional and tidy, with necessities like electric razor, toothbrush, toothpaste, shower gel and other toiletries all neatly laid out. Then, stacked in the base of the wardrobe, he found something odd.

'Note this,' he said to the Captain. 'One large suitcase, one small one, one large holdall and two small holdalls. The holdalls are bulging, with very few clothes hanging in the wardrobe. I'd say those cases are all full too, judging by their appearance. We will search them later. But would he not have hung all his clothes in the wardrobe?'

'That's what we might expect.'

'True. We've been at sea several days – why hasn't he unpacked?'

'It does seem odd.'

'It does, so I wonder what we'll find when we open that suitcase . . .'

'Perhaps he's been buying clothes on board? Or during shore trips? To take home. Many people do.'

'So why pack them now, long before the cruise has finished? But first let's get photographs of things as they are. Then I can consider moving the body, after I've inter-viewed the ship's doctor, of course.'

And so Pemberton's investigation got under way with all its limitations and lack of support services or modern scientific aids. It was like investigating a crime in the manner of detectives operating many years ago.

Chapter Four

Once Pemberton had absorbed a lasting image of the cabin's layout and contents, he asked the photographer to begin her work. She was a Scots girl called Morag McMillan; in her late twenties with beautiful short auburn hair, she wore the smart uniform of the shipping line. Then Pemberton recognized her – she was the girl who had photographed the passengers prior to boarding. It was unlikely she would remember the victim – he'd be just one of hundreds who passed before her every time the ship took on passengers.

As she entered, he expressed his concern at the state of the victim while quietly worrying that the spilt blood, little though it was, might cause her to vomit or faint. She responded by saying she had once worked as a civilian employee for a Scottish police force. Her duties had involved photographing road traffic fatalities, battered children and wives, seriously neglected animals and even murder scenes or serious assault victims. It meant she had no difficulty coping with her present task and, she added, she did not recognize the victim even when Pemberton pointed out she had taken his picture upon arrival. He reminded her about the bearded monk in the wheelchair.

'I was too busy making sure I got the right picture,' she smiled. 'I don't look at faces, we get so many coming through. I do remember Brother Luke though, he's one of our regulars.'

'Can you find that photograph in your records?' he asked. 'The one of his companion, name of Lionel Cooper. I need to compare it with the victim.'

'Yes, I'll find it,' she promised.

Pemberton thought fate must be on his side, with such an experienced crime scene photographer to assist him. Morag said she would be using both a still digital camera and a hand-held digital video camera; it meant still digital pictures could be transmitted ashore by computer in the blinking of an eye. She explained that the dreadful cases with which she had sometimes had to deal weren't the reason she'd left police work. She'd done so because she wanted to see the world beyond the Highlands and reckoned that working on a cruise ship would enable her to do that.

She seemed a feisty young woman which pleased Pemberton and although, in her strong Scottish accent, she chatted while working, he did note she was using her initiative and was clearly a competent professional. In addition to her shots, however, he directed her towards some of the particular pictures he wanted – such as the water heater, the sign on the doorway, the holdalls and suitcases.

Of major importance were photographs of the body taken from various angles, with the bloodstained shirt and its lack of damage by the murder weapon. He made sure she included shots of the position and style of bloodstains smeared on the wall. The shape and style of a bloodstain could indicate a great deal – it might show, for example, whether the victim had been standing up or lying down as the fatal blow had been struck. He asked her to take some external shots too, showing the cabin's relationship to the rest of F Deck and reception.

As Morag and Pemberton worked, the others waited in the corridor. When she had finished, she told him she would return to her studio to process them immediately, and would locate the boarding picture of Lionel Cooper. She added that all the passengers had been photographed before boarding and that the crew members' photographs were also in her records. All could be made available if required. Pemberton felt it was not necessary at this point but might become so later. He then rejoined the others in the corridor.

'Now,' he said, 'what would normally happen next on shore is that forensic Scenes of Crime Officers would take over. They would conduct a lengthy and meticulous examination of everything in here, even the tiniest piece of dust or fibre, hoping to find DNA samples apart from anything else. A forensic pathologist would also be called to examine the body, both at the scene and in the laboratory, and, of course, there would be a post-mortem with an inquest at a later stage. I'm therefore faced with a dilemma – do I secure the cabin and leave things exactly as they are until we either reach the next port or return to the UK so we can have the benefit of a forensic input? Or do I have the body removed, get your ship's doctor to carry out a routine post-mortem, and conduct my enquiry with the limited resources available in the hope that I can identify and detain the killer before we reach port?'

'We can secure the cabin and leave it untouched until return to the UK. That is not a problem.'

'And the body?'

'In view of the time we shall be at sea, it would be our policy to remove it, but leave the cabin sealed until the UK shore police were able to examine it.'

'I'd prefer to have the body left where it is, so that no forensic evidence is contaminated, but the delay could be too great. I need to move swiftly and I do need to know what caused this death, and how. I am very concerned we have a killer on board, one who needs to be caught before he or she can inflict further harm. In this case, I'd say the safety of passengers and crew takes precedence.'

'I couldn't agree more. If the death was premeditated, the killer might have made plans to vanish when we're in port. Such cruise disappearances are not unknown – some go ashore and never return while others disappear overboard, or give that impression! We always notify the relevant immigration departments but sometimes it's too late. The quarry has vanished – and we seldom know why.'

'All the more reason to continue, so it's back to some good old-fashioned police work. I need to talk to the ship's doctor, here in the cabin, then we can move the body and arrange a post-mortem. Do you have a mortuary?'

'Yes, in the medical centre. Natural deaths at sea are not all that uncommon even if murders are rare! We have somewhere to store and refrigerate dead bodies.'

'Good. So you'll call the doctor?'

'I'll send him as soon as possible. So do you need me any more now?'

'Not at the moment. I'm sure you have lots of pressing responsibilities which need your attention. Once the post-mortem's over, Lorraine and I will search the cabin and its contents in greater detail. I must also begin security checks and examine criminal records to see if we have any known villains on board, and, of course, I need to start interviewing witnesses – if we can find any.'

'So do you still need me?' asked Erika.

'Not for the time being, thanks. Lorraine and I have our own notebooks to make written records of what we find. We'll use black ballpoints so we can scan them. We'll give you copies if we need transcripts. I think you've enough to keep you occupied.'

And so Captain Hansteen gave Pemberton the master key of Cabin F150 and left him in charge.

'Right, let's get busy!' he said to Lorraine.

'Where shall I start?' she asked.

'Remember me watching this fellow sign a chit with his left hand?'

'Yes?'

'That made me think he was a replacement for the monk's helper.'

'I can't see how that could have happened. Surely Brother Luke would have noticed if he'd had a replacement.'

'That's the point, they didn't look different. Certainly, their differences weren't evident to a casual observer – but there were differences! I'm not saying they are as alike as identical twins, but their appearances were so similar they could pass for one another, at a casual glance and certainly among strangers. I saw both, remember, and their similarities were enough to make me comment upon them. That's why I need that boarding photo. But it wasn't their different appearances which alerted me, it was what they did and how they did it.'

'So what, in particular, am I looking for in here?'

'Names and addresses of contacts, next-of-kin and so forth, but especially evidence of a substitution, an impersonation. Someone assuming another person's identity. The ship's records show this man as Lionel Cooper which means Lionel Cooper booked the cruise and was allocated this cabin. So far as the Captain is concerned, this victim is Lionel Cooper. I have my doubts about that. Serious doubts. It's vital I establish who this victim really is.'

'Is that why you mentioned the luggage not being unpacked?'

'Absolutely. We know the man called Cooper came on board at the same time as us because we saw him when we got our photographs taken. I need to show that photo to Brother Luke to see if he knows him as Cooper. If there has been a substitution, surely Luke should know but he wouldn't be suspicious if he was expecting it – in other words, he might have been told to expect more than one companion, or even been given a plausible explanation to explain the second man.'

'Or he could be so old or ill that he doesn't know what's going on around him.'

'We can't ignore that possibility,' he nodded. 'But look at it like this. Once on board like the rest of us, Cooper would come to this cabin and, I guess, unpack his belongings fairly soon after arrival; he would put them in the wardrobe and elsewhere in the cabin. So, as I said earlier, what's in those bags and cases? Is this just one man's luggage, or more than one? That's the point I'm making, it's something you need to consider while going through the bags. If the victim is an interloper, he would not want Cooper's clothes around him – he'd pack them away, which is what seems to have happened. The luggage is all ready for collection upon disembarkation even if we're a long way from the end of the cruise.'

'It could contain things Cooper bought both on shore and on board, gifts, clothes and so on. Those he bought on board will be charged to his cruise card, so we can check to see what he bought,' she said. 'It might all be Cooper's.'

'So we need to examine his spending habits and the signatures on his cruise card chits. We can see if two men have used the same name in their signatures. And I need to speak to Brother Luke very soon, to find out how he acquired this helper and how much he can tell us about Cooper, but I'd like to clarify some other things first. If Cooper has been replaced we've got to ask why. And how. What was the motive? And, of course – where is he? If this isn't him, what's happened to him?'

'And who really was the intended victim?' she added. 'Did someone intend to kill Cooper, or this man? Or both? Or is Cooper the killer? Is he hiding somewhere on board, like a stowaway? Is he ashore somewhere? After all, there is a dead man in his cabin! And where does Brother Luke fit into all this? Is he a suspect?'

'Nothing's impossible, Lorraine, especially if the stakes are high enough. We don't know what those stakes are – we've no idea what the motive was. Let's first consider the possibility of identity theft, then we'll talk to Brother Luke and get the Captain's stewards to search the ship for a stowaway. If a substitution has occurred, it could have been at Andelsnes which is the most likely place. That was our most recent port of call; it ties in with my own observations and is closest to the time of death. When we were there, I saw Luke sitting alone near the mountain lodge, and assumed his companion was exploring the surrounds. Now I am asking myself – what actually happened outside that lodge? One thing is certain – the dead man and Cooper must have met each other when this fellow, by means foul or fair, acquired Cooper's cruise card. That's all he would need to get on board this ship and to live here. Either there was an agreement to do this swap, or else this victim did so illegally – if that happened, we must still ask the questions, where's the real Cooper now and what has happened to him? And did anyone see this meeting or exchange?'

'You're not suggesting another murder, are you?'

'Why not? I don't think it happened on board, but some-where like the vicinity of the Trollstigheimen Mountain Lodge. It's very remote up there, as you know, so is Cooper lying dead somewhere deep in a mountain gulley? Shot and left dead at the foot of a waterfall? In some other in-accessible place? Anyone could fall down these slopes. Or be pushed. And never found for years.'

'If you're right about the substitution, I agree that's how it could have happened,' she admitted. 'It must have been carefully planned in advance with someone checking the location as a disposal site for the body.'

'I'm sure there was a lot of advance planning but could Cooper and this chap have been in this ruse together? With Cooper still alive now, somewhere in Norway? Under another name? Think about our sojourn on that mountain top – there were plenty of places to do a swap, buildings to hide behind, vast areas of mountain scenery, space to bump off someone – and leave the body in a foreign coun-try without any means of identification, or with a false identity. With nothing more than Cooper's cruise card, though, and a remarkable physical likeness, chummy could come aboard, get into his cabin and spend money on Cooper's account by forging his signature. For the rest of his trip, he could become Cooper. Who'd notice? They are so very similar in appearance, I doubt if the crew would notice. Brother Luke might but Cooper and Brother Luke didn't mix with other passengers; they ate together and I've rarely seen them talking to anyone else.'

'I still think Luke would have noticed if a new person took over Cooper's duties. Unless he's involved in some way, particularly if there's some kind of plot.'

'I doubt if he's the killer, Lorraine. His age and infirmity almost rule him out. It requires strength and agility to stab someone to death. It means we have to find Cooper, dead or alive, wherever he is.'

'Aren't you jumping the gun a little, Mark? These theories are fine but that's all they are – theories. We've no proof this victim has replaced the real Cooper, have we? Apart from you seeing him sign with his left hand and order some wine. That's not proof. He might be ambidextrous and people can change their mind about ordering alcohol. You've said they are so very much alike, enough even to confuse you. You have to admit you could be mistaken; a trick of light, a new haircut.'

'I'm not mistaken, Lorraine. I'm convinced this fellow is an impersonator. Look, if Cooper went ashore with the monk on one of those excursions, what would he take with him? Not a lot. Certainly not his luggage, not his toothbrush or razor or spare socks and underpants. He'd leave them all in his cabin and take his wallet and camera. Tourist's things. Things for a brief visit.'

'Unless he intended staying ashore . . .'

'For the moment, let's consider he intended to return, like everyone else.'

'I see what you're getting at. It's back to the luggage! If an impersonator took Cooper's place and came on board to occupy the cabin, he wouldn't want to use Cooper's toothbrush or razor or socks and underpants. He'd bring his own luggage on to the ship, little though it might be, and put away the things he didn't want.'

'He would. He'd want to look like a passenger returning from a shore visit. He might have a small holdall, the sort of thing a holidaymaker might use to contain gifts or souvenirs. A plastic bag perhaps? Whatever he was carrying, his luggage and clothes would be scanned before boarding but those searches are only for bombs, guns, weapons and drugs, not to see whether they contain old clothes or new ones, or toothbrushes. Besides, he could say he'd just bought the stuff. I'm convinced the impersonator brought essentials with him, and packed Cooper's things ready for collection upon our return to Southampton. His passport, toothbrush, razor ... everything. To get rid of Cooper's stuff, all he has to do is wait until the cruise is over, the luggage is taken off by crew members. Bang goes our evidence.'

'So why not throw it overboard? That would get rid of it quickly, easily and permanently. That's where you think the murder weapon is. Somewhere under those grey waves. Or hidden in this luggage maybe?'

'It's not easy throwing large stuff like this overboard, not with other passengers likely to be wandering about and watching. There are security cameras on every deck and crew members walking about and looking out for odd behaviour day and night ... and, of course, there is a chance he might not have wanted rid of all Cooper's things. If this man is an impersonator, he might want to look even more like Cooper by wearing some of his clothes, a jacket perhaps. Having said that, we don't know why he came on board – perhaps he intended leaving at another Norwegian port before returning to the UK, and leaving the luggage behind so that people would be tricked into thinking Cooper had disappeared. Gone overboard even. A perfect vanishing trick. But whatever he had planned, he wouldn't expect to be murdered! So are we looking for Cooper as a victim or a suspect?'

'If the killer can avoid us and get ashore at the first opportunity, he can vanish. We'll never know what happened.'

'Right. And if this luggage was taken ashore and not claimed, it would remain in the luggage hall until somebody decided to do something about it. The crew would believe the owner had been on board until the last moment ... remember, his movements and presence would show up on his cruise card, even if somebody else had been using it. It's a neat way of disposing of a victim and escaping arrest too.'

'You've got to know how cruise ships function to carry out that kind of deception, Mark, but we've got to ask why would anyone do this? Why go to the trouble of impersonating another passenger and taking over his role in such a complicated way and killing him in order to do so?'

'I've no idea, except, as I said earlier, the stakes must be high enough. That's something we need to work on.'

'It all sounds very odd to me, and very unlikely.'

'Perhaps I am thinking aloud and getting carried away by my weird theories, but isn't that how detectives succeed? Get a daft theory and then set about proving it?'

'You're too experienced to go chasing silly theories, Mark. If you have a theory about all this, let's examine it carefully. I'm playing devil's advocate right now so that I can listen to your reasoning. So where do you want me to start?'

'We need to be very methodical and careful, noting everything we do and all that we find. Make a list of everything. Can you start by going through the pockets of those clothes in the wardrobe? Then the drawers. And finally the luggage, even if it means sorting through dirty clothes. You could get some plastic gloves from the medical centre if you need them. And we need to find out what was in that mug with the water heater. Look for evidence of identification, passports, cheque books, credit cards and so on, names of friends or family. You know the routine. I'll begin by going through the pockets on the body because the doctor should be here soon, and then I'll help you.'

And so they began their grim task.

The position of the body meant it was not difficult for Pemberton to conduct his preliminary search. Kneeling by the bedside and taking care not to touch any of the congealing blood, he bent to his task, first sketching the position of the body in his notebook. The man's shirt was of high quality and had a breast pocket; it was there that Pemberton found Cooper's cruise card for *Ringhorn*, but nothing else.

The left trouser pocket revealed nothing of interest, only a fresh white handkerchief and some loose coins, both sterling and kroner. In the right pocket, however, there was much of interest. It contained a small fold-over wallet of black leather which contained two charge cards – one from Austin Reed and the other from Marks and Spencer, but neither was in the name of Lionel Cooper. The name on both was R. W. Mansell. There was also a Tesco Platinum Mastercard, a Mastercard from Barclays and a Barclays Connect card, all in the name of R. W. Mansell and all signed in that name. There was also a cruise card for another cruise line, the *Velia*. The wallet contained fifteen £10 Bank of England notes and 500 kroner, plus a receipt from the *Velia*. There was also an English Heritage membership card in Mansell's name, current for a further ten months.

None of those cards, however, bore Mansell's home address. And then, tucked deep in a pocket of the wallet, was a small key, too tiny for a house door or motor vehicle. In the rear pocket of the trousers was a comb and a pocket diary with a black leather cover plus a slender pencil down the spine, but it did not contain any handwriting nor any addresses, telephone numbers or personal data. Maybe he kept it purely to check dates?

Pemberton entered all these details in his notebook, then placed the items aside on the dressing table until he could take them to the office he'd been allocated. Each would help in his further enquiries – to check with the banks, for example, or with the relevant stores. That should reveal a home address and perhaps more details. Having searched the pockets, he then conducted a swift check in other places which might contain personal effects. Some people concealed money or important documents in their shoes, for example, or in secret pockets on the inside of their trousers or even in belts and other places hidden under their clothes. But his careful, and rather delicate, search produced nothing further. So was this man's name really Lionel Cooper? And had he stolen these items from Mansell, whoever Mansell was? Or was his real name Mansell, now acting out his impersonation of Lionel Cooper even in death? If he had impersonated Cooper, why keep all these documents in the name of Mansell? Was it because he intended leaving *Ringhorn* and rejoining his former ship at one of the Norwegian ports?

'Any luck?' He sat back on his heels and turned to Lorraine.

She was also on her knees, going through the contents of the large suitcase.

'There's nothing of interest in the wardrobe or drawers, except a packet of teabags, that could explain the water heater,' she told him. 'Just the clothes we can see. These cases are all full, though, so I've no idea what I'll find here. How about you?'

He explained his finds, saying they supported his hypothesis that the deceased was an intruder. He helped her to go through the clothing in the large suitcase – it had not been locked and contained a suit, trousers, two jackets, shirts, spare socks and underwear, all clean. Everything appeared to have been thrust unceremoniously into the case, not packed with care.

They examined every garment and even unrolled the socks, but there was nothing of interest or value among them. It was all fresh clothing, not yet used on the cruise, so why was it so badly packed? Now it was the turn of the smaller suitcase. He decided to check its contents while she examined one of the holdalls but it was locked.

'Try this,' and he tossed the tiny key to her. 'It was in the victim's wallet.'

The key unlocked the holdall and she found it packed with more clothes, chiefly underwear and socks in plastic shopping bags – dirty washing in other words – but there was also a plastic bag with papers inside. She removed it first and found it contained details of the cruise with tickets, maps and schedules, a passport and other personal effects. Everything was in the name of Lionel Cooper although the passport bore a photograph which looked very like the man lying on the bed. Even a studied examination of the picture against the features of the victim could conclude it was the same person, although the picture was by no means recent. She realized she would not be alone in failing to notice the difference in their features. There was also a wallet and credit cards in Cooper's name, along with his home address.

'Mark, you should see this stuff now.'

He carefully studied the contents and nodded.

'So is this what happened? Cooper came on board as the legitimate occupant and this fellow later took his place, replacing Cooper's things with his own and packing Cooper's ready for unloading, never to be seen again. He's kept Cooper's documents in case he needed to show them. That's how it seems to me.'

'It does look like that.'

'What's the date of birth on Cooper's passport?'

She flicked it open. '23rd October 1952. He was born in South Africa. It's a South African passport.'

'We need to find Mansell's passport too, if it's here, so what else have we that might have belonged to Cooper?'

Her further searches revealed a toothbrush, electric razor, some shower gel and shampoo, a packet of Rennies, some spare cheap non-electric razors and even a plastic box containing a bar of soap. The second smaller holdall contained more clothes such as clean underwear, socks and T-shirts, and outdoor items including a sweater and a cagoule with a yellow hood. And then she found the passport in Mansell's name. It bore the same date and place of birth as Cooper's, and was also issued in South Africa.

'One person or two?' she asked. 'Twins?'

'Would twins have different surnames?'

'It's possible, through adoption. Or it's one man with two passports in different names. It's easy to think of a false name, but not a false date of birth.'

73

As they continued their searches, it became increasingly likely the combined luggage contained the belongings of two men. But were both dead? Or just one? And had one killed the other, or had another person killed both?

Then there was a knock on the door. A uniformed man was standing there; he had fair hair and a ready smile. Pemberton guessed he would be in his mid-forties, a fit and athletic-looking man who would have graced any tennis court.

'Dr Andrews,' he announced, extending his hand. Even in those few words, Pemberton thought he detected a Canadian accent.

'Ah, Detective Superintendent Pemberton and Detective Constable Lorraine Cashmore. Pleased to meet you,' and they shook hands warmly. 'You can come in, we've almost finished here.'

'A nasty business, Mr Pemberton. I've never dealt with anything like this on board, never.'

'Me neither! Now, you were called to examine the body earlier this morning. Can you tell me what you found?'

'It would be shortly after 9.30. The Captain called from his office to say a steward had entered a cabin a few minutes earlier to find a man lying on the bed, clearly dead with blood around. I hurried along; both the Captain and steward were there, waiting. I am familiar with Fleet Instructions and so, being careful not to interfere with anything else in the cabin, I examined him. He was dead, there was no doubt about it, and it was immediately evident it was not from natural causes.'

'You couldn't establish the cause of death though?'

'No, that can only be done through a post-mortem as you know. From what I saw I thought he had been stabbed in the area of the heart, but if a major blood vessel had been severed, then most of the escaping blood could have gone into his body cavities. Not a lot can escape through a knife wound and some was also absorbed by his clothing. The minute his heart stopped beating, of course, the blood would cease to be pumped out, although there might be some seepage.'

'There are no stab holes in his shirt, doctor.'

'I think his shirt was replaced or buttoned after the stabbing. It was probably open when he was stabbed. That would explain some stains on the walls, the killer using the wall to support himself as he rose from the bed. Killers who use knives almost inevitably become bloodstained even in a small way and some might have been spread on the wall and bed by the victim in his final moments.'

'You can see there are fingermarks on the wall, in blood.'

'Yes, I saw those but we can't check fingerprints, Mr Pemberton. I guess they are from the killer but one can never be sure. Perhaps both killer and victim.'

'So, doctor, can I put you on the spot by asking how long you think he had been dead when you examined him?'

'I'm sure you know that is virtually impossible, all sorts of factors present difficulties in determining the time of death, such as the temperature of the cabin . . .'

'I know, but he hasn't been dead for days, has he? Death is fairly recent, the blood in the stains is not yet congealed, and I'd guess *rigor mortis* has not set in.'

'That would suggest death within, say, the previous eight or ten hours.'

'That agrees with my prognosis, doctor. I am sure I saw this man alive just after midnight, around 12.30.'

'I would support your theory that he died between midnight and 9.30 this morning, I cannot be any more accurate than that.'

'That's good enough for me. Now, the bloodstains. You'll see the pillow, his clothes and the wall alongside the bed are all contaminated. Have you the means of testing them?'

'Testing them? What for?'

'I'd like to know if they all came from the same person, doctor.'

'Ah, yes. Well, I can carry out a simple test to determine blood groups. It's one we do if a patient doesn't know his or her own group, if they need a transfusion perhaps, but it's no more sophisticated than that.'

'Fine, that'll do for a start.'

'I can't find DNA, you realize that?'

'Of course. Basic blood analysis will help – it's important I know if anyone else was injured in this fracas. So, since midnight, have you or your staff treated anyone for cuts or other injuries which might have resulted from this attack? Or for any other kind of knife injury?'

'No, no one, I've checked the overnight log.'

'And do you think the assailant would be bloodstained? And his or her clothing?'

'A fatal stabbing using a single strike rarely if ever stains the assailant, particularly if it is delivered through clothing. This one wasn't. A repeated attack with several powerful blows could result in staining an assailant but in this case the killer fastened the shirt after stabbing the victim just once. That action – fastening the shirt – would mean the killer's hands would almost certainly be bloodstained.'

'Then we need to know whether anyone has been seen on the ship with bloodstains on either their hands or clothes.'

'Ask our security staff to check their records and films, Mr Pemberton. I note there is no sign of a disturbance in the cabin, no sign of a fight or struggle, no rucked carpets, broken chairs, simply a swift death by stabbing. I wondered if it might have been a nasty accident.'

'The killer could have straightened things before he left, it has been known!'

'Well, yes, I suppose so. Apart from the body, the cabin is very tidy.'

'Right, now I need to know what sort of weapon it was. A knife or dagger of some kind is highly feasible, but with one sharp side on its blade or two? And what was the length of the blade? What kind of knife was it?'

'I can only answer those questions through a post-mortem, Mr Pemberton.'

'And you are able to perform it fairly soon?'

'Yes, indeed. I'm busy for the rest of the morning – the sick can't wait even on a cruise – but I can do it this afternoon. You might like to know I have done this kind of work on previous occasions, usually if there is a sudden unexplained death on the high seas.'

'Not murder though?'

'No, most are due to natural causes, but I am familiar with the requirements. Shall I call you when I'm ready?'

'Yes, as investigating officer I must be present, but I'll be making enquiries elsewhere in the body of the ship so you'd better use the tannoy. Another reason for my being present is to fulfil a legal role, i.e. identifying the body on the operating table as the one I saw in the cabin. It's all part of the chain of evidence.'

'Ah, yes, of course.'

'Right, well, I think we can have the body transferred to your theatre as soon as possible, leaving it fully clothed.'

'I'll get two medical stewards to bring a trolley right away.'

'You'll compile a written report of your part in all this, will you? For the file?'

'Of course,' and the doctor left.

Pemberton turned to Lorraine. 'Once the body has gone, I want to search that bedding.'

'What do you hope to find?'

'Who knows?'

Chapter Five

Two white-coated stewards arrived with a stretcher and, under Pemberton's supervision, carefully lifted the body from the bed. They covered it with a white plastic sheet, a practice not allowed by forensic Scene of Crime experts due to the possibility of contaminating microscopic evidence. They then bore it to the medical centre, taking care to avoid passengers. Once they'd left, Pemberton conducted a meticulous search of the bed, its covers and surrounds, but found nothing concealed. Having thoroughly searched F150 and the contents of the luggage while recording their actions, he and Lorraine could now vacate and secure the cabin, albeit removing the documents relating to Lionel Cooper and R. W. Mansell. He popped them into plastic bags and labelled them. For the time being, everything else could remain untouched and under lock and key, although a replacement 'Do Not Disturb' sign was still needed; he'd remind Erika about it. Now it was time to investigate the background of the key players in this drama and interview witnesses.

When he entered the incident room Erika was working at a computer on her desk. It was a spacious, light and airy office on the starboard side towards the prow with two landscape windows, deep fitted carpets in the ship's colours of blue, gold and white, and three desks. Each was equipped with a computer keyboard and screen, telephone and intercom while around the walls were maps of the ship, showing the layout of each deck with cabin numbers and the site of every public room and other locations.

There were two four-drawer filing cabinets, empty and ready for use, and so he put the plastic bags of evidence in one of the drawers until it was required. There was also a stationery cupboard and a pair of large empty pinboards, ideal for notices.

'Coffee?' she asked as they entered.

'I'd love one,' said Pemberton, his plea being echoed by Lorraine.

As Erika went to fetch the coffee, Pemberton selected his desk after discussing it with Lorraine; she opted for one near a window even though it looked over nothing but the grey sea. Its gentle swell and a hint of mist in the distance were rather soothing. Each settled at their desk, opening drawers and finding paper, notebooks, pens and pencils, envelopes – all the basic necessities. When Erika brought the coffee, each was presented with an individual cafetière, jug of milk, bowl of sugar lumps in brown and white, and a pair of biscuits in wrappers.

'I've arranged for a new "Do Not Disturb" sign and Cabin F150 will be secured. I've got the lists you wanted too, Mr Pemberton,' she told them. 'They're very comprehensive, taken from our own records, but the passenger list is based on information provided by them. Sometimes, that is not entirely reliable! The crew list is also from our records, and may be more accurate even though many crew members are from countries other than the UK. There are a lot of people on board – 1650 passengers and 700 crew. And we're arranging a search for stowaways.'

'Well done, this is a good start. However, we can't interview everyone and only one has so far been eliminated from our enquiries!'

'Who's that?' asked Lorraine in her innocence.

'The man I believe to be R. W. Mansell. And only because he's dead. Right, Erika, this aspect of a murder investigation involves interviews to eliminate people from the enquiry. It means taking written statements and compiling a file of them, all indexed. They've all got to be read and analysed to see if any contain lies or inconsistencies, and to abstract relevant facts, often by cross-reference. For example, I'll be looking for accounts of witnesses who noticed the monk and his companion with dates, times and places, so any references to them need to be identified in the statements, and then checked. In particular, I want to know if anyone has been seen speaking to the monk or his companion, arguing with them perhaps. If so, I need to know when it was, and who it was and what they said. You need to look out for this sort of thing.'

'Our computer's word search system will help,' she offered.

'It will, but even so, there's a lot of reading involved! If there are too many statements to cope with, we may need to bring in a statement reader or two. Someone from the crew, from security. You might need another secretary to help process them – don't be frightened to ask for help. An enquiry of this kind is very time-consuming but I'm not going to waste precious hours and minutes interviewing and eliminating you, or the Captain or even Lorraine and the ship's doctor – that would only become necessary if we don't find the killer!'

She nodded her understanding as he suggested she print a full list of passengers in deck order and a list of crew members, preferably in fairly large lettering. They could be displayed on the pinboards for quick reference. He then added that as each person was questioned and positively eliminated, their name could be crossed off in a bold colour, say green; other colour codes could be incorporated beside the names, such as a red dot for anyone with a criminal conviction for violence, a purple dot for someone who was clearly lying or being evasive, and a black dot for a positive suspect. A blue one might be for someone who managed to avoid being questioned, and an orange one for someone who needed to be reinterviewed. A list of suspects would have to be drawn up too – that was the famous 'frame'. Suspects were said to be in the frame if they had not been eliminated – rather like the frame of runners at a race meeting. The noticeboard would also show every known fact about the deceased, including his facial photograph in death and that of Lionel Cooper for comparison. A selection of photographs of the murder scene in F150 would also be displayed. Visual aids of this kind were always beneficial to murder enquiries.

'I'll be making use of my own staff in Rainesbury CID office,' he told her. 'My chief contact there will be Detective Inspector Paul Larkin and so I think you should talk to him as well, to establish contact as well as to establish a secure email link. And I don't need to remind you that what transpires here is absolutely confidential.'

'Of course – but I must say it is quite a change from my normal routine.'

'I know you'll find it both enjoyable and memorable, especially if we find the guilty person. Right, my first call is to Paul Larkin. I can call the shore from here, can I?'

'Yes, it's a radio telephone so there may be a slight time lapse between conversations and sometimes a little static interference.'

'Good, then I think you should make the introductory call to Paul,' and he told her his direct line number. She dialled and asked for Paul Larkin.

'Mr Larkin, my name is Erika Lampes, speaking from the cruise ship *Ringhorn*. I am the Captain's secretary but am currently seconded to Mr Pemberton. He wishes to speak to you. Hold the line please.'

When his own handset sounded, he lifted it. 'Pemberton.'

'Did I hear that right, boss? You've been given a secretary?'

'Yes, Erika's right. I am working!'

'I thought you were on holiday!'

'So did I! But I've a job to do. Now listen. I'm investigating a murder on board this ship . . .' and he provided all the details, adding, 'I'll need all sorts of help from you and the team, but right now I need to know as much as possible about Lionel Cooper and R. W. Mansell and any links they might have with a monk called Brother Luke. At this stage, I know nothing much about any of them. Can you run the usual checks? I need to know the names and addresses of next-of-kin and anything about their backgrounds that might be relevant. Erika can provide you with a lot from the ship's records, but we need to confirm things for ourselves.'

'Right, I'll liaise with her.'

'We can email you anything you want to know, just ask Erika. And can you check with the Norwegian police authorities to see if the body of an unknown middle-aged man has been found? It might coincide with this ship's visit to Andelsnes, the victim might have turned up in that area. It was one of our stopping points. We had lunch at Trollstigheimen Mountain Lodge yesterday and explored the area. Bags of space for someone to get lost or bumped off. The fellow might still be alive, of course, and he may have legitimate access to Norway. Whether he's alive or dead, he is Lionel Cooper but he might have documents on him in the name of R. W. Mansell. Both have the same place and date of birth – there's food for thought. Both men's passports are with me now; both are South African and white. Cooper boarded this cruise at Southampton. The details he supplied when booking the trip can be supplied in an email from Erika but we've nothing much on Mansell so his banking details will help. She'll send them to you. We're talking identity thefts or swaps here. I'll hand you back to her now, but in the meantime, I also need, asap, CRO checks on all the passengers and crew. I'm about to start interviews, there'll be a post-mortem sometime today as well, but I'm sure we'll be in touch as we go along. Oh, and Lorraine is helping me.'

'You don't half drop yourself into the mire, boss! So what's the rush with this one?'

'We're at sea for the next three days. I'd like to get this sorted before we dock at Spitzbergen – that's the first chance for the killer to walk ashore and vanish – not that he can get far on Spitzbergen. The weather or polar bears would probably get him! And I don't need to highlight the risks involved with a killer still on board.'

'Got you. And you're a long way from anywhere, aren't you? Too far to fly a helicopter out?'

'Too true! North Pole next stop after Spitzbergen, besides we don't have helicopter-landing pads on this ship. Spitzbergen's a remote island inside the Arctic Circle with a lot of ice and a few wooden huts, populated with scientists, reindeer, Arctic foxes and polar bears. We don't know what kind of plans the killer might have made before joining the ship. He might have organized some means of getting off at Spitzbergen and returning to civilization – realistically, though, that would have to involve an aircraft which suggests this is no ordinary murder. Nonetheless, we'll alert the authorities on Spitzbergen, if there are any.'

'Right, got you so far. Put me back to Erika and we'll get her side of things sorted.'

While Paul was discussing his requirements, Pemberton reminded Lorraine they would have to establish a system for interviewing any witness who might be vital to the investigation. There was insufficient time to call in every-one and if they relied on the public address system, there would be the inevitable delay between summons and response. It took about twenty minutes to walk from one end of the ship to the other, notwithstanding all the stair-cases and lifts that would have to be negotiated. And some people ignore or never hear such a summons – the killer in particular.

Pemberton did not have the luxury of time. He would have to go out and find his witnesses – just like a murder enquiry on shore. He waited until Erika had finished her chat with Paul Larkin, then said, 'I need to call in people for interview, Erika. How can I do that without knocking on the door of every cabin? That would be tantamount to door-to-door enquiries but I don't have the detectives to do that. In this case most will be out of their cabins and doing something on the ship – and not easy to find.'

'I can call in any crew members you want to talk to but for the passengers the only way is to use the public address system. If they don't respond, it will mean knocking on cabin doors, or finding them somewhere on board.'

'I could make a nuisance of myself by contacting them at dinner, couldn't I? All their seating places are in your records, aren't they?'

'Yes, you could do that. And it might be possible to find out who has made advance hair appointments and so forth. As you know, whenever we have a shore excursion, they are pre-booked so we know who they are; they gather in the theatre in groups at pre-arranged times – you could always address them there.'

'Thanks, I'll consider it. One snag is I don't know precisely when I'll need to interview particular people. Questioning of one might lead very quickly to another I'd never considered, so I can't use the queue and wait system.'

'That's where the PA system would help.'

'Yes, I agree. In addition, though, I could visit the public areas and talk to anyone I find there, and cross them off our list. I might even try that on occasions, by talking informally to people. Like those at our dinner table. The only way to start is at the beginning, so let's call in the steward who found the body.'

'That's no problem.'

'After him, I'll want to talk to Brother Luke and the occupants of cabins at either side of F150. And any night duty crew members around between midnight and 9.30 this morning. I also need to interview any security staff patrolling the ship through the night. I'll wait until after they've had their sleep. Both Lorraine and I will be present at these early interviews, to establish the basic facts, and then we'll divide the load.'

'I understand. So shall I call in the steward who entered F150 this morning? His name is Altivey, he is Indian, from Goa in fact.'

Normally, the person who finds a body is the first suspect until he or she has been eliminated, some killers

84

mistakenly believing that by reporting the discovery of a murder victim, they present an air of innocence. In this case, the circumstances suggested it was unlikely Altivey was the killer. He was about six feet tall, a handsome dark-skinned man with a thick head of black wavy hair, beautifully kept. He wore the uniform and name badge of a steward. Pemberton introduced himself and Lorraine, then settled him down to explain why he had been summoned.

Altivey understood, he spoke good English. Under gentle questioning by Pemberton, he could not elaborate upon what was already known. At the sound of the heat alarm, he had been urgently dispatched to F150 with a portable fire extinguisher and, even though he had noticed the 'Do Not Disturb' sign on the door, had unlocked it with a master key card. No one else was in the corridor at the time. It was daylight when he had entered, the lights were not switched on and there was no sign of forced entry. Immediately, he'd noticed the man on the bed with signs of bleeding. At that point, he did not know whether he was dead or alive, or how long he had been lying there. He spoke to him but got no response and decided to seek urgent help. There was no one else in the cabin, he was sure of that even though he had not searched the shower room. He agreed with Pemberton that someone could have been hiding there. In spite of the trauma of that discovery, Altivey had recognized the source of the alarm as the water heater which had overheated and so he had switched it off. He'd noticed the mug was empty. That action, even with the casualty lying there, took a fraction of a second. He did not touch anything else, not even the cabin telephone, and did not put his extinguisher down anywhere.

After trying again to rouse the victim, without success, he ran to reception to raise the alarm because it was close by. He said a doctor was needed immediately in F150. As he had run out of the cabin, the door had automatically closed and locked itself; he had waited outside until the ship's doctor arrived. He then explained what he had found.

The doctor, using Altivey's master key, had entered to examine the body, telling Altivey that the occupant was dead under suspicious circumstances and the Captain must be told. The doctor said he would remain until the Captain arrived, asking that Altivey summon him via reception. He had done so, and then returned to his normal duties, leaving the key with the doctor and returning his extinguisher to its storage point. And that was all he could say, except that afterwards the crew had been warned not to discuss the incident, particularly within the hearing of any passengers. Pemberton thanked him and allowed him to leave. Erika had recorded the statement and it would be transferred into her computer.

'He confirms what we already know,' he said to Lorraine. 'But he hasn't given me anything new, has he? Now we must find Brother Luke. We've got to consider him a suspect at this stage. What time is it?'

'Quarter to twelve,' she said. 'Why does that matter?'

'There's a classical music concert – a pianist playing Chopin – in Forseti's Hall up on D Deck, I saw it in the daily newspaper. It will finish at twelve. I've noticed Brother Luke attends most of those concerts, he positions his wheelchair at the back. I can catch him as he leaves. I'll go and see if I can find him. Coming?'

'Of course.'

Leaving Erika to look after the incident room, they hurried into the corridor to make their way via lifts to D Deck. They arrived at Forseti's Hall just as the sound of applause was filtering through the closed doors, and waited.

The audience of about fifty emerged looking happy and content, most heading for a bar or coffee lounge. Pemberton and Lorraine would try and interview some of them before lunch, but first he must talk to Brother Luke. When the audience had dispersed, the monk emerged, his wheelchair guided by a steward.

'Excuse me, Brother Luke,' said Pemberton. 'Might I have a word?'

The old man peered at him rather short-sightedly, then asked, 'Who are you?'

'Detective Superintendent Mark Pemberton, of Rainesbury police in North Yorkshire,' he said. 'And this is Detective Constable Lorraine Cashmore, my partner. We are fellow passengers, but I need to talk to you about an incident in the cabin adjoining yours.'

'Ah, my helper, Lionel. He didn't answer my call this morning, and when I emerged from my cabin, I saw a notice on his door saying he must not be disturbed. The letters were big enough for me to read. So I got this young man to help me until Lionel decides to rejoin me. I fear he might have drunk too much wine last night. He's not used to heavy drinking so I hope he's not been making a nuisance of himself.'

'What makes you think he might have been a nuisance?'

'Well, nothing really, except as a rule he doesn't touch alcohol but he had a bottle of red last night, all to himself. Most uncharacteristic.'

'Look, we can't talk here in the corridor. Can we find a quiet corner? And I would like your current assistant to join us, I need to ask him questions too.'

'Why, what's happened?'

'Do you know your companion's full name? Lionel, I mean.'

'Lionel Cooper,' he said. 'He told me to call him Lionel rather than Mr Cooper, and so I do.'

'Where did you recruit him?'

'Oh, I think it was someone in the home knew of him, there are good people out there, true saints who help people like me. At the moment, I'm spending time in the diocesan care home, it's for retired and sick priests, monks and nuns who've nowhere to go and no one to care for them. It takes lay people too. It's kind and thoughtful people such as Lionel who escort the aged and infirm to places like Lourdes and Fatima, go on pilgrimages with them, and help them on jaunts like this. Lionel is wonderful, nothing is too much trouble. When I said I was taking this holiday, Lionel said he was willing to come along and care for me. It's in the ship's rules, you know. It's not an easy task, I might add, being stuck with me all day every day.'

Pemberton asked if the current helper, a uniformed steward called John, knew of a quiet corner where they could talk at length in confidence, and he assured them he did. Staying on the same deck, he led them to the cinema. 'There's no film showing until this afternoon,' he said. 'It will be quiet and private in here.'

John manoeuvred the wheelchair into the cinema and wheeled it down the sloping aisle to the front where there was ample space, along with room for Pemberton, Lorraine and John to occupy nearby chairs.

'So what's all the mystery?' asked Brother Luke when they were settled.

'It's not easy and I don't want to alarm the other passengers, but I have some dreadful news. It's a shock, I know, but I'm afraid your helper has been murdered in his cabin. Sometime during the night. He was found this morning.'

Luke sat in shocked silence for a few moments before replying. 'Lionel? Are you sure?'

'Your helper,' said Pemberton, not wishing to confuse the old man with the likelihood of an alternative name. 'Yes, sadly it is true. And you, John, had you been informed?' he asked the steward.

'No,' he stammered. 'No, no, I had no idea. I was called to help Brother Luke because his friend didn't want to be disturbed . . . I had no idea this was the reason.'

'I understand that most of the crew have been notified, but you must have been out of reach while you were looking after Brother Luke. The others have been told not to speak about the crime, certainly not in front of any passengers.'

'That's the normal procedure when something happens, assaults, thefts and so on, we haven't to alarm the passengers but we've never had a murder before, not that I know of.'

'So what happened, Mr . . . er . . . what did you say your name was?' Brother Luke had now grasped the enormity of the situation.

'Pemberton. Detective Superintendent Pemberton, and this is Detective Constable Cashmore. We are from North Yorkshire but happened to be on board, enjoying a holiday. We have been asked to help with the enquiry.'

'Oh dear, poor you. Our priests rarely get a holiday either, not a real one. They're on duty all the time, like you. They must say Mass every day, even if it's in their rooms, but I am not ordained. I am not a priest even if I wear this collar and look like one. I simply help out at a monastery. But this is dreadful news. I shall pray for Lionel. Thank you for telling me.'

'I'm afraid there is more, Brother Luke. I need to ask you a lot of questions. First, I need to know all about Lionel. What can you tell me about him?'

'Very little,' and the monk spread his hands in a gesture of helplessness. 'As I said, he's one of those volunteers who come forward to help old crocks like me. I know nothing about his personal life or circumstances.'

'How long have you known him?'

'Well, the home recommended him. I've never met him until this trip, we got together a few days before we set off and liked each other. Then he came to the home to collect me and take me down to Southampton from Teesside. He has one of those vehicles which have been adapted to carry wheelchairs. He left it on the docks, in the care of one of those companies who do that sort of thing.'

'You travelled alone? Just the two of you?'

'As always, yes. He's a very good and steady driver. Was, I should say. Oh, this is awful, trying to remember he's no longer with us. Anyway, when we arrived we were given a trolley for our luggage and he wheeled me to the boarding point where our luggage was taken away, later to reappear at our cabin doors. He was allocated the one next to me, you know, very convenient. He has been most attentive throughout. I couldn't wish for anyone better.'

'He must have told you something about himself, surely?'

'Not a lot, Superintendent, not that I can recall anyway. My memory's not what it was, you know. The penalty of growing old, like being rather deaf and more than a bit short-sighted. I am eighty-two, not long for this life, I fear.'

'You've years left in you! So what *can* you recall? Any small snippet will help. I need to know as much as possible about him. His home situation, whether he has relatives, enemies, a job, his background, anything that might help me decide who might have killed him. His address is in the ship's records and I have arranged for my colleagues to check his background, but it's his private life that interests me.'

'That's a tall order. He never told me much about himself although from his chatter I did gain the impression he had been on cruises before, he was familiar with the routine which I found helpful. He was more interested in me, how I first realized I had a calling for the religious life, where I was working before retirement, what my leisure interests are. I do like good music, as you might have guessed. That kind of thing. He always made sure I got to my concerts. I do enjoy my music, you know, now that my eyesight is not so good. Reading is hard work.'

'Do you know anyone who might help us to research his background?'

'All I can suggest is that you contact the home where I am staying at the moment. They know Lionel. It's called St Bede's Diocesan Rest Home and it's at Acklam on the outskirts of Middlesbrough.'

He provided them with the full address and telephone number, and the name of the resident warden, a Mrs Agnes Kitching.

'Thanks, I'll organize some enquiries. Now, let's talk about last night. I believe you and Lionel stayed up to watch the midnight sun? In Hraevelg's Hall?'

'Yes, it's something I always enjoy. One of God's miracles.'

'So what time did you leave?'

'I can't be completely sure, but it would be around half past twelve, perhaps a little later.'

'Both of you?'

'Yes, we had enjoyed dinner, the second sitting, and I asked Lionel if he would take me up to Hraevelg's Hall to watch the sun literally dancing on the sea. He said he would love to, and would buy us a drink of wine, but as I don't drink, I think he downed the lot himself. He's never done that before. That's why I wasn't too surprised when he didn't turn up this morning.'

'He never drank?'

'Well, I thought not. I'd never seen him do it until last night. He'd never bought one for me either. Not that I am against alcohol, I'm not, but I'm on medication at the moment, for my heart, and have to avoid strong drink.'

'So around half past twelve, he took you back to your cabin?'

'Yes. He used my card to unlock the door and once I was inside, he returned my card and left me. I can cope on my own really but it's a rule of the ship that crocks in wheelchairs have to be accompanied. So I went inside, the door closed and locked itself, then I prepared for bed.'

'Did that take long?'

'No longer than usual. I said my prayers and would have been in bed by about 1.15. Went to sleep almost straight away.'

'And where did Lionel go?'

'Well, I don't know but I suppose he went to his own cabin, next door to mine.'

'Could he have gone elsewhere?'

'Well, yes, I suppose he could. I would never know, would I? Unless I tried to call him on the phone.'

'But you didn't?'

'No, I had no need to.'

'So did you hear anything in the night? Noises? Voices? Shouts? Cries? Doors opening and shutting? The sounds of someone else in Lionel's room?'

'No, absolutely nothing. Those cabins are very sound-proof and my hearing is not as sharp as it was. I had a peaceful night and woke this morning just after 7.30, did my daily offices and got ready for breakfast. When I rang for Lionel to say I was ready for him there was no reply, then I remembered his bottle of wine last night, so thought he must be still asleep. I let myself out about 8.30 to go and find help from reception to escort me up to breakfast, and then saw the notice on his door which, as I said, didn't surprise me.'

'You thought he'd over-indulged and overslept?'

'Yes, I wasn't angry, not when he's supposed to be on holiday too. Surprised, perhaps, but not angry. I asked reception to get someone to escort me up to breakfast, because it's one of the ship's rules. That's when John arrived.'

'And throughout all that, there was no reason to think anything untoward had occurred?'

'No, not at all. I assure you I had no idea until you told me just now . . . really, I can't believe it . . .'

'Brother Luke, thanks for that but I'm afraid I must give you another shock. You told me you were surprised when Lionel ordered a bottle of wine. Was there anything else that surprised you last night? About Lionel. I'm interested in the period following your shore trip to Andelsnes. I want you to think carefully about this, it is most important.'

'Well, yes, now you come to mention it. I thought Lionel wasn't himself. Yesterday evening that was. Before dinner. I wondered if he'd had bad news of some kind, and had bought the bottle to make him feel better.'

'In what way was he not himself?'

'Well, he seemed to have lost his bearings on board, he was somewhat disorientated. Not that I'm too bright myself nowadays, I'm a bit blind and even a bit deaf and daft, it's all due to my age, you know. Even so, I got the impression he wasn't behaving normally because he didn't seem sure where to take me, where things were. I had to remind him. I thought he'd had some kind of shock – his voice was different too. I think it might have been the drink.'

'And what about your time at the mountain lodge? How was he then?'

'Not really himself, I must say. Someone came to talk to him and they went off together. They left me alone for a while, then when he got back, I thought he'd had something to drink with the other chap ... he wasn't used to drink, you see. I didn't mind being left alone. The scenery is wonderful and I was chatting to some other passengers after lunch while he went for a look around. When he returned he was alone and escorted me back to the coach. That's really when I thought he wasn't himself, he seemed uncertain of things, like how to handle my wheelchair. Drink can do that, can't it? Make you fuddled.'

'That's one of its effects, yes. Now did that man tell you he was taking over from Lionel? Even for a short while? Did he give any explanation for the differences you noticed?'

'No, nothing. But I didn't know Lionel all that well, I didn't like to pry.'

'Can you describe the man who spoke to Lionel?'

'Not really, he was just a man – he was very like Lionel in some ways, height, colouring, age. He never spoke to me then.'

'Would you recognize him if you saw him again?'

'I doubt it. I didn't take much notice of him. There were lots of people about and my sight is very poor.'

'Do you think he was a passenger from *Ringhorn*?'

'Oh, I have no idea, Superintendent. I can't say I've noticed him around the ship, though.'

'So who were the passengers you spoke to? Can you remember them?'

'Sorry, no. They said they'd seen me around the ship – I think I'm the only person wearing a dog collar, wheelchair or no wheelchair, but I can't say I recognized them either.

I don't know their names, if that's what you're going to ask. I'm not being very helpful, am I?'

'Clearly, they are on *Ringhorn*, so I'd like to talk to them at some stage, about what transpired at the lodge. If you see them again, try and get their names or cabin numbers, then contact me.'

'Yes, all right, I'll do my best.'

'You can always contact me through the Captain's office or reception. So how long were you left alone at the mountain lodge?'

'It's hard to say, Superintendent, with all that lovely scenery to enjoy, and talking to the other passengers.'

'I was there too, we had only about an hour and a half at the lodge, and about an hour of that was taken up with lunch.'

'I'd guess I was alone for half an hour maybe, perhaps a little longer.'

'After lunch?'

'Yes.'

'So that would be from around half past one to two o'clock? Roughly?'

'I would think so, yes.'

'Thank you. Now I have to say that I noticed Lionel too, in the restaurant last night when he ordered the wine. He signed the chit with his left hand, something he'd not done before. You know what I thought?'

'Go on, surprise me.'

'I thought it was another man. I thought you'd got a replacement companion – which wouldn't have surprised me. I could understand a helper wanting a break during a long engagement, and so it wouldn't have surprised me if a deputy helper was also on board.'

'Well, no, I don't think he had a deputy, he would have told me. No one said I was going to have a replacement. Certainly, though, I thought there was something different about him, but with my eyesight, I never studied him closely. As I said, his voice wasn't the same – and he was by no means as attentive when we returned from that trip.'

'English, was he? His speech, I mean?'

'Oh yes, very English, no trace of a foreign accent. I'd have noticed that. I'd say he came from my part of England too, the north-east that is. Lionel is – was – from the north-east. But his voice was different, I know. I'm good with voices.'

'Simple things like a change of hairstyle can alter an appearance, but I thought this man looked very similar to Lionel. Even with my police training, I didn't notice any physical difference – not that I was looking closely, of course. But voices rarely change.'

'As I said, I didn't spot any major difference in his appearance, but if he had replaced Lionel, you'd think one of them would have told me, wouldn't you?'

'I think Lionel would, if he'd known. Now, does the name R. W. Mansell mean anything?'

'Mansell?' The monk paused for a long time, frowning as he tried to recollect the name and then shook his head. 'No,' he said adamantly without looking Pemberton in the eye.

Chapter Six

Pemberton decided not to interrogate Brother Luke any
further at this stage, neither did he wish him to view the
body for the purposes of identification. He preferred to
wait until he had more information about Lionel Cooper
and R. W. Mansell. In any case, it was doubtful whether
Luke would be able to make a positive identification.

Pemberton then questioned the helper-steward, John
Osbourne. He said he had been working until midnight at
the cocktail bar in Forseti's Hall and had returned to his
cabin about 12.15 this morning. He had walked from the
bar to his cabin with another steward, Simon Rogers,
who'd also been working late in Forseti's Hall. Simon's
cabin was three doors away from John's on G Deck and
John said Simon could confirm his story. They had used the
lifts down to G Deck and had not therefore been on F Deck
during that journey. John said he had not left his cabin until
7.30 this morning when he breakfasted in the crew's mess
before reporting for duty. He had not noticed anything
untoward during the return to his cabin. Pemberton
thanked him and released him, albeit making a mental note
to interview Simon as confirmation of his account.

And, of course, the post-mortem was expected this
afternoon.

Leaving the cinema and watching John steer the monk
away for lunch, Pemberton decided he and Lorraine
should now eat before resuming their investigation. They
had the entire afternoon ahead and, over a quick lunch,
could determine their course of action.

They opted for a light buffet-style meal in Vingolf's Hall, the huge conservatory-like dining room on the Lido Deck. After queuing to select their food they sought a table and were hailed by Rob and Helen, friends who shared Table 36 in the Folkvang Restaurant.

'Come and join us,' invited Helen whose table enjoyed superb sea views.

'Thanks,' said Pemberton even though he would have preferred to be alone with Lorraine. But now the bonus was that he could surreptitiously interview this couple and hopefully eliminate them! As they settled down with small talk over their meal and glasses of wine, Rob eventually asked, 'So what have you been up to this morning, Mark?'

'I'd better be straight with you both,' he smiled somewhat ruefully. 'We're investigating a sudden death on board. Both of us.'

'Good God! A real one, you mean?'

'Yes, the victim was found in his cabin this morning. The Captain has asked us to help with the investigation.'

'They kept that quiet! So are you in the police?'

'Yes, I'm a detective superintendent and Lorraine is a detective constable, both in North Yorkshire. The Captain knows that, which is why he asked us.'

'Rob, you can't!' said Helen suddenly. 'Not you as well . . .'

'Why not? It would keep me occupied for a while . . .'

'Does that mean you've links with the police?' smiled Mark. 'I've noticed we've all studiously avoided any reference to our professions at dinner!'

'I'm a retired forensic pathologist,' smiled Rob. 'For a time, I was a Principal Scientific Officer with the Home Office Forensic Service, based at the lab in Gooch Street North, that's in Birmingham. I retired about seven years ago but keep up to date by reading everything I can lay my hands on, especially all that wonderful new stuff on DNA, and I'm called in from time to time by West Midlands police in an advisory capacity. Even though I'm retired,

I rarely mention it on holiday, it prompts all manner of silly questions!'

'Don't I know it! So you can appreciate why neither Lorraine nor I talk about our work! Anyway, back to business. I can tell you I suspect this is murder, but we're not telling everyone. A passenger was stabbed. The post-mortem's this afternoon. I'm waiting for the summons by the ship's doctor.'

'Well, if you think I can help, I'd be very willing, it would only be an hour or so out of my holiday, but I don't want to get in anyone's way. Do you think the ship's doctor is up to it? Conducting the post-mortem on a murder victim, I mean.'

'It doesn't seem to bother him, he's done this kind of thing before, on routine sudden deaths but not a murder.'

'Would my experience be of any value? Both you and I know that performing a forensic post-mortem on a murder victim is vastly different from a routine examination into the cause of a sudden death.'

'I'm aware of that and yes, your input would be most valuable. I'd also like you to look at the murder scene, that's Cabin F150. I have the key, it's sealed now against any other person entering but the body has been removed to the mortuary. It's almost certain the victim was stabbed in the heart area and an artery probably severed, the aorta more than likely. The weapon was not left at the scene, I suspect it has been thrown overboard. Nonetheless, I'd like to know what sort of knife was used – two-sided, one-sided, long blade, short blade; was it wielded by a right-handed person or a left-handed one? Was extreme force used, or was it an unfortunate accident? A suicide even, with someone removing the weapon to make it look like murder? You know the sort of detail that's needed if I am to determine precisely what kind of weapon it was and how the murder was committed. Once we've answered those questions, the next will be who used the knife and how was it smuggled on board? Where was it hidden until it was used as the murder weapon? And where is it now?'

'Look, Mark, you know your job but I'm here if you need me. I don't want to be pushy and I don't want to poach on the ship doctor's territory or insult him by suggesting this case is out of his league.'

'If I need you, I'll use the tannoy system – but I don't know your surname!'

'Easton. Dr Robert Easton.'

'Right, thanks.' Pemberton recognized the name. During his tenure at the Birmingham laboratory, this man had been one of the leading forensic pathologists in England.

Helen Easton now interrupted. 'Right, you two. No more shop talk and discussions of post-mortems over lunch! So, Lorraine, what did you think of Trollstigheimen?'

The call to attend the post-mortem came immediately after lunch.

Because Pemberton had not been able to discuss his plans with Lorraine over lunch, it meant he must do so after witnessing the post-mortem. Meanwhile, he suggested Lorraine could begin questioning a random selection of people in Vingolf's Hall, taking their names to ensure they were crossed off the elimination lists. As some were elderly ladies and gentlemen, probably from refined backgrounds, she decided not to mention the word 'murder'. Instead she would say there had been an unexplained sudden death in Cabin F150, and then she would ask people about their movements and possible sightings or knowledge of odd events last night. She reckoned that would keep her busy in Vingolf's Hall until Mark returned; this popular place with its superb views of the restless waves was always busy.

Pemberton made his way down to the medical centre where Dr Andrews was waiting. The Captain had arrived too, but said he would not stay for the actual operation, merely wanting a progress report. Mark provided a brief summary, stressing his belief that Cooper was not the victim but that further enquiries into his role and disappearance were being made by his officers on shore. Captain Hansteen remained unconvinced the victim was someone other than the lawful occupant of F150 – he thought Cooper might have been using an alias and the fact that there were two passports bearing the same date and place of birth in two names supported that argument. The presence of another ship's cruise card was no proof either.

Pemberton admitted there were still some doubts in his mind but mentioned Dr Easton and the help he could provide both at the post-mortem and in a re-examination of the murder scene. Without hesitation, both Captain and doctor agreed – they wanted the best help available. Captain Hansteen said he must now leave as he had duties on the bridge, but would arrange for a tannoy call to be put out for Dr Easton to attend the medical centre immediately.

'Could you also ask a ship's photographer to attend?' Pemberton reminded him. 'Preferably Morag McMillan.'

When everyone was assembled in the mortuary and the necessary introductions had been completed, it was decided Dr Andrews would conduct the operation, with Rob Easton as observer but for consultation if required. Then the two doctors, each dressed in sterile operating gowns, and accompanied by Pemberton and Morag, moved into the operating theatre of the small mortuary.

'First,' said Dr Andrews, 'I will remove every item of clothing very carefully, all the time looking for evidence, especially that which might be in the turn-ups of trousers, pockets or even sewn into linings.'

'A good start,' beamed Rob Easton, relishing this challenge. 'Right, off we go.'

'Before we begin,' said Pemberton, 'I ought to state, for the official record, that I have doubts about this man's identity. The ship's records show that F150 was occupied by a Mr Lionel Cooper – ostensibly this man – but I have reason to believe Mr Cooper has been replaced by someone else.'

'But that's impossible . . .' began Dr Andrews.

'I am making the necessary enquiries,' stated Pemberton. 'Nonetheless, we must know how this man died. It is possible his name is R. W. Mansell. I found that name on personal effects in Cooper's cabin. At this point, I know nothing more of Mansell but I shall use that name when asking my questions.'

'In view of the doubt, I will record the post-mortem under both names, until the matter has been clarified,' said Dr Andrews. 'I will refer to this deceased as Cooper-Mansell, a male.'

'Fine,' said Pemberton. 'Let's hope we can soon get a positive identification.'

As Dr Andrews started his work, he spoke into a tiny microphone clipped to his gown; this formed a direct link with his secretary who would record his words and then prepare her files. Wearing lightweight rubber gloves, Dr Andrews began by carefully removing the clothing item by item and, with advice from Easton, checking each for evidence.

Nothing was found; Pemberton's earlier search had been thorough. Both he and Dr Easton declined to handle the clothing in case the items were later required on shore for DNA testing. Each piece was then stored in a separate plastic bag and labelled. Even if the murderer was identified on board, it would be necessary to retain the available evidence if a prosecution was to follow. Prior to the clothing being stored, the locations of bloodstains were noted and photographed, with samples being retained for analysis. Dr Easton advised that the blood samples be examined to establish more evidence about those present at the time of death. A control sample of the victim's blood was also required to make that comparison. Andrews said that could be done.

At this stage, the body had not been washed or cleaned as this would have destroyed valuable evidence, and so the operation got under way with Dr Andrews showing his skills as a surgeon, Dr Easton watching and commenting on the forensic elements with Pemberton looking on. After being visually examined back and front, the body was described as that of a white-skinned adult male, five feet ten inches (178 cm) tall and of average build. His age was estimated to be around fifty, he had grey hair neatly trimmed and thinning on the crown and temples, grey eyes and good natural teeth. He was clean shaven and not wearing spectacles or any kind of jewellery, not even a ring on his finger, although he had an expensive Longines watch which was showing the correct time. His dead weight was not specified but the body was described as being well nourished and maintained, clean and with no signs of violence other than the stab wound in the chest. There was some bruising around the entry point and lots of recently clotted blood, making it difficult to see the entry hole or holes. Any hole would be tiny, not because the weapon had been small but because the flesh and skin would naturally stretch as the knife went in, then close once it had been removed. Removal of a knife from a deep stab wound is often very difficult due to the suction of the flesh, and so a twisting movement is usually necessary. That would be revealed in the appearance of the wound or wounds – twisting movements opened the flesh but with little time for blood to spurt out.

'I believe there was just one strike of the knife,' observed Rob Easton. 'It is clear the shirt was not pierced by the murder weapon. I would say it was open to the chest at the time of the stabbing. That makes me wonder why. Was he merely too hot in his cabin, or was he entertaining someone? Whatever the reason, the shirt was on him at the time of death, it was not replaced afterwards. That would have been too difficult and messy. It seems to have been closed and the buttons fastened after death, perhaps to staunch the blood or conceal the wound.'

'He has cut marks on both hands.' Pemberton felt he should mention this. 'You can just see them beneath the clotted blood.'

'Classic defence wounds,' said Easton. ' In murder cases, or serious wounding, the victim invariably tries to defend himself or herself, often with bare hands. With just a single wound, it seems he tried to grab the knife.'

'So would the killer be heavily bloodstained?' asked Pemberton of Easton.

'Not especially heavily, not much blood would come from this wound, but yes, there would be staining on the killer's hands and perhaps his clothes. It would show where his hands and fingers came into contact with the buttons and flowing blood, and I'd venture a guess that if he wore a long-sleeved garment, the cuffs might also be stained. It seems odd, however, that he took the time and trouble to fasten the shirt buttons.'

'There were no bloodstains in the bathroom,' Pemberton noted.

'The killer could have rinsed his hands and lower arms and flushed away the stains but that would show in a scientific analysis. If he was bothered enough to fasten those buttons, he might have taken time to remove other evidence.'

'So he could have cleaned himself in the cabin?'

'Superficially, yes. He could probably hide the stains on his clothing until he returned to his own cabin just by rolling up his sleeves – that's if he wore them long. I say he but, of course, I am not ruling out a female killer.'

The precise nature of the stab wound would become evident once the chest cavity had been opened and layers of skin and flesh peeled off, but first the scalp and face must be cut and peeled back, and the skull sawn open to examine the brain. Then would follow a deep cut of the flesh from the neck down to the groin with the flesh being peeled back and all the innards being examined in detail with special emphasis being placed upon the heart and the vessels surrounding it. This was to decide whether or not death was from any cause other than the apparent stabbing. Morag, unfazed by the scene being revealed before her, continued with her photography as the operation continued, sometimes being directed by either of the two doctors.

'There is a knife wound near the heart,' said Dr Andrews eventually. 'Deep enough to slice through the aorta, and that is almost certainly the cause of death. There is a lot of blood in the chest cavity too.'

'If it's possible, I need to know the length of the blade which caused the death,' said Pemberton. 'And whether it was two-sided, or any other information.'

'I think this is for you,' said Dr Andrews, standing back so that Easton could conduct that examination.

'Thanks,' said Easton. 'I must stress that giving a precise measurement and description of the blade is difficult. Flesh does not behave like clay or plasticine, it doesn't stay in the same position when it's cut; it tries to return to normal once the foreign body has been removed, as it has in this case, but I'll do my best.'

With the relevant parts of the chest cavity, heart and skin fully exposed he studied the corpse for a long time, peering very close and at times moving portions of flesh, lungs and innards to gain a better view. He carried out a running commentary which was picked up by Dr Andrews' microphone, and told them that a knife with two sharp edges would produce acute angles in a deep stab wound whereas one like a sheath knife, with only one sharp edge, would produce a deep wound with one angle acute and the other blunt. A knife with a single serrated edge would tear the flesh and skin. Then he dug deep into the body, separated the dead flesh near the wound and introduced a small ruler provided by Dr Andrews.

'In my opinion, and it is an opinion not a guaranteed fact, the wound which caused this man's death was caused by a knife with a blade about five inches long, or thirteen centimetres. I'd say at its widest point it was about an inch wide, near the hilt that would be – or two and a half centimetres, and narrowing towards the point. And it had one serrated edge, clearly very sharp. That is not in doubt.'

'So we can rule out a sword, a bayonet or a double-sided blade like a stiletto?' said Dr Andrews.

'Yes, we're thinking of something more like a vegetable knife,' confirmed Rob Easton. 'The sort you might use to slice lemons or tomatoes.'

'A chef's knife?' queried Pemberton. 'They're often used by attackers during Saturday night brawls, sales are not restricted like flick knives and they can be legally bought almost anywhere. A lot of domestic stabbings are done with kitchen knives, some with smooth blades and others with serrated edges.'

'They'd never get a knife past our security systems,' said Andrews. 'Every person, and all their luggage, is electronically scanned before they come on board. You'd have difficulty getting a pair of scissors or a Swiss army knife on to this ship without permission.'

'Would that apply to a knife destined for the galley?' asked Pemberton. 'I'd like to bet your galley is full of chef's knives, in all sorts of sizes, and all sharpened to perfection. Razor sharp as a good chef's knife should be. And remember, we talked of disposal of the murder weapon. Where did it come from and where is it now? Was it taken from the galley at some time before midnight – even on another day – and returned afterwards? Can you think of a better place to obtain a murder weapon, and then conceal it! So how good is the security of the galley, Dr Andrews?'

'You'll have to ask the head chef about that! So you're not suggesting a member of the crew did this, are you?'

'I'm not suggesting anything,' said Pemberton. 'After all, several passengers have already visited the galley. It's one of the highlights of any cruise. I wonder if someone might have stolen a knife during one of those visits? It's a possibility.'

'I can't say I like the idea of a murder weapon being used to kill someone and then being returned and used for food preparation in our galley!' said Dr Andrews.

'Then my guess is that it will have been sterilized. The galley in this ship, and all its equipment, is meticulously clean at all times,' smiled Dr Easton wickedly. 'Even my former colleagues might have difficulty tracing human blood on such a well-cleaned weapon!'

'All of which makes it very difficult, even impossible, to identify it as the murder weapon,' said Pemberton. 'Or it might have been thrown overboard. But we must do our best to find it, or to find someone with access to it.'

'The killer might still have it in his possession,' added Rob Easton. 'Because he's the murderer, he might feel threatened, particularly if he's likely to be exposed. He might want to protect himself against arrest, which means he might not have disposed of that knife. And that means he is still very dangerous.'

'A fair point, thanks for the warning. Now, Rob, I have some other questions while we're all here.'

'Yes?'

'First, I believe you and Helen had a tour of the galley? Would you accept that a chef's knife, with a serrated blade, might be the murder weapon?'

'Yes, it's very likely. I can't be more specific.'

'So could anyone steal such a knife during one of those organized tours?'

'A determined thief will steal anything, Mark. Yes, it's possible. And if he did so, then it suggests a strong degree of premeditation, a planned killing.'

'That makes sense. Now, back to the galley. Can you remember the names of the others who went around with you? I need to talk to them.'

'The monk and his companion were in our party, I remember seeing them, but I can't recall the names of the others. I think I could point them out to you, if any of them happened to walk by while I was with you! Maybe I could spot one or two in the restaurant tonight? Or on other parts of the ship?'

'Let's hope so. Give me a nudge if you do. And I mustn't ignore the crew who work in the galley. Now, can you suggest how the blow was struck? I got the impression it was very deep, it must have been a powerful thrust to reach the heart area, it would have to pass through skin and flesh even if it missed the shirt.'

'It was a powerful strike – so what do you read into that, Mark?'

'That the victim could not back away from the attack?'

'Right, and you told me he was found on the bed?'

'Yes, with bloodstains on the wall and floor.'

'Almost certainly he was stabbed on his bed, by someone close to the upper body. The wound's angle suggests that – as the blade entered while horizontal but at an angle, from left to right. If he was lying on his bed, I'd say the killer was standing or kneeling on his left, close to his head, and the fatal blow struck from that position. It suggests the killer is right-handed. That is supported by the angle of the wound.'

'So he must have known his assailant? To let him get so close?'

'Yes, and that tallies with the fact he let his assailant into the room late at night. You said the room had not been forcibly entered.'

'True. Right, thanks, both of you,' said Pemberton. 'I've learned a lot. Now, I must continue with my enquiries, but first, Rob, I'd like you to see the scene of the crime and if you need to see a photo of the deceased on the bed in the position he was found, then I can arrange it.'

'Thanks, we'll see how things go. So lead the way.'

'Will you need me there again?' asked Morag.

'We might, if I see something that's not already been noted,' said Rob Easton.

Leaving Dr Andrews to deal with the body and to preserve it by refrigeration for possible future examination, they returned to F Deck where Pemberton admitted them into F150. Standing in the corridor, they allowed Rob Easton to examine the room before entering. He asked one or two questions which Pemberton answered, such as the significance of the water heater and luggage which might belong to two men instead of just one occupant.

Then he said, 'Fine. I think you've got it right, Mark. Those blood marks on the wall and bedding correspond with your theories – even though his shirt, and the natural closure of the wound once the knife was removed, must have stemmed some of the spurting blood, a few drops obviously got through. If you look carefully at those on the wall, I think some were made by the victim's bloodstained hands, in his dying moments perhaps, rather than by spurts of blood. It looks as if he was trying to struggle on to his feet, clutching at the wall for help – and failing. Without the ability to take fingerprints, we can't be sure whether they were made by him or his assailant – his assailant might have used the wall as a prop to get off the bed after the deed, that's always a possibility.'

'You've already said the assailant might be blood-stained?'

'Some do get stained, others don't, Mark. If this character did, then it might be restricted to that part of the body nearest the dagger, the hands and lower arms, in other words. Or sleeves.'

'There are several launderettes on board, he could already have washed any bloodstains out, but he would still have to run the gauntlet of getting from here to the nearest launderette or to his own cabin, with bloodstains on him. That would surely attract unwelcome attention.'

'It depends whether the stains were large enough for people to notice them. Stains on one cuff could be concealed with the other hand perhaps, or even by rolling up the sleeves. Hidden long enough to get into the security of his own cabin. And yes, a launderette could wash them out sufficiently to deceive the naked eye but not to defeat a scientific test. And don't forget, Mark, unwanted things are easily disposed of here – you throw them into the sea. It doesn't take long to remove a bloodstained shirt or jumper and replace it with a clean one.'

'I'm aware of that but with crew members and passengers always around the place, and security patrols at night

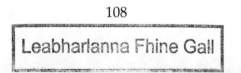

with the added benefit of closed-circuit cameras, anyone doing something dodgy would be spotted.'

'Perhaps they have been?' smiled Rob. 'And you aren't aware of it yet?'

'That's one of the questions we'll be asking everyone,' returned Pemberton. 'I'll get the security team to check their tapes for last night but if they're anything like the usual films on CCTV, they'll be fuzzy and indistinct in black and white, certainly not good enough to identify anyone.'

'But enough to tell you that someone – man, woman, big, little or whatever – had been around at the material time, in circumstances of some suspicion? Like being close to the murder scene, or apparently throwing something overboard.'

'Sure. Now, Rob, this luggage is as we found it,' and Pemberton explained his theory about it belonging to two men. He outlined his reasons, listing the contents of the cases and bags.

'You said earlier you felt the dead man is not the true occupant of the cabin?'

'Right. I think the occupant – Lionel Cooper – has been killed or kidnapped in Norway, and our deceased is an interloper.' And he gave his reasons.

'Well, I must say I agree with you, Mark,' said Rob. 'This looks like one man's luggage packed and ready to be removed, the other's containing very little stuff, also ready to move out quickly. It would support your theory. But why would anyone do that?'

'That's what I need to find out, I need a motive!'

'Well, if it's any consolation, I think you're on the right track. Do you need me any more right now?'

'Not immediately, thanks, but I might want to pick your brains later.'

'You mentioned photos of the scene with the deceased on the bed. I'd like to see them – it would be useful to know the position of the body before it was removed, and pics of the cabin at the time would help.'

'I'll arrange that.' Morag had been silently recording the progress. 'I think there are copies in the incident room.'

'There are,' Pemberton confirmed. 'I'll make sure you see them, Rob.'

'Excellent. So what are your plans now, Mark?'

'I've got my office on shore checking passengers and crew for previous convictions and other related matters which might interest us, and they're also checking as far as possible the backgrounds of Lionel Cooper, R. W. Mansell and Brother Luke. I've asked them to contact the Norwegian police too, to see if Cooper's body has been found, and the ship is being searched for anyone who might be hiding. Now, of course, in view of the post-mortem result, I need to check with the galley to see whether any of their knives have gone missing and if so, when. And by whom! I want to see the overnight security camera shots too. Meanwhile, Lorraine and I will be quizzing passengers.'

'I'll keep my ears and eyes open,' smiled Rob. 'One never knows what one might overhear during an unguarded conversation. And if I have any bright ideas about all this, I'll let you know. See you at dinner?'

'I'll be there,' smiled Pemberton, thinking dinner time seemed an eternity away. 'Now I must find Lorraine to see how she's progressed.'

Pemberton found Lorraine still in Vingolf's Hall. Helen Easton had gone to her cabin for an afternoon nap, which left Lorraine free to chat with others who remained. She went from table to table, introduced herself as a detective and said she was investigating, on behalf of the Captain, the sudden death of a passenger in a cabin on F Deck.

As she moved patiently among the passengers with her questions about where they had been between midnight and half past nine this morning, and whether they had noticed anything untoward or suspicious during the night, she was recording their names and cabin numbers so they could be eliminated. Lorraine wondered about the advisability of concealing the truth in this manner but did consider it might be wise when coping with more than 2000 people in such a confined space. She had no wish to start a state of panic on board – panic was like a disease, it could spread with dramatic speed and awful results. And, of course, she was aware that any of the people she interviewed could be the killer – she was acutely aware that she could be in danger.

As Pemberton entered the vast hall, he noticed Lorraine talking to a couple at one of the tables but did not intrude; he was prepared to wait until she had concluded her interview, and then he and she could enjoy a cup of tea and a cake together. He went to the self-service counter, organized a tray for two and gathered his requirements, then headed for a table near the window. She spotted him and waved to acknowledge his presence, then joined him a few minutes later.

'So how's it going?' was his first question.

'People are willing to chat and help, but I've got no useful information out of them.' She sipped her tea. 'Nothing to point towards a suspect, but everyone has said they'll keep their ears and eyes open, and let me know if anything turns up. I've no prime suspects or good witnesses, if that's what you're hoping. How about you?'

He told her about the outcome of the post-mortem and of Rob Easton's contribution, saying he was heading next for the galley. He knew from the map of the ship that a single galley, staffed by dozens of crew members, served both dining rooms, but was its security sufficiently good to notice the absence of one knife? He also told her about his intention of checking the overnight security tapes, particularly the one for F Deck.

'He confirmed that the assailant would be bloodstained, especially on his hands and arms or that his clothing might be,' he reminded her. 'The cuffs of his sleeves for example, so if you're questioning anyone who used any of the launderettes after, say, 12.30 this morning and before 8.30, they might have noticed someone washing bloodstained clothes.'

'We were up until one o'clock ourselves,' she reminded him. 'We never noticed anything out of the ordinary on our way back to the cabin.'

'But we weren't anywhere near the launderettes, or on F Deck, although we did use the lifts and staircases, and passed through several public areas. We need to find people who were up later, and using those places, F Deck in particular.'

'There's no reason for anyone to go down to F Deck at night, Mark, except to their cabins. There are no public rooms down there, apart from reception.'

'That's the problem, it'll make it difficult to us to find witnesses and reception isn't staffed right through the night either. So my next task is to go back to the incident room and update Erika. I'll tell her Dr Easton wants to see the photos of the murder scene and ask her to obtain the F Deck tapes for us, then while she's doing that, I'll call at the galley. We can see about viewing the overnight security tapes later.'

'And I'll continue to interview people up here. I'm attracting some interest from the curious, I'm sure they think I'm doing some kind of survey. If I give you a list of the names I've spoken to, Erika can cross them off the list – as being interviewed that is, not eliminated!'

'We've a long way to go, so when shall we meet?' He glanced at his watch. 'How about 5.30 back at our cabin? I reckon we'll have earned ourselves a drink or two by then!'

In the incident room, Erika confirmed she had arranged to have last night's security tapes made available, with due emphasis on the one featuring F Deck, and she would mark Lorraine's interviews on the list of names on her pin-board. Already, the post-mortem results, in all their gory detail, had been emailed from the medical centre and so she had found enough to occupy her. Pemberton asked if she could contact reception to see whether any phone calls had been made from F150 during the previous night.

'I need to know if anyone was called to the cabin,' he said. 'People like friends, crew even. Is that possible? To find out if calls were made and if so, to whom? And the time?'

'I'm not sure internal calls can be traced. I'll find out and let you know later.'

Pemberton dictated a short account for the file, then said he was heading for the galley. It was on E Deck and occupied more space than both the main restaurants combined and comprised row upon row of glistening stainless steel units, wooden work surfaces, sinks, cupboards, refrigerators and storage space, all with air-conditioning. Everything was spotless, everything had its place and everyone who worked there knew the importance of efficiency, scrupulous cleanliness and an enduring rapport between all the staff. Temperamental outbursts were not tolerated, however intense the pressure. As Pemberton entered, the debris from lunch was being dealt with, afternoon tea with its freshly made cakes and biscuits was under preparation near the centre, while across to his right work was already starting on preparations for dinner.

The galley produced more than 8000 meals every day – breakfast, lunch, tea and dinner with snacks available around the clock. All were to the standard of the best hotels and yet there was an air of calm efficiency with everyone knowing precisely what he or she was supposed to be doing. What appeared to be hundreds of white-clad staff in immaculate overalls were at work in almost total silence, save for the clatter of crockery and utensils, and the whirring of mixers and washing-up machines.

As he entered through the door used by the waiters coming into the Folkvang Restaurant, a young woman of oriental appearance approached him. 'I very sorry, sir, but galley not open to passengers.'

'I know, but I wish to speak to the head chef, please. It is most important. I am Detective Superintendent Pemberton.'

'A policeman?'

'Yes.'

'One moment please, wait here.'

She disappeared behind a barrier of stainless steel units and after a couple of minutes returned with a fair-haired man wearing a chef's tall white hat and crisp white overall. He would be in his mid-forties, clean-shaven and surprisingly calm. Pemberton had always thought chefs must lead a frenetic life but this man looked cool and relaxed.

The girl bowed ever so slightly after saying, 'This is Ian McAllen, the head chef,' and departed.

'Detective Superintendent Pemberton,' he introduced himself. 'I am investigating a death on board, under the command of the Captain.'

'Ah yes, he called all senior crew members for a meeting and told us. I know it's a murder enquiry. You'd better come into my office.'

McAllen led the way into a small but neat office, offered Pemberton a chair and a cup of tea from a pot already on his desk. Pemberton accepted.

'So, Superintendent, how can I help?'

After outlining the circumstances of the death, Pemberton said, 'We are convinced the murder weapon was a knife. Judging by the nature of the wound, we believe it was a kitchen knife with a serrated edge and a blade about five inches long.'

'Good grief, you mean the killer took it from here?'

'That's what I need to find out. I understand it is virtually impossible for a passenger or crew member to smuggle a knife, or any kind of weapon such as a firearm, on to the ship. Your security inspections cater for luggage as well as people.'

'We have very sophisticated means of searching, yes, using modern electronics and radar systems. So what else can you tell me about the knife?'

'It was obviously very sharp as modern knives tend to be. Almost certainly it has a five-inch blade, blunt on one side, and widening to almost an inch where it joins the hilt. And the cutting edge was serrated.'

'It certainly sounds like the type of knife we might use. Not difficult to conceal up a sleeve either – or in a sock!'

'So would you know if one was missing from here? Or had been removed temporarily? And replaced?'

'Almost certainly not, Mr Pemberton. I have no idea how many knives there are in the galley, the place is full of them. There are sets for most of our working surfaces, suspended from hooks. We don't store them in wooden blocks – that's ruinous to good blades. And the chefs have their own personal knives – they guard them and care for them as if they were the crown jewels! In here, knives are either in use, being cleaned or sharpened all the time – hundreds of knives of all kinds, not merely dozens.'

'A real armoury! Is it possible for anyone to smuggle one out of here?'

'If I said no, I'd be lying, even if I hope it would never happen. As I said, all my staff take a great care of, and deep pride in, all their utensils, the tools of their trade, but, yes, a waiter could smuggle a knife of some kind out on the tray which carries a meal . . . under a serviette perhaps or even up his sleeve, and I suppose other crew members, like cleaners, food preparers, butchers, washers-up and others could get one out of here if they were really determined and were familiar with our routine.'

'So there is no daily inventory check on them?'

'Sadly, no. Bearing in mind that chefs look after their own, we don't count the knives every day. I'm sure some get thrown out with waste food and vegetables too – inadvertently, of course, to be lost forever in our waste disposal unit.'

'And could a passenger steal one?'

'During their official tours, you mean?'

'They'd not be allowed in at other times, would they?'

'Certainly not. If one tried to get in other than during an official tour, someone would know. I'd say that was impossible. But when passengers are admitted, the crew members who work here keep them under close supervision, that is one of our priorities. You'd be amazed at what some try to do, anything from pinching an apple to trying to purloin a bottle of best claret. As I said, most of our official-issue knives are up on hooks, well away from thieving hands, but inevitably some are vulnerable, particularly during busy periods. So yes, a determined passenger could steal a knife from here – but probably not from a chef's personal set. I have to admit I cannot rule out theft.'

'But you can't tell me whether this has happened during this cruise? Or even since midnight last night?'

'Sorry, it's impossible. I just do not know, and there is no way of finding out. If a chef lost a knife, he or she would make a fusss and I'm sure we'd know about it, but if it was one of the ship's official stock, I doubt if we'd know.'

'Thank you – at least I know the murder weapon *could* have been a knife from here. At some stage too, I will need to question all your staff as to their whereabouts between midnight and half past eight this morning.'

'I could save you a lot of time by providing a list of those who were working late, those in here all night and those who were having a break during those times.'

'Thanks, then we can check them against our master lists.' They agreed that the head chef would email his lists to Erika.

Then Pemberton was taken on a quick tour of the galley where he examined all the storage points for knives and noted the locations of each chef's personal set. He agreed it would be difficult for a thief to remove one from anywhere – but not impossible. He was still in the head chef's office and about to leave when the phone rang.

'McAllen,' responded the chef, listening and then saying, 'Yes, he is here, Erika.' A pause, and then he said, 'Sure, right.

'That was Erika, from the Captain's office, Mr Pemberton, she thought she might catch you here. There is an urgent email from your office in Rainesbury. She thinks you should see it straight away.'

Chapter Seven

Paul Larkin had emailed the results from the first search of CRO records. A secondary search would be conducted through the auspices of Interpol and Europol, with particular emphasis on those who were not resident in the UK. Further checks would also be made through the Police National Computer to check for names considered to be 'of interest to the police' even though the persons concerned had no convictions. The names of all passengers and crew, even natives of foreign countries, had been fed into the computer and the results had been swift. An exercise which once would have taken days or even weeks had now been completed in minutes.

'Mr Larkin has highlighted those of immediate interest.' Erika handed over a long printout. 'He thought you would want to have this information immediately although he says he has no photographs of the people referred to. They can be obtained if you require them.'

Pemberton settled down to read the first list; it comprised the ship's own complete manifest, or schedule of passengers. It was in alphabetical order but without cabin numbers or complete home addresses. It was now endorsed with CRO's additions where appropriate. Of the passengers, three men and one woman were shown to have convictions for violence; three had used knives against their victims and the fourth had been found guilty of using a firearm with intent to endanger life.

Pemberton made a note of those names; in view of the gravity of their convictions, their photographs would be in police records. It was a good beginning because it provided four possible suspects whose movements must be traced. He noted that several others had convictions for minor offences such as careless driving, shoplifting, burglary, theft and drinking alcohol on licensed premises outside permitted hours but none of those concerned him at this stage.

Those in whom he was now deeply interested – and who were currently on board the *Ringhorn* – were:

1. John William Hume, aged thirty-seven, of Manchester – a self-employed bricklayer/window cleaner, unmarried, convicted of wounding a prostitute who had stolen his wallet while he was in her flat. He had used one of her kitchen knives. The crime had occurred five years ago and he had been sentenced to two years' imprisonment. He had previous convictions for assault, theft and burglary but no further criminal record since being imprisoned for the stabbing.

2. David Charles Roberts, aged forty-nine, of Nottingham – an electrical appliance retailer with a shop near the town centre. Married. He was convicted of shooting at a youth he found in the yard at the rear of his shop in the early hours of the morning. The shot, from a .22 pistol, had missed but Roberts was given a suspended sentence of two years. He was also found guilty of possessing a firearm without a certificate. The incident happened four years ago. Roberts had no previous convictions and in mitigation the court heard that his premises had been a regular target for burglars and thieves in spite of the various security measures he had installed. He had no convictions since that incident.

3. Ian Taylor, aged twenty-nine, from Milton Keynes – a greetings card salesman. Unmarried. Convicted of wounding a man in a brawl outside a club, he had used a knife. The incident had occurred six years ago and he had been sentenced to eighteen months' imprisonment. He had previous convictions for assault, theft, criminal damage and arson. Since that crime, he had been charged and convicted

of causing death by dangerous driving. No details of that offence were given.

4. Geraldine May Norris, aged forty-two, from Swansea – married and part-time supermarket checkout assistant. Attacked a female neighbour with a carving knife in a dispute when she thought the neighbour was trying to seduce her husband. Sentenced to probation for two years. No previous convictions and none since.

Pemberton explained to Erika that when a murder investigation team received this kind of intelligence, with convicted people whose crimes closely matched the one under investigation, then those people were immediately regarded as suspects, i.e. they were 'in the frame' and would remain so until formally eliminated. All four must be interviewed without delay and asked to explain their whereabouts at the material time, if possible with proof. Personal assurance alone was rarely sufficient although much depended upon what they stated during the interview.

'They'll complain about the police harassing them because of their past records, saying we never let convicted people live down their past, but we've a job to do. You'll see from these records that some are regular offenders. That says a lot about them and it must always be borne in mind when we are accused of harassing them – we know a leopard never changes its spots, as they say. Interviewing them is my next job, so can you obtain their cabin numbers for me? And their home addresses?'

'Yes, no problem. They'll be in our records.'

'Good. I need to know if any live near the victim or near Lionel Cooper or could have had any contact with those men or with Brother Luke. You supplied your details of Luke to Paul, didn't you?'

'Yes, as much as we've got. So do you want me to call them in for interview? Via the tannoy?'

'I might ask them to meet me somewhere, preferably not in here, but only if I can't track them down elsewhere. I'd like to see where their cabins are in relation to that used by the victim and I need to know how long it might take, and which route would be taken, to walk or run from one to the other.'

'If one of them is the killer, won't it be dangerous, going into a cabin alone? They might still have the knife. I can give you their cabin numbers and a map of the layout of the ship, if that will help.'

'It will help, but I had no intention of going into the cabins alone – if I go I'll take someone with me. But thanks for the thought.'

And so, from the ship's own computerized manifest, she produced their cabin numbers and personal details which had been supplied when making the reservations, along with a quarto-sized file of deck plans, showing all public places, every cabin with its number, the offices on board and crew's quarters. It would be of enormous help when questioning people's movements.

'Right, thanks, I'll go and find Lorraine and then start knocking on doors.'

'When would you like to see the security tapes?' she asked. 'I've arranged for them to be ready whenever you need them. We can fast-forward them to save looking through hours and hours in times which don't apply and our security staff will help too, they are familiar with interpreting them.'

He paused, his mind racing over the benefits of seeing the films at this stage of the enquiry, then said, 'Yes, right, I'll see them now, they might contain one or other of our four suspects. I might recognize him or her. It's amazing how a person's gait or the way they hold their hands or head helps in identifying them. And their clothes of course, bearing in mind that people change their clothes! I might need more viewings, depending upon what the pictures reveal.'

'They're in our security office along the corridor, together with a monitor,' she said, and so he allowed her to lead the way, locking the door of the incident room as they left. A member of the security staff was present and had been primed to expect such a visit and so tapes from the cameras supervising F Deck were already to hand. Each had already been examined by the security personnel who had acted as filters, identifying those tapes of particular interest. This was part of their daily routine, and so those covering the period from midnight until 9.30 this morning were now awaiting Pemberton's attention. There were a dozen cameras for each deck, covering the port side, starboard side and central aisles of each of the four component parts of a deck, staircases 1, 2 and 3 along with the nearby lifts marking the divisions. And there were thirteen decks. More than 150 cameras in total. They were neatly concealed at strategic sites and would not be readily noticed by the passengers, but they operated on an automatic sweeping motion, constantly moving to cover as wide a range as possible. By doing so, of course, they could miss taking important pictures – especially if someone knew how to avoid the direction of the lenses. That might be the situation so far as the crew was concerned – though not most of the passengers.

Pemberton began with the tape covering F Deck in the vicinity of F150 and the reception area. The tapes contained a timing mechanism and displayed the relevant date and time. At midnight, the corridor outside F150 was clearly deserted, then at 12.32 he saw the distinctive figures of Brother Luke and his companion heading the same way, identified because of the wheelchair, dark suit, beard and clerical collar. They paused outside F152 as the companion used the cruise card to unlock the door, then the monk entered, took back his card, and allowed the door to swing shut behind him. But Pemberton was surprised when the companion did not enter his own cabin. He paused for a moment, apparently listening to see if the monk needed any further help, and then turned on his heel and retraced his steps. The camera moved away from him before he vanished and so Pemberton had no idea whether he had entered another cabin on that deck or gone to another area of the ship. Perhaps he had returned to Hraevelg's Hall for another viewing of the midnight sun? Or for a final drink?

Or to meet someone? That action meant the time of the victim's death would have to be reviewed – and films for all the decks would have to be examined to see if the fellow made a reappearance in any other area. And, of course, this camera might have picked up his return to F150. On the other hand it could have missed him completely due to its ranging lens.

And then there was another surprise. At 12.35 a woman walked from fore to aft and let herself into F138. There was insufficient clarity to recognize her facial features but judging by her height in relation to the cabin doors, she was a small rather dumpy woman wearing a T-shirt and light jeans. The black-and-white film did not show her colouring but her hairstyle reminded him of the beehive fashions of the 1960s. As she walked, he noticed her distinctive waddling style, perhaps due to a problem with her legs. Surely she must have seen Mansell in the corridor? The times alone and directions they had taken suggested they must have passed one another at some point. Pemberton made a note to talk to her.

Even allowing for the fact that some films could be omitted, at least in the first instance, it looked like being a long session of viewing.

One benefit was that the films showed people entering their F Deck cabins between midnight and 9.30, and clearly distinguished between port and starboard, as well the inner cabins. Numbers on the cabin doors were very legible and so their occupants could be quizzed, as they might have seen or heard something out of the ordinary. One problem was that, apart from reception and Odin's Garden, F Deck did not have any public areas. It largely comprised cabins which suggested that once their occupants were inside, they would not hear or see anything.

Nonetheless, Pemberton noted those cabin numbers and watched the film, speeded up during blank periods, until it showed 9.30 a.m. He was aware that the monk had noticed the 'Do Not Disturb' sign at 8.30 but the killer could have been inside while the notice was on display.

The body had not been found until an hour after Brother Luke had left. At least he now had the numbers of some doors upon which to knock. Lacking sufficient time to view every film for every deck at this stage, he must try to ascertain the destination of Brother Luke's companion after he had escorted the monk to his cabin. The security staff, more experienced than he in the interpretation of these films, could do that for him. He turned to the attendant, whose name was Ian Hadfield.

'Ian, your staff have done a good job eliminating hours of stuff that's of no value, but I've got some good information from this section,' he said. 'Cabin numbers to check and so on. Now I need to go back a little.' And he asked Ian to rewind the film until it showed Brother Luke at his cabin door. When it showed his companion hesitating outside the monk's cabin, and then walking back the way he had come, he halted it.

'That man outside the monk's cabin is our victim. He was killed sometime between then and 9.30 this morning. He was killed in his cabin, that is not in doubt. It happened sometime before 9.30 and probably before 8.30. So when did he return to his cabin? It's vital I establish that, and I need to know whether anyone was with him. We know the monk saw the "Do Not Disturb" sign about 8.30 but the killer could still have been inside. Highly unlikely but not impossible. We can almost certainly say the victim died sometime after 12.32 but before 8.30, assuming the killer placed the sign on the door as he left. So where was Mansell and who was he with between 12.32 and the time of his death? That's where I need your help to scan all the decks. Will your cameras show where he went after leaving Brother Luke?'

'Not necessarily, he might have been out of camera shot for some of the time. That's always the case, our cameras operate in a sweeping motion, they don't record everything.'

'I appreciate that but there's a fair chance he might have been caught at more than one location. I realize he's not easily identifiable but can you do that check for me? You know the layout of the ship and locations of the cameras, and how to interpret the films.'

'Sure, we can tell a lot from them. It helps having seen the victim.'

'Great. I'd like a note of each place he was spotted, such as entering or leaving a lift, in one of the bars, entering another cabin ... anything at all, along with the precise time. When retracing his movements back to his cabin, I need to know who he was with, or if he was alone. And I need to know whether he met anyone else away from his cabin, and if so, who and where.'

'It will give me something interesting to do!' smiled Ian. 'So yes, I'll do my best.'

'While you're examining the films, I also need to know if anyone tossed anything overboard – clothing, a knife, anything else. That would be after 12.32 and probably before 9.30 this morning, although it might have been later. Unless there is any other place things can he hidden?'

'Sure, I can do all that in one go. Leave it with me, Mr Pemberton.'

Pemberton was now free to find Lorraine who would probably still be in Vingolf's Hall, and then try to locate the first of his four suspects. It would not be easy finding them at this time of day; very few people would be in their cabins, particularly as afternoon tea was being served. Vingolf's Hall, with its massive conservatory appearance, was one of the most popular venues although tea was also served elsewhere. It meant people would be scattered throughout the huge ship, resting, taking tea, playing sport, visiting the gym, sleeping, sunbathing, swimming ... doing all sorts and making it almost impossible to locate anyone. As expected, he found Lorraine in Vingolf's Hall where she was sitting at a table and talking to four middle-aged people, two men and two women; he caught her attention and settled on a nearby chair to await her. After three or four minutes she joined him.

'Any luck?' he asked.

'Still nothing.' She shook her head. 'I've interviewed dozens of people but no one can help, no one heard anything or saw anything out of the ordinary. One problem is that not many have cabins near Brother Luke's so there's no reason to go down to F Deck in the early hours of the morning. If passengers urgently want anything, all they have to do is pick up the telephone, especially when reception is closed. I did find one couple with a cabin on F Deck but they attended the theatre and went straight to their cabin afterwards, they were in bed before midnight and never heard or saw anything out of the ordinary.'

He told her about the woman caught on film entering F138 at 12.35 and said she must be interviewed – at this stage, he had not yet obtained her name. That cabin was only four doors away from F150, all the even numbers being on the port side. F140 was an inside cabin, not one of the outside sequence which included F150 and F138. Then he told her about his four prime suspects.

'I don't think you should enter any of their cabins alone,' she cautioned. 'If one of them is the killer, he – or she – might still have the knife.'

'You're the second person to warn me! But that's why I'm here, to ask you to accompany me.'

'Thanks a million, Mark! Look, I know you like to interview people in their natural habitat, but these are all anonymous cabins, so why don't you get them to meet you in a public place? Somewhere like the library or one of the gardens. I'd be happier doing that – they could meet you in the reception area, Odin's Garden is very suitable. It's easy to find and is always open. So why not put a personal message over the tannoy?'

'Whichever way I do it, I will be recognized thereafter,' he said. 'If the killer doesn't get me in his cabin, he could wait for me elsewhere – from the moment I interview him, I'll be a target.'

'Don't say that . . .'

'Well, it's true. That's why it's so important to get this thing sorted out as quickly as we can. All right, I appreciate your concern so I'll use the tannoy system and get them to meet me in Odin's Garden. I want you there too, to know them for the future and hear what they say. Right, let's start with John William Hume. We can get a cup of tea while we're waiting for him.'

Pemberton asked for the tannoy message to be broadcast, requesting Mr Hume of Manchester to report to reception as soon as possible. No reason was given. He and Lorraine settled down in Odin's Garden with a cup of tea and cakes with Pemberton wanting to have a good look at Hume before approaching him. It took a quarter of an hour for the man to respond and when Pemberton saw him approach, he realized it was the thick-set man who had been watching Brother Luke in Hraevelg's Hall late last night.

Of average height, Hume was not yet forty though his hair was greying; he had a round face which was clean shaven and slightly tanned, and was dressed in casual slacks and a short-sleeved T-shirt, hardly the sort of clothing in which to conceal a knife. Pemberton watched as Hume approached the receptionist and gave his name; she indicated Pemberton and Lorraine in Odin's Garden and the man then made his way towards them.

'Jack Hume,' he said in a Lancashire accent. 'You wanted to speak to me?'

'Thanks for coming, yes. Sit down, please,' invited Pemberton. 'Can I get you a cup of tea?'

'No thanks, I've just had one,' and he eased a chair to their table and settled down. 'So, what's all this about? I don't know you, do I?'

'No,' said Pemberton. 'My name is Pemberton, Detective Superintendent, and this is Detective Constable Cashmore. We are interviewing all passengers to ask their help – a man was found dead on board in suspicious circumstances this morning and we have been asked to assist the Captain in making enquiries.'

'You think I did it? Is that it?' The man's eyes flashed in a sudden show of anger and concern. When he saw Lorraine taking notes, he was quickly on the defensive.

'No, nothing of the kind. We're questioning everyone, crew and passengers. Now the dead man was in Cabin F150 – that's along the corridor behind us, on the port side. We want to know whether anyone saw or heard anything suspicious since about 12.30 this morning.'

'Why are you picking on me?'

'We're not picking on you.' Pemberton did not want to inflame this man's prickly disposition. 'As I said, everyone on board is being interviewed, passengers and crew. Some we can visit in their cabins, others we have to find on board.'

'So what do you expect me to say?'

'I don't expect you to say anything. I'm trying to establish who might have known the deceased, who might have been on F Deck after midnight and into the early hours of this morning, and who might have heard or seen something out of the ordinary. Nobody is being accused of anything.'

'Well, I didn't do it, no matter what they say. Who is the dead chap, then?'

'I believe his name is R. W. Mansell, but I know very little about him. He is companion to a monk in a wheelchair. Brother Luke. I believe you were in Hraevelg's Hall last night when Brother Luke and his companion were there.'

'You watching me, were you?'

'No, I just happened to be there as well, enjoying the midnight sun.'

'Why? Why spy on me?'

'I was not spying, Mr Hume. I am a professional police officer and I notice things. It's my job to notice things. I saw you there, alone. Just before half past twelve this morning.'

'There's no crime in being alone.'

'Mr Hume, you are not under any kind of suspicion. It's my task to interview everyone so that I can eliminate them from this enquiry –'

'Sounds like a murder enquiry to me, that's the sort of lingo they use.'

'The death is suspicious, Mr Hume, otherwise I wouldn't be asking these questions. I repeat I'm not making accusations, it's help I'm seeking. I need to trace Mr Mansell's movements after 12.30. First, did you know Mr Mansell? Or a man called Cooper? Or Brother Luke? Have you ever met them?'

'No, only seen them about the ship. The monk and his pal, I mean. I never knew their names.'

'So did you see them around 12.30 this morning?'

'You know I did, you just said so.'

'Did you see them leave Hraevelg's Hall?'

'Yes, a bit before me. Half-twelve like you said, or thereabouts.'

'Alone?'

'As far as I could see, yes.'

'Did anyone follow them out?'

'Can't say I noticed really, I wasn't watching them that close.'

'So what time did you leave?'

'I got myself another drink, a pint, and watched the midnight sun, wonderful stuff, then went to my cabin.'

'Which is?'

'C Deck, 241. Starboard side, a single. I'm not with anyone so no one can give me an alibi, can they?'

'So what time would that be?'

'One-ish, I can't be more precise.'

'Did you go direct from Hraevelg's?'

'Yep, down the stairs. Never went anywhere near F Deck though, Mr Pemberton. You have my word.'

'Did you see the monk and his companion, either together or alone, whilst returning to your cabin?'

'Nope, never set eyes on them.'

'Have you seen anyone taking a close interest in them?'

'Nope, they seem to keep themselves to themselves. Like me. And if you want to know why I was watching the monk it was because I was thinking of having a word with him, on the quiet. I can't get my head round this religious stuff and thought, one day, I might see if he could put me right. Didn't have the guts last night, didn't want to make myself look like a charlie in front of others. Besides I didn't want to spoil his midnight sun.'

'That was thoughtful of you.'

'I dunno about that, I think I was more scared of looking some sort of twit. Anyway, I did see the monk at breakfast this morning without his usual minder, he'd been boozing a bit heavy last night, the minder I mean, so I wasn't surprised. He had a steward with him, the monk I mean, at breakfast.'

'Yes, he has to be accompanied on board, it's one of the ship's rules.'

'Life's run by rules and regulations, eh? Well, you'll know about that, doing your job.'

'And the more rules there are, the more we're likely to break. Well, I think that's all for now, Mr Hume, and thank you.'

'You know I've done time, don't you? Isn't that why you are quizzing me?'

'It's not why I am quizzing you. As I said, I intend speaking to everyone.'

'Well, so long as you know I've done time, I don't want to hide anything from you lot, I don't want to seem like a liar. I've been a bit of a villain, Mr Pemberton, but not now. I've turned the corner, going straight, which is why I wanted to talk to the monk. We had visits in prison, from a priest . . .'

'Good – and are you enjoying the cruise?'

'It gets a bit lonely at times, not knowing anyone, but it's early days. I'm not very good at making friends, no conversation, not among these sort of folks.'

'Well, if you see me in one of the bars, come and join me. I'll buy you a pint!'

'For a copper, that's a real treat! Right, and I'll keep my ears to the ground, eh? About this matter. You never know, I might learn something to your advantage!'

'I could do with a bit of help, I've not got very far yet. So is this all to do with your change of direction?'

'You could say so, yes. I've got a decent job now, good money, and I'm trusted. Maintaining fruit machines and gaming machines. First time in years I've had a regular job, I don't want to blow it. Earned enough to come here, nice, eh?'

'Thanks for talking to me. Now I must speak to a Mr Roberts. David Charles Roberts. Do you happen to know him?'

'Sorry, no. Has he got form as well?' grinned Hume as he left them.

When he'd gone, Pemberton asked Lorraine, 'Well, what do you make of him?'

'He's accustomed to being questioned by the police,' she smiled. 'And he knew that we knew he had previous convictions. He's not daft, Mark.'

'I know that. But is he in the frame?'

'I'd say no. He was too open – and he didn't deny watching Brother Luke. He could have denied that, making it sound like a figment of your imagination.'

'But he has no alibi, he can't prove he went straight back to his cabin. He could have met Mansell somewhere later – remember, Mansell did not return to his cabin after delivering the monk to his. So where did he go? And why? And remember he wasn't the monk's real companion, it's almost certain he was an interloper. I know I haven't proved that yet, but I've got to bear the likelihood in mind. And we mustn't forget that some suspects try to ingratiate themselves with the police in the hope we'll think they're innocent. That man could be trying it on!'

'If you've doubts about him, maybe something will show up on the security films?'

'That's always possible. And he wasn't entirely truthful, was he?'

'Wasn't he?'

'No, he said he was employed maintaining fruit machines. His criminal record said he was a self-employed bricklayer and window cleaner.'

'Maybe he was, when he was arrested for that stabbing. It was some time ago, remember.'

'Right, he did say he's reformed himself. Now, let's pull in our next customer!'

Mr Roberts of Nottingham arrived with a woman, his wife as it later turned out to be. Looking around fifty, he was small with greying fair hair and sharp foxy features while his wife was equally tiny, albeit with nice blonde hair and sunglasses.

'Mr Roberts?' Pemberton approached him and used the same introduction as he had with Hume, making reference to the suspicious death in F150. In return, Robert introduced his wife, Shirley, and somewhat nervously accompanied Pemberton to his table in Odin's Garden. He declined a drink of any kind.

'So how can I help, Superintendent?'

'Everyone on board is being interviewed,' Pemberton stressed while making no reference to Roberts' past. 'What I need to know first is whether you and Mrs Roberts have any links with a Mr Mansell, a Mr Cooper or Brother Luke? You may have seen Brother Luke around the ship in his wheelchair, with a companion.'

As his questioning intensified, it was clear they were a quiet devoted couple who had no such links. They did not resort to the bars of the ship but last night had stayed up late to watch the midnight sun from the Sun Deck, returning to their cabin – B104 – shortly after midnight. They made no reference to their secret past and neither did Pemberton; both he and Lorraine felt they had absolutely no links with the murder.

Next for interview was Ian Taylor, the greetings card salesman from Milton Keynes. He swaggered up to the counter, gave his name and asked what it was all about. The receptionist pointed him towards Pemberton who stood up to meet him. He was a stocky man, clearly fit and active with wide shoulders, a slender waist and tanned skin. His dark hair was cut very short and he had a few days of whiskery growth around his chin and cheeks. Clad in a tight-fitting white T-shirt and shorts, he looked as if he could handle himself in a roughhouse.

'Ian Taylor?'

'Who's asking?' He sat on a chair opposite Pemberton and beamed cheekily at Lorraine.

'Detective Superintendent Pemberton and Detective Constable Cashmore. Sit down, please. I'd like a chat.'

His cockiness evaporated, at least momentarily. 'I've done nothing, honest, it wasn't me, whatever it was.' And he tried to laugh it off.

'No one is suggesting you've done anything, Mr Taylor. Now listen, this is important. I am interviewing everyone on board because a man was found dead in his cabin this morning, and there are suspicious circumstances.'

He named both the monk and his companion as Taylor sat in stunned silence; all his bravado had faded rapidly.

'Oh, God, you don't think I'm responsible? Is that why you're talking to me? You think I did it?'

'We're just trying to establish the movements of everyone on board, Mr Taylor. Now, you might have seen Mr Mansell around the ship last night, he was accompanying the monk in a wheelchair.'

'Oh, right, I have seen him. Them.'

'As I said, everyone on board is being questioned, it's not because we suspect you of being responsible, it's so that we can find out exactly what happened. Now, he died after 12.30 this morning but probably before 8.30, 9.30 at the latest, in Cabin F150.'

'He was in Hraevelg's, I saw him. The chap in the wheelchair with his mate.'

'What time was that?'

'After second sitting, ten mebbe, onwards. I saw his mate with a bottle of wine. The priest or whatever he is had an orange, I think.'

'Did you see them leave?'

'No, we went down to the casino, elevenish, me and my mates. There's six of us, me and my girl, and pals. We all went to the casino, lost a packet but it was fun, you can ask them.'

'And your girl? Who is she?'

'Lucy Stockton, she's sharing my cabin.'

'So what time did you get to your cabin?'

'Late. After the casino, we went up to the Sun Deck to watch the midnight sun, it would be getting on for half-two when we got to the cabin. Me and Lucy.'

'Did you visit F Deck for any reason?'

'No, none of us. No need, was there? It's way off our territory down here, there's nothing at night, even reception's closed.'

'So while you were in the casino, did you see the monk with a companion? Anywhere else on board?'

'No, never set eyes on them in there but other folks were about, walking, chatting, not doing anything unusual.'

'Did you see the companion later? Without the monk? We think he stayed up later after seeing the monk back to his cabin, but we're not sure where he went.'

'Can't say I noticed him about the place, not after he went home with the monk. Not that I was taking much notice with my eyes on the roulette table most of the time. As I said, before we packed in for the night we all went up to the Sun Deck but never saw the priest or his minder up there.'

'Where will you be tonight? I'd like to ask your friends if they saw anything.'

'Sure, we're second sitting so you'll find us either in one of the bars, or the casino. Mebbe Hraevelg's or even on the Sun Deck if we want to see the sun again before we pack it in. Look for me, I'll look out for you.'

'We'd like a chat with your girlfriend too.'

'No problem, she'll be with me.'

And then it was time to interview Geraldine May Norris who had attacked a female neighbour over a dispute about her alleged seduction of Mrs Norris's husband.

Chapter Eight

The moment Geraldine Norris walked into the reception area, Pemberton realized she was the woman from F138, the one caught by the security cameras. Her dumpy appearance, hairstyle and distinctive manner of walking left him in no doubt. Now he could see that her hair was very auburn, her skin very pale and she wore a white T-shirt and blue jeans, both rather tight. He studied her as she approached the counter, thinking she looked younger than she had appeared in the security film, but now she was heading in his direction. He stood up to greet her.

'Mrs Norris?'

'Yes.' She sounded nervous and unsure of herself.

'Sit down,' he invited. 'Tea?'

She shook her head.

'My name is Detective Superintendent Pemberton and this is Detective Constable Cashmore. She will be taking notes of our chat. We are investigating a suspicious death on board, a man was found dead in his cabin this morning. We believe his name is either Mansell or Cooper, you might have seen him accompanying a monk in a wheelchair. Brother Luke. We believe he died between half past twelve and half past eight this morning.'

She nodded, even if she was frowning heavily at this unexpected news.

He continued, 'We are interviewing everyone on the ship in case they heard or saw anything which might be relevant. We especially want to hear from passengers occupying cabins fairly close to his.'

Once again, she merely nodded her understanding.

'Now, your full name is Geraldine May Norris, you are forty-two years old and from Swansea. Is that correct?'

She nodded again, not questioning how he knew such details.

'Mr Mansell occupied F150 which is only four doors away from you, he was alone. Are you alone on the cruise?'

'No, my husband is with me, a double cabin. David is his name.'

'Then we would like to chat to him in due course. But in the meantime, can you tell us whether you heard or saw anything suspicious last night?'

This time, she shook her head.

'Did you know Mr Mansell? Had you ever come into contact with him? Or with the monk in the wheelchair? Brother Luke?'

'No, I didn't,' and her voice had a strong Welsh accent. 'I never spoke to either of them, and neither did David. We never saw them before this trip, although we have seen them around the ship, you know. Very distinctive they are, him a priest and in a wheelchair.'

'Have you noticed anyone else talking to them? Either together or alone? Anyone being angry with them perhaps? Or a confrontation of some kind?'

She shook her head. 'Sorry, no.'

'Can I ask you about last night, Mrs Norris. Whereabouts did you and your husband go, for the evening? Say after dinner.'

'Oh, we had our meal, a lovely one it was too, second sitting and then we went up to the Sun Deck to watch the sun, the midnight sun it was. Beautiful you know, quite beautiful. It was cold up on that deck that time of night, we had to wrap up well, but we stayed quite a while, with a nice drink or two.'

'And then?'

'Well, David wanted to play poker with a man he'd made friends with. In the casino. He said he wouldn't be very long but I was tired so I came back to the cabin on my own. I'm not one for the cards.' She now seemed to be gaining her confidence and was becoming very chatty.

'What time would that be?'

'Oh, I dunno for sure. After midnight, getting on for one maybe. I can't be absolutely certain.'

'So what time did David return?'

'No idea, I went to sleep and when I woke up this morning he was there at my side, snoring his head off. We have our own cruise cards, as you know. To get in with. I think he had had a good night at the poker because he was happy when he woke up, in fact he was so happy we went up for breakfast together.'

'Now, Mrs Norris, when you returned to your cabin, between half-twelve and one, did you see anyone? I am thinking in particular of the area near F150 – those are the cabins on your deck reserved for people in wheelchairs, they're screened off from reception.'

'Well, yes, I know where they are. But as you ask, I made my way down from the casino – that's on the Promenade Deck – and used the staircase which took me almost to my cabin door. I don't like lifts, you see, and didn't use the corridors on F Deck. As I said, the stairs take me almost to my front door, if you know what I mean. Mind, even at that time of morning there were people about, some in the bars, some in the quiet areas and lounges, but I got the feeling most had been up watching the midnight sun. Quite a lot were heading home, like me. But I never saw anyone near our cabin. Dead quiet down there, it was.'

'And your husband? Did he mention he'd talked to anyone on his way home?'

'He never said a word this morning, not a word. It made me think he'd won because he was in a good mood when he woke up.'

'We'd like to talk to him, to see who he noticed on his way home.'

'Shall I get him to come down here now?'

'Thanks, we'd appreciate that. Now, is there anything

else we should ask Mrs Norris?' He addressed this question to Lorraine.

Lorraine smiled. 'The man with the monk, Mrs Norris, you said you'd noticed him around the ship?'

'Here and there, yes, always together. Nice, I thought. Such devotion.'

'Would you have recognized him if you'd seen him without the monk?'

'Oh, I dunno about that. I mean there's such a lot of people on the boat and one middle-aged man's just like any other when you don't know him very well. But as you ask, I don't think I ever saw the monk on his own, or his helper on his own.'

'It's one of the rules of the ship, that people in wheelchairs have to be accompanied.'

'Oh, I see, that's nice though, isn't it? Always together, and so they were.'

'There are several people on their own, though. Men and women.'

'Oh, I know, I do feel sorry for them, not having anyone and it must be so hard to make friends, nice friends, I mean. You can never be sure, can you? You've got to be careful who you pal up with.'

Lorraine paused, not being able to think of another pertinent question at this stage, and so Pemberton said, 'Thank you, Mrs Norris. It was good of you to come so quickly.'

'I'll send David down, shall I?'

'I'd appreciate that.'

When she left them, they sat for a few moments without speaking, each alone with their thoughts, then Pemberton said, 'We're not getting very far with this, are we? We've interviewed our only prime suspects without any of them raising our suspicions. I've not interviewed one person I feel is guilty. Normally when you interview a suspect you can sense when they're hiding something, but not these people. I have no gut feeling that they're hiding anything about this morning's events. So where do we go from here?'

'Back to the beginning? Isn't that what you say, Mark, when you need a breakthrough in an investigation? Go back and start all over again?'

'It can work sometimes. Often in the early stages one tends to overlook something very basic and simple which throws the investigation completely off course. I hope that's not the case here. The thing that intrigues me is that we have a murder victim but I don't know whether it was intended that he should be the one who died, or whether someone else was the intended victim. And where is that other chap? Cooper? I don't think he's the killer, so is he dead? If so, where? Have we had a vigilante at work, killing a killer? If so, someone knows more than us! Furthermore we haven't a motive. Why would anyone kill a monk's companion, real or phoney – and not a full-time companion either. He's not one of those live-in house-keepers that Catholic priests used to have, one to leave all his money to and so upset his family. Nothing makes sense, Lorraine.'

'Let's see what David Norris can tell us. He's one person we know who was out and about during those early morn-ing hours, moving from near the top of the ship almost to its bottom, almost to the victim's door in fact. And maybe the cameras will tell us something? Either about him or about Mansell.'

'We need to concentrate on F Deck. The problem is that, other than reception, there are no public areas down there. At night, there's absolutely no reason to use F Deck, other than to leave or enter one's cabin. You'd not expect to see crowds of people milling about, as you do on D Deck, the Promenade Deck, or the upper two. They're always busy.'

'That's where we'll find people when they're away from their cabins.'

'Exactly. It's in direct contrast to A, B and C which con-sist entirely of passenger cabins, albeit with a launderette on C. So people walking about on those decks are either coming or going from their cabins, or passing through en route to another deck. For that reason, they're hardly likely to know what's happening down on F Deck. Certainly they'd never hear anything, not even the loudest scream. And I'd say F Deck is the quietest of those with public access – so is that why the murder was committed there? You'd hardly get a murder in one of the busier areas, would you?'

'So you're saying we should obtain a list of all passengers and crew with cabins on F Deck, and interview them systematically, every one of them?'

'I think we'll have to. Do we have that kind of information?'

'Yes, Erika has arranged passenger lists in deck and cabin number order – and alphabetically deck by deck.'

'Good, and in addition we've a full alphabetical list of all the passengers?'

'It's on the noticeboard in our incident room. Erika's making a good job of things and keeping a check of those we've interviewed.'

'Excellent. We need the same exercise for the crew. Don't forget we've 700 crew on board, most of whom will know the way past all the security cameras! We can't forget that one of them could be the killer. With a knife from the galley.'

They ranged across the current information but failed to spot anything significant, other than Mansell's unexplained departure from his cabin. The security cameras remained their best hope of securing more evidence, especially concerning Mansell's whereabouts after 12.32. They hoped David Norris might add something worthwhile too. When he arrived, he appeared to be a warm and friendly person, a tall and handsome Welshman with a ready smile.

'Oh yes,' he beamed when Pemberton asked about sightings of Mansell. 'I saw him, I thought it a bit odd he wasn't with the monk then I thought if I was looking after somebody full-time day and night, I would welcome a break for a bit of fun.'

'So where did you see him?'

'I went to the casino for a game of poker with a chap I met in one of the bars, name of Brian something-or-other, and we decided not to play later than two o'clock. We stuck to that agreement and when I left the casino I went through the bar adjoining it, drinks weren't being sold by the way, there was no staff but the doors were open. When I emerged into the corridor, I decided to go to the Gents. It was quite a long walk home back to our cabin and I'd had a few drinks so I thought I'd better go right away, didn't want to be taken short midway along a deck! That's when I saw the monk's helper. He happened to be walking past the bar entrance as I was coming out, striding along the corridor at a fast pace, then as I went into the Gents, he turned into Fjorgyn's Hall.'

'The nightclub?'

'Yes, it was still going strong. Music thumping, lights flashing, folks dancing, young men and women, drinks flowing and so on. Not for me, Mr Pemberton. I watered my horse then turned for home and went straight back to our cabin.'

'Arriving when?'

'Dunno precisely. However long it takes to do that walk. Quarter past two, something like that, give or take a few minutes either way.'

'So did you see anyone during that return journey?'

'Well yes, people were about all the time. Not many, but some were coming down from higher decks and even Hraevelg's where they'd been watching the midnight sun, I could hear them talking about it. And some had been clubbing or to the casino, or just walking around the Promenade Deck in the sunlight. Don't ask me who they were, I have no idea.'

'So the public areas were still quite busy?'

'Most of them, yes. Not as busy as they are earlier in the evening but not deserted by any means.'

'And what about the passenger decks you'd have to pass through? A, B and C?'

'I didn't see much of those, to be honest. I trotted down the staircases, top to bottom, although I did walk the full length of C Deck to get to Staircase 1, it leads down to reception as you know, only a yard or two from our cabin door.'

'When you saw those people moving about the various decks, did anything strike you as odd or unusual about any of them? Suspicious perhaps?'

'No, nothing.'

'No one being objectionable, furtive, drunk, anything out of the ordinary?'

'Nope, nothing. Just a happy home-going few who weren't pressed for time, as you'd expect on a cruise.'

'Did you see Mansell again? During your homeward journey?'

'No, never set eyes on him again. I got in and went straight to bed, Gerry was asleep and didn't wake when I went in so I crashed out until this morning.'

'So you can definitely say that the monk's companion was alive about two o'clock this morning? And entering the nightclub?'

'I'd swear it,' he said.

'A long way from both his own cabin and that of the monk?'

'Yes, but it's always quiet on F Deck. You hardly see a soul, except when reception's open.'

'Did you hear him return? Or hear any unusual noises or activity after you entered your own cabin?'

'Not a thing. I dropped into bed like a stone, and was asleep in seconds. I was happy, you see, I'd won a few quid!'

'Your wife said you'd won.'

'Came away fifty-five quid better off than when I started. A good game.'

They continued to talk to David Norris for a further twenty minutes or so without eliciting any further information and thanked him for his public-spiritedness. He left them to return to his wife.

141

'So does this sighting mean we can be confident that Mansell was alive at two – in the nightclub?' asked Lorraine.

'I'd say reasonably confident,' smiled Pemberton. 'As reasonably as one can be without seeing him for ourselves. But because David Norris was one of the last to see him alive, does that put him in the frame as a suspect? You know how these things work – the person who finds the body and the person who was last to see a murder victim alive are automatically in the frame until they're shown to be innocent.'

'He wasn't the last though, was he? There were others, those people in the nightclub, whoever they were. Did he go there to meet someone or did he go merely to pass the time, being temporarily free from his duties?'

'So all I need to do now is find out who was in the club at two this morning!'

'Clubbers tend to be of a sort,' she said. 'If some were there last night, then the chances are the same lot will be there again tonight. Like gamblers in the casino.'

'So you're saying we're going to have a late night?'

'What other option is there? Unless something turns up in the meantime.'

'True. So if we go to the nightclub, it would be helpful to have a photograph of Mansell to show around – that's if we had one, but we haven't. He's not officially a passenger. But because he looked very like Lionel Cooper, we might be able to use *his* photo. It would be better than nothing. Morag was going to find it for me, the one taken just prior to boarding. I can check with Erika to see if they've turned up. In fact, I'll do that now, it'll be an excuse to check whether anything else has developed in there, if you'll excuse the awful pun.'

'Shall I return to Vingolf's Hall and continue my enquiries?'

'Good idea, try to get the passengers to discuss it among themselves. I'm sure some will be doing so already, but we need the sort of widespread gossip one gets in a village or town when a murder occurs. I appreciate it won't be so likely here, almost everyone is a stranger to everyone else! In small towns and villages, everyone knows one another, they gossip and exchange news. It's different here. Now we have a little puzzle to answer. If Mansell was seen on camera leaving his cabin just after 12.30, and entering the nightclub at two, where was he in the meantime? And who was he with? I think we need to ask questions from anyone out and about until two. If I get no new leads in the incident room now, I'll call at the photo gallery for a word with Morag, then rejoin you.'

When Pemberton returned to the incident room, he was pleased to learn that Morag had left half a dozen copies of her photographs of both Brother Luke and Lionel Cooper. The one of Brother Luke was instantly recognizable and it bore his name, the time it had been taken in hours and seconds, and the number of his cabin plus the identifying letter of the deck. That of Lionel Cooper was equally clear. Both were in full colour. Pemberton studied the picture of Cooper; beyond doubt, it was a remarkable likeness to the man lying dead in the ship's mortuary. Even Pemberton, with his detective's skills, could easily mistake one for the other. The man in the photograph, named as Lionel Cooper and undoubtedly checked and verified with passport and boarding documents, was around fifty years of age, with grey eyes. Not wearing spectacles in the picture, he was sporting a neat and fairly short haircut of grey hair swept back off his brow but was clean-shaven with no scars or other marks on his face. There was a faint smile, almost as enigmatic as that of the Mona Lisa, and he was wearing a dark blue T-shirt with a crest-type badge in the area of the left breast. The crest comprised two silver-coloured crossed keys with embellishments and what appeared to be a tiered crown above them in the centre. There was no lettering on the shirt, however; it looked like the sort that a football supporter or member of a pub darts team might buy, especially if they played for a pub called the Mitre or

Cross Keys. The detail was difficult to see due to the small size of the image.

After studying both photographs for a few minutes, he pinned one of each to the noticeboard. There were also copies to show to the clubbers. He explained his thoughts to Erika, commenting upon the remarkable similarity of the two men and pondering whether they could be related. Then he said both he and Lorraine would carry copies to show to people they interrogated. He hoped some of them had noticed the deceased other than when he was accompanying Brother Luke – even if this was not a photo of Mansell. He told Erika of the sighting by David Norris, thus narrowing the time of death to between two and 8.30, with the puzzle of where Mansell had been between 12.30 and two, and also after two. What time had he returned to his cabin? Perhaps the security cameras might help again? Erika said she would check on progress with the security team, and inform them of this development.

She told him there had been no further messages from Paul Larkin and so he said his next task was to pay a short visit to the mortuary, to examine once more the features of the dead man alongside the picture of Lionel Cooper. He would then ask Morag to take another picture of the deceased's face so that the two portraits could be closely compared.

'With regard to the alphabetical lists of passengers and crew,' she asked, 'would it help to have their photos alongside? The photo gallery arranges its proofs in full alphabetical order. I'm talking of the photographs which were taken as the passengers boarded. Would that help? That will already have been done for this cruise, and the gallery produces more than one copy.'

'That's an almighty lot of pictures!' he smiled, but even as he spoke he could see the benefits of having a named photograph of every passenger.

'There's a master copy for every cruise. About thirty to a page in an album of about sixty pages. They can produce more if necessary. I can get a copy for you.'

'Two would be better,' he said. 'One for me and Lorraine, a sort of reference book of those we speak to, and one for here so that you can check and identify those we've spoken to, and mark them off our various lists.'

'Right, I'll speak to Morag about it.'

'Good. Now, your own security staff are checking the movements and duties of crew members at the material time, and meanwhile they're checking films for movements I've already discussed, but in addition we need to find Mansell's missing hour and a half. I'll have a word with Morag because I need her to take a photograph of his face, so can we call her down here?'

'I'll do that, and you'll mention the albums to her when she comes?'

'I will. Now, another thing. I've come to the conclusion we need to publicize this crime, we need to get the passengers gossiping about it. We needn't describe it as a murder, merely a sudden and unexplained death, a mystery for them to think about. I think it's only fair to everyone that I do this but I realize the ship's owners are wary of bad publicity.'

'If I were you, I'd clear it with the Captain first. He's very fastidious about company rules, maritime regulations and our public image!'

'Of course, that's his job. So how do I go about getting the details into the ship's newspaper?'

'You've plenty of time for tomorrow's edition,' she said. 'It's compiled and published every day by the Purser's office, and is delivered by our night crew to each cabin's letter rack before six each morning. It's only four A4 pages. I'm sure you've seen a copy – with permission, we use extracts from the *Daily Mail* and *The Times* to keep abreast with UK and world news, but we also include events and news affecting the ship. It's compiled by a crew member called Giles, shall I call him in? He'll be in his office now.'

'Yes, let's do that. How about informing Captain Hansteen?'

'I'll call him in too.'

'Right, well, can you ask Morag to come to the mortuary straight away if she can spare five minutes – I can then get the photograph of Mansell. While you're organizing all that, I'll pop into the mortuary to prepare our victim for a photo shoot.'

'What time shall I say you'll be back here?'

'About twenty minutes.'

While Erika began her tasks, he headed for the medical centre down only one flight of stairs; Dr Andrews was in the office and spotted his approach.

'Ah, Superintendent, how's it going?'

He provided Andrews with a summary of his rather limited progress, and then asked permission to view the body once more, this time with the photograph of Cooper alongside. Andrews said he would accompany him – he was still doubtful that a passenger could be replaced by someone else – and Pemberton said he welcomed his presence on the grounds that two minds were often better than one.

In the brightly lit and strongly disinfected mortuary, Dr Andrews drew the chilled remains of the victim from the fridge cabinet. He allowed Pemberton to examine the body at close quarters, especially the face. Clutching the photograph of Lionel Cooper in his left hand, Pemberton moved around the head, comparing the flare of the nostrils, the arch of the eyebrows, the shape of the lips, the appearance of cheeks and chin and the hair, along with its colouring, style and line. He also checked for differences such as moles, scars and blemishes of any kind. Andrews did likewise.

'So what do you think?' asked Pemberton.

'Amazing,' said Andrews. 'I'd say we have the same man here – if I didn't know your views on this, I'd say this body is the same person as the man in that photograph. I don't have to remind you that I'm still not convinced anyone could bypass our security systems and board this ship as an interloper by replacing an existing passenger merely through using the cruise card.'

'The dead man was left-handed, the man in the photo isn't – or wasn't.'

'People can be ambidextrous. I know a man who plays golf and cricket right-handed, but who writes with his left hand. I know another who deals cards and fastens his ties with his left hand and does everything else – writes, plays sport and so on – with his right hand.'

'In the good old days,' laughed Pemberton, 'you could always tell which hand a person used to write with – the fingers were ink-stained. Not any more. But I have further checks to make. In spite of this likeness, I'm still convinced this man is not Lionel Cooper – but the boarding photograph is. And we found documents in both Cooper's and Mansell's name, even though Mansell's not on the passenger list.'

'One man using a false name? Or two men?'

'Members of the same family perhaps? Twins?'

'You'd never get one twin killing another, would you?'

'Wouldn't you?' asked Pemberton. 'I'd say it would depend on what's at stake. Siblings have been known to kill one another.'

As they talked, Morag arrived and, at Pemberton's direction, photographed the dead man's face so that, when reproduced, it would be in the same format as the photo of Lionel Cooper. With her digital camera, she could show them the finished result on the camera's screen, albeit in a reduced version.

'They do look alike,' she admitted. 'I'll print some copies immediately and get them sent to the incident room.'

Pemberton explained his need for an album of all the passengers' portraits, and she said it was no problem. Some had already been printed for the ship's own use and she would send a couple to the incident room along with Mansell's photo; she'd also deliver the extra photos of the murder scene to Dr Easton's cabin. Pemberton returned to the incident room where Captain Hansteen and Giles were waiting. He updated them on his progress, adding he had no idea of the identity of the killer at this stage while stressing there was still a huge amount of work to do.

'I need the passengers to become involved, Captain, talking and speculating. Many people love a mystery and like being in the position to help solve one. Positive publicity of a murder mystery is one of the biggest aids in helping the police to detect crimes, especially major ones, so I'd like to put a note in the ship's newspaper.'

'I don't want a mass panic on board, Superintendent, nor do I want the company's good name to be tarnished by this.'

'It didn't do much harm to the Orient Express!' smiled Pemberton. 'Certainly not in the long term.'

'*Touché*! So what approach are you considering in the newspaper?'

'Something simple and very basic.' He glanced across at Giles who already had a notebook ready. 'I think we should say that a male passenger has died unexpectedly in tragic circumstances, and the police are making enquiries. We could add that it happened on F Deck between midnight and 8.30 this morning and so the police are anxious to trace anyone who saw or heard anything suspicious during those times, either on F Deck or elsewhere. I think also we should say that two police officers are on board, conducting enquiries. We might add that if anyone has any information, they could leave their names at reception and a police officer will contact them. I don't think there is any need to identify either us or the victim at this point. In fact, it might be wiser not to, particularly as the killer is still amongst us.'

'All right, I can't see any harm in that suggestion. Giles, include a paragraph on those lines. What about a photograph?'

'We could include a photo of Lionel Cooper without his name, it might jog a memory or two. It's not ethical to publish a photo of the dead man's face.'

'Without mentioning the monk's name?'

'I think not at this stage. I want the information, if and when it comes, to be spontaneous and willingly given.'

With Captain Hansteen agreeing to his proposal, Pemberton stressed the remarkable likeness of the victim to the photograph of Cooper, explaining he now had images of both. He gave Giles a photograph of Cooper, Giles saying he would go away now to compile the news paragraph and submit it for approval by both Pemberton and the Captain before publication.

'Can I ask you this?' Pemberton put to Captain Hansteen. 'Is there any record at all of Mansell ever being on this ship? On a previous cruise?'

'I did a thorough check on that point, and we have absolutely no record of him. Nothing at all, either on this cruise or any previous one.'

'The mystery deepens!'

When they had gone, Pemberton turned to Erika. 'We have another task, Erika. I need all the chits signed by Cooper, and those signed in his name last night. The handwriting should be different. That might help determine whether we have an ambidextrous victim, or whether two men are involved.'

'I can get those from the Purser's office.'

'Good, and thanks for all your help. I hope you don't think you need to work all night! What time do you normally finish work?'

'It depends, we're all very flexible with our hours of work, we have to accommodate things like time changes in international waters, but I'm happy to work late – there's not much else to do on board!'

'Well, I won't demand you work after five o'clock! You're free to go when you feel it right to do so.'

'Oh, I'll be here some time after five, and you'll be working late, I'll bet!'

'I need to visit the nightclub and the casino, but that will be after dinner tonight. Both Lorraine and I will be questioning people in the meantime.'

'I might see you around the ship, then. I don't spend all my free time in my cabin!'

'Then let me buy you a drink – cocktail of the day perhaps? As a small appreciation of what you've done so far. Suppose Lorraine and I arrange to meet you in the cocktail bar? Quarter to eight? We eat at 8.30.'

'Yes, that would be really nice. I'll be there.'

'Good, and if you need to contact me in the meantime, I'll be in my cabin for about an hour before dinner – six until seven perhaps or you could put out a tannoy message if it's urgent. But now I'll return to see how Lorraine is getting along in Vingolf's Hall.'

Chapter Nine

Lorraine had now interviewed several passengers who occupied cabins on F Deck but had not learned anything useful from them. Like those who slept in other areas of *Ringhorn*, none had noticed anything unusual in the behaviour of their fellows either last night or that morning. In particular, none had heard or seen any unusual activity in or near F150 and all had alibis for the period between midnight and 8.30 this morning. Even though most had watched the midnight sun, they had returned to their cabins either alone or with their partner from around one onwards. None could offer absolute proof they had remained in their cabins the whole time – they acknowledged it was possible for a partner to leave for a while without arousing the other, although none was aware such a thing had happened. As she questioned couple after couple, and several individuals, she felt none was guilty of the murder – she did not experience any of the gut feeling that often surfaced when a person was trying to hide the truth or conceal their guilt.

Because this huge conservatory was popular with everyone, it sustained a continuing interchange of passengers, some remaining only long enough for a cup of tea while others read or chatted with friends while watching the rolling grey sea beyond. It meant Lorraine could catch a considerable number of passengers. When Pemberton arrived, he found her getting another cup of tea to slake the thirst she had generated by dozens of interviews and so he obtained one for himself. He spotted an empty table a discreet distance away and made for it. Already, people were drifting away from Vingolf's to begin their leisurely preparations for the first sitting of dinner, inevitably with additional time to enjoy a relaxing preprandial aperitif or cocktail.

Pemberton and Lorraine settled down to reappraise their day's efforts, recognizing that their apparent lack of progress was no different from any other murder enquiry. Inevitably, there was the dull routine plus the chore of constant interviews and questions, the regular assessments of progress, the laborious cross-indexing and checking of information and sometimes a boss who wanted results rather too quickly. In this case it wasn't a boss wanting results – it was the relentless progress towards port and the likelihood of the killer's escape. In fact, it was often late into an enquiry before possible suspects emerged – and this was still a very new investigation.

After the refreshing tea, they decided to spend another hour or so in Vingolf's, interviewing more passengers. Sadly their efforts produced no useful information and so they returned to the incident room.

Erika was still there and said, 'Morag has brought more copies of Mr Cooper's photo and some of R. W. Mansell's face, and also a couple of albums with all the passengers in them. They're in alphabetical order with cabin numbers. I've put them in your in-tray. You wanted them tonight, I believe?'

He examined the pictures of Cooper and Mansell side by side. 'Look at this, Lorraine. Talk about two men looking like twin brothers! Let's see what tonight's efforts bring.'

Erika continued, 'Also in your tray is the draft article for the newspaper. The Captain has approved it – if you can give it the OK, I'll get Giles to make sure it's in tomorrow's edition, complete with photo. I haven't got the chits you asked for, they're still working on those so I'll check later, but I've got some stills from the security cameras for F Deck and from some of the others. Our security team believe they will interest you. And there's another email from Inspector Larkin. Do you want to see them all now?'

'You have been busy! And you bet I'd like to see them!'

He read the draft article, initialled it to show his agreement and Erika said she would return it immediately to Giles. Lorraine and Pemberton settled down to view the stills and found they showed a man whose somewhat blurred and grainy image appeared very similar to that of Mansell when caught leaving F150. It had been captured at 12.44 on Staircase 1 on C Deck, a quarter of an hour or so before Pemberton and Lorraine had used that same flight. That staircase, like the others in public use, comprised a series of interconnecting flights which gave access to each deck, the complete staircase leading from Deck G right up through the ship to the Sun Deck. The lift shafts were beside the stairs. The camera had caught the man as he was about to ascend from C Deck, and he was alone. The next frame was outside Hraevelg's Hall. It showed the same figure striding towards the entrance at 12.50; he was still alone but the camera did not reach into the interior.

'We were in there at that time, with the others. Everyone was busy watching the sun so probably no one noticed him arrive. Certainly I didn't. But it does seem that Mansell, without Brother Luke, went back to watch the midnight sun, like lots of others,' suggested Pemberton.

'Or to buy some more drinks!' smiled Lorraine, recalling the monk's comments.

'You could be right, although he could get drinks elsewhere or even in his cabin. The chits will tell us whether he bought anything, but that's all. Our trail ends there, none of the other cameras picked him up and there's nothing to tell us when he left Hraevelg's. Or who he was with. So if he entered Hraevelg's at ten to one and was then seen alone about two, entering the nightclub, where was he in the meantime? What was he doing? And who was he with? Or was he doing nothing more than sipping wine in here while watching the midnight sun?'

'That's very likely, but we are narrowing things down, Mark,' said Lorraine. 'It means we must question anyone who said they were in Hraevelg's between those times. Like us, they'd be concentrating upon the midnight sun and might not have noticed Mansell unless he drew attention to himself.'

'People are not as observant as we might wish, Lorraine. We need words with the steward who was on bar duty. They might have noticed something, we can talk tonight, it'll probably be the same person. So we have made progress of a sort. Now, what's Paul sent us?'

The email from Paul Larkin contained some preliminary information about Lionel Cooper and R. W. Mansell. Police officers had visited Cooper's home address, a modest terrace house in Middlesbrough, but it was deserted. A neighbour said that Mr Cooper lived alone and that he had gone on a cruise to accompany an elderly invalid monk from the diocesan rest home. She described Cooper as a man in his fifties and of apparent independent means or in receipt of a good, early pension. She added he had lost his wife from cancer about five years ago and now spent much of his time helping others. He often went to Lourdes, Fatima and other places of Catholic pilgrimage with organized parties, always to help invalids and those less capable than himself. He had also been on several cruises with disabled people, including the present monk, and always paying his own way. He was an ardent fundraiser for his local church and assisted with Sunday Mass and other events. He was a very good man, according to the neighbour, and this was supported by a CRO check which revealed that Lionel Cooper had no convictions of any kind, nor was he considered of interest to the police for any reason. Enquiries at the rest home had not produced anything further about Cooper – they confirmed he was a volunteer who was widely respected and well known within the diocese. Paul's email stressed this was a very early report; further enquiries were being made into Cooper's background. It was not known, for example, whether he had any close family. There were lots more questions to ask and Paul said he would try to trace any early 'customers' of Cooper's to see whether they had experienced problems whilst in his company.

So far as R. W. Mansell was concerned, even less was known. According to Barclaycard's officials, he had a permanent address in Northumberland but spent time travelling overseas, including two cruises to Norway on a ship called *Velia*. That was evident from the purchases and withdrawals made on his credit card. His permanent address was given as Church Cottage, Kirkwell near Hexham.

Because this was a murder enquiry, Barclaycard was prepared to provide more information and added that Mansell always paid his borrowings in full before the due date. Three days ago, he had drawn 600 kroner from an ATM in Bergen, a fact which clearly established his presence in Norway while *Ringhorn* was nearby on the high seas. Most of it was with him when he was found dead – 500 in notes and the rest in coins. It meant theft did not appear to be a motive. He also had a personal account with Barclays Bank in Hexham into which a regular sum of money – £950 or so – was paid every month and it was not overdrawn. It appeared this was an army pension but the reason for the pension was not known to bank officials and, to date, no one had been traced who could provide information about his personal affairs. Like Lionel Cooper, he did not have any convictions and had not come to the notice of the police. His full name was Richard William Mansell and his date of birth corresponded to that on his passport. Paul added that Northumbria police were making detailed enquiries into his background. They had been informed of the urgency of this investigation and a response was expected soon. Paul added that the request for the Norwegian police to search for Lionel Cooper, either dead or alive, in the region of Trollstigheimen Mountain Lodge, had not so far produced a result.

'All this convinces me even more there are two men,' muttered Pemberton. 'One was on board this ship while the other had gone ashore in Norway from another ship, drawn cash and sought an opportunity to come aboard *Ringhorn*. To do a swap! All these cruise ships visit the same ports. It suggests Mansell had planned it all very carefully, he'd need to if he was to join *Ringhorn* at a Norwegian port armed only with a cruise card! He'd know Cooper would have the card on him – it was needed to return on board. What I want to know is why do all this? Why go to all this trouble and why be so devious? And is Cooper still alive? If so, was all this done with his agreement or knowledge?'

'Or with the agreement of Brother Luke!'

'We can't ignore the possibility he could be involved but we don't know whether Cooper and Mansell knew one another, do we? Or whether Brother Luke knew Mansell. He says not, but he might have reasons for denying it. It's another area for research, we need to ascertain if there are any links.'

'Do you regard their personal backgrounds as material evidence?' Lorraine asked Pemberton. 'It's just that, on a cruise, most of the people are total strangers to one another, unless you get a family group, or party of friends. I'm just wondering whether we need to delve very deeply into their backgrounds, as we would for a normal murder enquiry? In a town or village, you get personal animosity, revenge, love triangles, anger over inheritance and wills, drunken rages, all that kind of thing. That sort of motive might not feature here where people rarely know one another.'

'Maybe but I think we must learn as much as possible about those three gentlemen. To effect an exchange like this, someone must have known in advance that Luke and Cooper were intending to cruise on *Ringhorn* and there is nothing to prevent an enemy joining the ship, even at the last moment. You can get a full itinerary of the cruise – the internet will supply that. Mansell had done his homework

– all he had to do was go ashore from his own ship and wait to catch Cooper somewhere. He knew how to find his cabin because he had the cruise card. But why? Why dispose of Cooper and then get yourself killed?'

'Remember the killer was admitted to his cabin, Mark. The victim must have known his caller, or it could have been someone pretending to have an urgent message . . . so was he expecting to find Cooper?'

'It's hard to be sure about anything at this stage. We can't even be sure the murder was planned – it might have erupted at very short notice. Even so, we can't forget the killer went to the trouble of obtaining a knife then made his way down through all the decks to F150, was admitted to Cooper's cabin for reasons we don't yet know, and carried out the crime. Then he left a note on the door in what appears to have been an attempt to delay the finding of the body until after the next port of call. That suggests he intended to leave the ship and disappear – which makes sense if the killing was premeditated. This has some of the hallmarks of a well-planned murder and some which suggest a sudden attack, but it was done for a very important reason. And on top of all that, we have an illegal switch of passengers with one of them being the victim. With the killer still on board, don't forget. Cooper is probably not the killer, unless he's hiding somewhere like a stowaway.'

'Then we might persuade the Captain not to call at Spitzbergen? Not to give the killer the chance to flee the ship? That would give us more time to get this sorted out.'

'I doubt he'll agree to that, he's already pointed out that fee-paying passengers call the tune – that halt is one of the main reasons for the cruise. And don't forget – trapping him on board might make the killer more dangerous . . . so we've a lot to think about. At least we can warn Spitzbergen of what might happen when we do dock there! Come along, it's time to get back to our bolthole to have a nice long shower before dinner.'

'What about Brother Luke? Is there any more about him?'

'Not really. The rest home has confirmed his story, he's not a permanent resident but has been staying for short breaks over several years, sometimes up to three months. He doesn't have any family but Paul said further enquiries are under way.'

At this point, Erika returned after delivering the draft article to the newspaper office, but also said she had called at the Purser's to collect Cooper's purchase chits. Pemberton decided to make a swift examination of them because they might be relevant to tonight's enquiries. It was easy to flip through them because they were in date and time sequence, all in a file for Cabin F150. When he checked those for yesterday, he found several signed by L. Cooper. It was a strong and distinctive signature in black ballpoint, the pen being provided by the relevant steward. These chits were used for all on-board expenditure and every chit was timed. This provided a good means of knowing where a passenger had been at a particular moment.

Cooper's distinctive signature appeared on chits until the day before yesterday, chiefly for soft drinks purchased in the bars, along with some postcards and stamps. Brother Luke would have used separate chits if he had made any purchases of his own. There were no chits during the daytime yesterday, probably because both Cooper and the monk had gone ashore. Pemberton was interested in evening purchases – and for the evening meal, the chit had been used to buy a bottle of red wine in the Folkvang Restaurant. Pemberton remembered seeing that transaction – it was the left-handed signature which had alerted him. And sure enough, the signature was different, backward-sloping and in a totally different hand, but signed as L. Cooper. And when he checked for later purchases, 'Cooper' had bought another bottle of wine in Hraevelg's Hall at 12.56 this morning.

So the security camera had been correct; the replacement 'Cooper' had gone into that bar where many were watching the midnight sun and there he had bought another entire bottle. So how long had he remained before entering the nightclub about an hour later?

'This adds to my belief that Cooper was replaced by Mansell,' he told both Lorraine and Erika. 'It doesn't tell us why, or why he got killed.'

He thanked Erika for her help so far and she said, 'If we can now be sure Cooper isn't on board, we could notify the Norwegian immigration authorities to say he's left the ship. That would add power to the police search; Immigration would get the police to carry out checks.'

'Good, I think we should do that if Captain Hansteed will agree.'

'I'll mention it to him.'

Pemberton left now, taking the albums so that he and Lorraine could use them during their enquiries tonight and tomorrow, and reminding Erika that he was looking forward to seeing her for cocktails. He added that after dinner he and Lorraine would be visiting Hraevelg's Hall, the nightclub and perhaps the casino to continue their enquiries. They returned to their cabin to prepare for this evening – the dress code for tonight's dinner was formal, an opportunity for the ladies to dress stunningly in their finest gowns. The men would also look resplendent in their dinner jackets and black ties and so tonight's dinner would be memorable and festive.

It was inevitable, over cocktails in the bar called Alfheim's Hall, that Lorraine and Pemberton would discuss the investigation with Erika. Normally discussions about work were banned in their house and during their leisure time. Today, though, things were different, and as soon as Pemberton ordered the cocktails and signed his chit, showing his cruise card to verify his name and cabin number, Erika began to explain that well-tried system.

'We include the time, date and place on each chit because of past disputes,' she told them. 'It's inevitable that some people can't remember what they bought or where they bought it, and some will blatantly disagree with what is written down even if they've signed it. Others will add someone else's cabin number to try and dodge payment, so we try to make each chit as foolproof as possible. One way is to tie the customer down to a precise place and time. And, as you've just seen, we ask to see the cruise card too, to verify the name and cabin number. Even so, some claim they've forgotten them, not realizing they need them to re-enter their cabins; we can then press them to search pockets and handbags! In all, though, the system seems to work very well.'

'Credit card payments are similarly timed and dated,' Pemberton said. 'It's amazing what we can learn from their records; we can follow a credit card user around the country, shop by shop, petrol station by petrol station, restaurant by restaurant. They leave a wonderful trail . . . Ah, here's Rob and Ellen.'

Pemberton's table companions were entering the bar and so he hailed them, inviting them to join the party.

'I'd like to buy you a drink, Rob, for helping out this morning. Much appreciated. And one for you, Ellen, for putting up with us!'

As the couple joined the party, the necessary introductions were made, drinks were ordered and it was Rob who asked, 'So, Mark. Any developments?'

Ellen piped up. 'I don't want any talk of dead bodies or murders at dinner, thank you very much!'

'Right, let's get it over now,' grinned her husband.

Pemberton therefore updated Rob Easton with the latest news of his investigation, adding that Mansell was known to be alive at 2 a.m. and concluding with his intention, after dinner tonight, to visit Hraevelg's Hall, the casino and the nightclub to make more enquiries.

'We know the victim was in Hraevelg's in the early hours of this morning. He arrived at 12.50 as near as I can tell.'

'While we were still there, with you and Lorraine, and the others?' Rob pointed out.

'Right, but I didn't notice him come in. How about you?'

'Sorry, no. I suppose we were too engrossed in other things.'

'I was fascinated by the sun,' said Pemberton. 'I think most others would be too. Anyway, after Mansell left Hraevelg's, he was seen entering the nightclub at two. To get there from Hraevelg's he'd have to descend through seven decks, but no one seems to have seen him doing that, neither did the security cameras pick him up. That's not surprising – the cameras don't pick up everything and there are several staircases and lifts out of vision. I know he bought a bottle of wine in Hraevelg's too, almost as soon as he arrived, so clearly he intended staying a while, but I don't know whether he was alone or not. He'd already drunk a full bottle of red at dinner, according to the monk – and I saw him buy it. And there were no bottles in the cabin.'

'If we'd been ashore, I could have had his stomach contents analysed to see how much alcohol he had consumed,' grinned Rob.

'Did he take his bottle or even just a glass into the nightclub?' asked Lorraine.

'We didn't ask the witness whether he was carrying anything,' admitted Pemberton. 'But at the time we had no idea he'd been to Hraevelg's. Is it important?'

'Well, if he was alone he might have had some of his wine left and taken it with him. If he was with someone else, they might have drunk it all. He was alone when David Norris saw him though,' said Lorraine.

'So are we thinking of a lonely man? Someone seeking solace in a bottle and in loud company in a nightclub? Someone wondering how to pass the time while alone on a cruise ship full of people who all seemed happier than him?' asked Rob.

'Could be, which is why I'm going to ask a few questions tonight. I'd welcome another chance to examine the scene with you too, tomorrow morning. Shall I fix a time?'

'Ring me,' said Rob.

'Look, I must go, I'm meeting a friend.' Erika stood up. 'Thank you for the drink, Mr Pemberton, I'll see you tomorrow, unless anything urgent crops up.'

'You could join us for dinner if you wish.'

'No thanks, we have our own mess and besides, your table places are all allocated.'

'Right, I'll see you after breakfast, hopefully with some developments after tonight.'

Over dinner, no one referred to the murder investigation and that alone supported Pemberton's theory that a high proportion of the passengers had no idea it had occurred. If the twin women and their husbands who shared their table had known about the crime, then they would surely have made some reference to it, even if they had no idea of Pemberton's role, or that of Lorraine.

This was not what he wanted, however; he wanted everyone to be aware of it, to discuss it over drinks or while sunbathing, talk about it with friends and acquaintances. Then some snippet might come his way, something he might otherwise miss. Tomorrow, though, the story would appear in the ship's newspaper so by breakfast time the ship should be buzzing with the news.

As Pemberton looked around, he saw Brother Luke sitting with a steward, and recognized other faces he'd interviewed or noticed among the passengers. Surely some would be talking about the murder? He wished he could eavesdrop on the conversations and was confident some would be referring to him and Lorraine, recognizing them as the on-board detectives. On those tables, therefore, there would be chatter and gossip and he hoped it might prompt some of the participants to come and talk to him.

'So where did you get to last night after we'd gone?' Ellen was speaking to the twins, Sue and Josie, and their husbands.

Brian responded. 'They all went to the nightclub except me. I went off for a hand or two of poker with a chap I met in the casino, and then joined them later.'

'In the nightclub?' asked Pemberton.

'Yes, it was noisy and dark, but we had a few dances then packed it in. We all left for bed.'

In spite of their earlier discussion, Pemberton knew he must raise the subject of the murder – these people had all been in the relevant places at the relevant times and he could not let the moment evaporate. It was highly possible they had seen something of interest.

'I'd like to talk to you all about those places,' he began, not quite knowing how to phrase this request. 'Perhaps not now. Later, up in Hraevelg's perhaps?'

'Whenever you like!' said Brian. 'Is there some kind of mystery about it? You sound rather guarded, Mark.'

Pemberton was aware of Ellen watching him but she flashed her eyes across the table and said, 'Mark, do it now. You must, you know that.'

At her remark, the others fell silent, all watching Pemberton as if he was going to make some astonishing announcement.

'There was a suspicious death on board in the early hours of this morning,' he told them. 'A passenger was found dead on F Deck, in F150. He was the man who has been accompanying Brother Luke, the monk in the wheelchair.'

Instinctively, all four turned towards the monk.

'So what's that got to do with us going to watch the mid-night sun?' asked Brian.

'The victim is known to have visited Hraevelg's just before one, he bought a bottle of wine and later called in at the nightclub around two.'

'Victim?' asked Russell, picking up on the word.

'We're talking of murder. Lorraine and I have been asked to investigate it.'

'You in the police then, Mark?' grinned Brian.

'Yes, we both are, CID. We're supposed to be on holiday but the Captain has asked us to help with the investigation.'

'Great stuff!' said Brian. 'I've always wanted to be a detective. Well, we'll all help, won't we?'

'You're not in the force, by any chance?' smiled Pemberton.

'Not us, mate. I'm in insurance and Russell's the marketing director for a large construction firm. The girls are both artists. So how about you, Rob and Ellen?'

'We're retired,' said Ellen. 'But Rob used to be a forensic pathologist, he's already been helping Mark and Lorraine with this.'

'So why didn't we know about it earlier?' asked Sue. 'You can't let a murder happen and keep it secret like this!'

'It's not being kept secret, we learned about it only this morning and have been busy all day, asking questions. It will be in the ship's newspaper tomorrow morning so I hope that prompts everyone to chat about it. A lot has been going on today, but because the victim was seen in the places I've mentioned, I need to talk to everyone who was there – and finding them isn't going to be easy.'

'Well, Mark, this is a turn-up for the books, but I'm an insurance investigator, so if I can help share the load with you, then just ask. I can always go around sparking off gossip . . .'

'I'm a former journalist,' said Russell. 'I got made redundant in a takeover of my regional newspaper, so I got this job in marketing. I'm used to asking questions too . . . I think we should get our heads together after the meal and devise a plan of action to get this sorted out. Right, everyone?'

'Right,' they said.

'And not another word over dinner!' laughed Ellen.

After the meal, they found a corner table in Hraevelg's Hall as Pemberton prepared to address his new-found team. He was very aware that none had been formally eliminated from the investigation but, as the normal rules were not applicable in this case, he decided he could use some extra help. He reasoned that he need not admit them to the incident room on the grounds of confidentiality, nor did he wish them to behave as police officers, partly due to the danger it presented and, of course, there was the question of personal insurance if any of them was attacked.

But they could go around asking questions of their own free will – after all, who could forbid them? And Pemberton did want lots of eyes and ears helping him. With his team gathered around a large table in a quiet corner of Hraevelg's, he bought them all a drink, provided them with the facts as he knew them and then showed the photographs of Lionel Cooper and Richard William Mansell.

'This is our victim,' he said, pointing to Mansell's picture and giving a verbal description. 'And this other man, Cooper, has vanished, he went ashore yesterday and has not returned. Mansell has taken his place for reasons we don't know and in circumstances we don't know. He was using F150, on Cooper's cruise card, having adopted his identity. I don't need to say how alike they look too! There's lots we don't know but my main purpose at this stage is to trace Mansell's movements while on board last night and into the early hours. I need to know his contacts, any arguments he might have had . . . anything at all, however trivial.'

'He wasn't on board very long before he died, was he?' noted Brian.

'Long enough to get himself killed,' said Russell.

'The point I'm making is that we are interested in a very few hours, it's not like tracing everyone on board to check their movements since they boarded,' said Pemberton. 'We think Mansell died between two and 8.30 this morning. That's the critical time, when most of us were in our cabins, with some still watching the midnight sun or enjoying the night life on board. I appreciate your offers of help but must remind you we haven't recovered the murder weapon, probably a chef's knife from the galley. The killer might be tempted to use it again, if we get too close to him. Or her.'

'We can look after ourselves,' protested Brian. 'It's our job too, Mark, it's not only coppers who need to watch their backs!'

'If you two are going to do your own investigating, we need a rendezvous point,' Pemberton suggested. 'The obvious one is the dinner table each evening.'

'We could meet for coffee at eleven, say, in Vingolf's Hall, over lunch in the bistro and over tea again in Vingolf's . . . or we could put out a tannoy for you, Mark, if it's something urgent.'

'And you could always leave messages for me or Lorraine at reception,' said Pemberton. 'Sealed, of course.'

'Right,' said Brian. 'Let's not waste any more time. Come on, Russell, you start with Idun's Garden and I'll do Frigg's.'

'What about us?' chorused Sue and Josie.

'You can come with us, we might need your wisdom. You can't beat a good man-and-wife team for getting results!'

'Thanks,' said Pemberton. 'I'm going to chat with the steward in here, talk to a few of the regulars and then go to the casino and nightclub. Catch me and Lorraine in there, otherwise I'll be in bed.'

'Anything I can do? I'm rather limited in the investigative field!' said Rob.

'Your role is to take that second look at F150,' said Pemberton. 'But not tonight. I'll be in touch tomorrow about that. In the meantime, go and enjoy yourself, and look after Ellen!'

And so Pemberton's team warmed to its task.

Chapter Ten

'Is it wise to recruit non-police helpers?' asked Lorraine when they were alone.

'I've been studying them over dinner and I'm sure they're honest enough – their conversations hinted at their professions and I'm sure none is a killer! I've no intention of inviting them to use the incident room though; all I want is for them to get among the passengers and pick their brains. And if one of them is the killer, then he or she will make a slip – so I'm really putting them in the proverbial firing line. You could say it's my way of testing them!'

'Obviously you know what you're doing. So what's next?'

'A word with the barman,' said Pemberton. 'Then we need to get among these customers to see if they noticed anything last night.'

When the bar steward, a Dutchman called Jan, saw the photograph of Lionel Cooper he nodded. Clearly, he could not see the difference between Cooper and Mansell. 'Yes, he came in late. I am supposed to shut the bar at one o'clock, Mr Pemberton, even though people remain later, and he came in just before I closed. He bought a bottle of red wine and went over there.'

He pointed to a small table just inside the second entrance. It was almost out of sight when the door was opened; it closed automatically so never remained open to obscure the table. It was not the best of locations but it was very secluded.

'Alone?'

'Yes, he was quite alone. I gave him a glass, just the one, and he settled down with his wine, he didn't seem concerned about the midnight sun. He just sat quietly watching the people while he drank. The place was very full, there weren't enough seats for everyone so most were standing to get a good view of the sun, although some were dancing.'

'I recall it being full, we were here too, but I must admit I didn't notice this man. We left around one o'clock too. So was he alone all the time?'

'I didn't take much notice of him, I was busier than normal. We get quite a lot of loners on our cruises, Mr Pemberton, and some like to be left alone. Others try to strike up relationships, sometimes with crew members I might add, so I was not really aware of that man once he'd settled down with his wine.'

'Does that mean you weren't aware of the time he left?'

'Sorry, no. As I said, I closed the bar at one and so I left a few minutes after he arrived. I'm almost sure he was still here when I left the room.'

'Still drinking alone?'

'I couldn't swear it, but I think he was still alone, sitting at that little table with his wine and a single glass.'

'Did you see him afterwards? Elsewhere on the ship?'

'Sorry, no. I went straight to my cabin, that's on G Deck, I took the lift down because I was due to start early this morning with breakfasts. I never saw him again. I didn't clear the glasses from the tables, that's done by the overnight crew, they clean the place for the following day, so I don't know whether he left any wine.'

'I see. Now, did you notice me or Lorraine?' smiled Pemberton. 'We left around the same time as you, heading for C Deck.'

'The ship was busy, Mr Pemberton, I was busy, so I'm afraid I don't remember you.'

'It just shows how easy it is not to notice people even though we were moving around at the same time in the same place. Well, thanks, Jan, I appreciate your help.'

Pemberton and Lorraine then split and approached several tables of drinkers, identified themselves and their purpose, but received no useful information. Their presence, however, and the fact they were investigating a serious crime on board did generate a lot of discussion afterwards and so Pemberton's desire was coming true. Passengers were beginning to discuss the crime; before long, he hoped, it would become a topic of regular conversation.

Then it was time to visit the casino. It was on the starboard side of Deck 7, otherwise known as the Promenade Deck. Entry was via a darkened doorway, the casino itself being dimly lit to provide an atmosphere of opulence broken only by the whirring of the roulette wheel and the clink of chips being placed on selected numbers. Several card tables were in use; blackjack was being played on some with others hosting games like brag and poker. There was little or no conversation, save for the whispering croupiers and dealers deftly displaying their skills. Every table appeared to be busy, men and women were concentrating upon their tasks, nervously fingering piles of chips and wondering whether tonight was going to make their fortune or lose it.

As Pemberton and Lorraine stood for a few minutes to observe the scene, a smartly dressed young man approached them. Dark-haired and immaculate, he wore a curious mixture of the formal dress of a senior naval officer and evening dress, but it looked right in this hallowed and moneyed place.

'I'm sorry, sir and madam, but every table is booked. If you wish to make use of our facilities, you are advised to make an early reservation.'

'No thanks, we don't want to play. I am Detective Superintendent Pemberton and this is Detective Constable Cashmore, you may know that we are helping your Captain to investigate a sudden death on board.'

'Ah, yes, we have been informed. How can I help?'

As Pemberton eased the photograph of Lionel Cooper from his pocket, the man invited him to come into the office where the light was better and where they could conduct a private conversation.

'Thanks,' said Pemberton when they were in the small office with the door closed. 'Now, I'd like you to look at this photograph. Were you on duty early today?'

'Yes, we close at three.' He took the photograph and examined it, nodding. 'Yes, I remember him. He came in very late last night but we could not accommodate him. As I said to you, it is wise to make a reservation either for a place at cards or at the roulette table.'

'How late was he?' Pemberton recalled David Norris saying Mansell had entered the nightclub around two o'clock.

'I can't be certain, around two, I'd say.'

'So what did he do?'

'He asked if he could remain a while, just to watch. I had no objection to that, so I allowed him to remain even though there was nowhere for him to sit.'

'Was he alone?'

'Oh, yes. I thought he was one of those lonely people who sometimes join us, even at that time of the morning. He was no problem.'

'Did he talk to anyone?'

'I don't think so, although I couldn't be sure. I was busy and the punters wouldn't want to be interrupted, then when I looked up he'd gone.'

'Any idea what time that might be?'

'It's hard to be precise, but I'd say quarter of an hour or twenty minutes later, something like that. Half past two at the latest. He didn't stay long. It gets boring after a time, watching people being parted from their money!'

'So while he was in here, you think he never spoke to anyone, and that he left alone?'

'I'd say so, yes.'

'Did he have a drink with him?'

'Yes, a glass of red wine. A full one, he brought it with him.'

'And a bottle?'

'No, just the glass. We don't allow drinks at the tables, but because he was standing some distance away, I allowed him to retain it.'

'Have you seen him in here on other occasions?'

'Not to my knowledge. Most of the people in here are regulars, they come night after night, this kind of gaming for big stakes is not for the faint-hearted, Mr Pemberton, it's not like a whist drive or a game of dominoes in a pub. Some hardened gamblers do nothing else while on board, it's like a drug for them.'

'I was going to interview the punters but having spoken to you, I don't feel they could add anything at this stage. Now, what time did you leave here?'

'As I said, we close at three, so it would be about quarter past when I locked up and left. I lock the doors when everyone has gone.'

'You returned directly to your cabin? With no diversions en route?'

'Yes, it's on G Deck, 211.'

'And your name?'

'Anderson. John Anderson.'

Lorraine noted the name and cabin number; this man could be crossed off the list of crew members if they were satisfied with his account.

'So on your way home did you see him again?' Pemberton continued. 'I am anxious to know where he might have been between leaving here at, say, 2.15 or thereabouts and returning to his own cabin. That's on F Deck, 150.'

'No, I didn't see him again. Can I ask if he is the victim you're asking about?'

'It is the victim I'm asking about.' Pemberton was careful in the words he used and did not reveal that the photograph was of another person. 'As you might have been told, he was found dead this morning about 9.30, and our

171

first intimation was that he died between two and 8.30. Now I can amend that to between 2.30 and 8.30.'

'Yes, it would take him about fifteen minutes to get from here down to his cabin whichever route he took, assuming he didn't stop on the way.'

'Where might he have stopped? Any idea?'

'At that time of day, not many places are functioning, the bars are shut although the lounges remain open. The Prom Deck is open if people can't sleep and want some fresh air, they can walk the entire way around the ship, or you can always go up to the Lido Deck or even the Sun Deck, just to watch the sea.'

'We believe he went to the nightclub before coming here, that's my next destination.'

'That also shuts at three,' said John Anderson.

'Thanks. So he could have been anywhere on the ship before returning to his cabin – and he could have spoken to anyone or accompanied anyone, or even been accosted by someone . . . I might add we are checking the security cameras for sightings of him during the night.'

'There's always somebody about at night, you'd be amazed how many passengers wander around, usually alone, and with the boat being bathed in the light of the midnight sun, you could forgive some for thinking it was daytime. If they want food or drink when the bars and restaurants are shut, all they have to do is ring from their cabins or even an on-board public phone, it can be delivered anywhere on board.'

Pemberton thanked the steward for his help and they next moved to the nightclub, located on the port side of the Prom deck, close to the photo gallery. Even though it was well insulated against noise, they could hear the smooth dance music as they approached. People were still sitting in some of the bar areas even though they were closed, and several lounges continued to have groups sitting and chatting. The midnight sun had that effect – people didn't want to go to bed.

As they entered Fjorgyn's Hall, venue of the nightclub, the band was playing soft music for a foxtrot and couples were on the dance floor in the dim light, holding one another in the old-fashioned dancing mode. They were middle-aged people enjoying a dance from their past. The place was by no means packed and several people were sitting at tables around the edge of the dance floor, this bar still being open and serving. Pemberton and Lorraine moved through the darkness to find a table, but did not obtain a drink.

'All we can do is visit each table,' he said, 'and show them the photo, asking if they were in here last night – or to be precise, in the early hours of this morning – and whether they saw our victim.'

As the music drifted lazily into the night, he and Lorraine went from table to table showing the photo of Lionel Cooper but succeeded only in getting shakings of the head when asked if he had been seen in here around two this morning.

And then Lorraine found a couple who had seen him.

'Yes,' said the girl, a pretty brunette with a Lancashire accent. 'I saw him come in, he was alone. He went across to that table,' and she indicated one on the edge of the floor. 'He just sat here watching.'

'What time would that be?'

'After two, I can't be absolutely sure.'

'Did he talk to anyone?'

'No, no one, and no one came to join him. I expected his wife or girlfriend would join him but no one did. He didn't buy a drink, he had a glass and a bottle with him when he came in, and then the next thing I knew he'd gone. He left the bottle on the table. I don't think he was there more than five minutes.'

'Do you know which way he went? I'm wondering if he went up to the Lido Deck or Sun Deck to see the sun . . .'

'Sorry, I've no idea. '

They thanked her and obtained her name and cabin number to cross her off their list, and then approached the band during a break in the music. The five-piece group and their girl singer all examined the photograph, and it was the singer who nodded. Like the girl witness, she had noticed the man's lonely arrival shortly after two, and she confirmed that he disappeared five minutes later, having spoken to no one.

'Come on, time to go home,' said Pemberton.

Before going to bed, and in the privacy of their cabin, Pemberton decided to write up his notes for Erika to process and record in the morning. He wanted to record his impressions now, otherwise he might forget something important. The strong message from tonight's exercise was that Mansell had left F150 at 12.32, entered Hraevelg's at 12.50, the nightclub around two and then the casino where he'd remained until 2.20–2.30. Then, if he had returned directly to his cabin, he would have arrived not later than 2.45. But had he gone elsewhere? Met someone? Or had someone been waiting near his cabin?

Had someone noticed him moving around the ship alone in the early hours? Someone waiting to kill him? Someone who had prepared for the event by obtaining a knife? That did not seem feasible. You didn't go to the trouble of stealing a knife on the off-chance of finding a victim.

In Pemberton's view, the killing had all the appearances of being a sudden attack and yet some elements indicated advance planning, such as the lack of a break-in at the cabin, and the use of a knife which had somehow evaded the security system. So how did the late-night wanderings of Mansell fit into the overall pattern of events? If the murder had been planned, the killer must have known Mansell was going to board the ship and he must have known which cabin he had occupied. Unless the intended victim was Lionel Cooper? How significant was it that Mansell, during all those wanderings and visits in the early hours, had always been alone? With a drink?

'It's becoming increasingly important to learn more about the family backgrounds of both Cooper and

Mansell,' he said when he had written up his diary. 'And Brother Luke. Somehow, I think they're all linked to this affair.'

But Lorraine didn't hear him; she was already in bed and fast asleep.

Pemberton and Lorraine had a break from enquiries during breakfast in Vingolf's Hall. Not wishing to conduct any interviews or answer quesions at this early stage, they secured a table for two, fully aware that most of the people would now be aware of the mysterious death, even if the identity of the victim was not stated. That could not be done until he had been formally identified. The news item was prominently displayed in the ship's newspaper which had been delivered to every cabin; Mark had read the piece in his own copy and it said that passengers and crew must expect to be interviewed by police officers. With the passengers now aware of the death, he hoped their enquiries on day two would be more productive.

After breakfast, they went immediately to the incident room where Erika was eagerly waiting. He told her he was pleased the death had now been made public and explained the events of last night.

'What we need is a time chart,' he told her. 'Can you make one for me? Either on the computer or on graph paper which we can pin up on the noticeboard.'

'What's it for?'

He explained how, in a murder enquiry, time charts are used to note the whereabouts of the victim, and possible killer or killers, at any particular time and place. The times are taken from the statements of witnesses and it is a highly visual method of plotting the paths of the key players in the drama, as reported both by the players themselves and by reliable witnesses. He explained how she could show the time along the base of her chart, in blocks of, say, half an hour, from the time Mansell was known to have boarded the ship to when he was known to be dead. Locations could be in a vertical list, perhaps by deck number. He drew a rough sketch to explain his idea and she understood immediately, saying she would enjoy the exercise by abstracting data from the material already amassed.

'So might it help us to see where and when the killer and victim might have met away from the cabin?' she asked.

'That's exactly what I hope it will do. Now, I need other things too,' he continued. 'Can you contact the security staff and ask them for more checks of their cameras until 2.45? That's cameras on all decks. It's clear that Mansell was wandering around the ship alone until the early hours. Why, I wonder? We're still anxious to know whether he met anyone and whether anyone accompanied him back to his cabin or joined him later – but I must stress we don't know what time he returned. All we know is the time he left the casino. Was he a homosexual looking for a partner? Wanting to invite someone back to his cabin? We mustn't forget that the ship's records don't mention Mansell, so any official records could make it appear the deceased was Lionel Cooper, simply because he was the occupant of F150. Even the photographs might support that! The purchase chits are in Cooper's name too, even if they are signed by a fake. We still need to get Mansell formally identified as soon as possible. I'll ask Paul Larkin to get a CID officer to obtain specimen fingerprints from the homes of both Mansell and Cooper, he can send them here by computer. I can check them with the body, I know enough about fingerprints to carry out a simple check, enough to establish an identity for our purposes even if it's not enough to be official.'

Erika said, 'The Captain still needs a lot of convincing! He can't believe there's been a switch of passengers, he believes our security cannot be breached like this. He needs more proof before he contacts the Norwegian immigration authorities.'

'Oh, crumbs! I need all the help I can get from Norway. So if I can get fingerprints, that should settle it. Now I need you to contact Paul Larkin and ask if he's found anything more about Mansell, Cooper and Brother Luke. They are our eternal triangle! I know he's already busy doing that, but a nudge might help speed things up. Someone knows more about this affair than they are admitting. I'm increasingly sure we're dealing with a complicated and well-planned killing here, not an opportunist murder. I find that very odd indeed.'

'It is very peculiar,' Lorraine admitted. 'All this skulduggery . . .'

'Because there's more to this than is obvious to us, we must establish a motive. There's bound to be one. A complex murder of this kind doesn't happen without a reason, and if it's not linked to anything which has happened on board, then the backgrounds of Cooper and Mansell, along with Brother Luke, might offer a solution. Something must have happened ashore, but what? To find out, we need to know more about their families, and we should talk to their neighbours again.'

'They don't appear to have families, do they?' Lorraine reminded Pemberton. 'That initial information from Paul suggests they are all loners, even if Cooper has been married.'

'We need to dig deeper, but time's against us. I'm not satisfied they have no one. Someone must know them and what they do in their private and working lives. And don't forget, we might have two murders, Lionel Cooper hasn't been found yet, so we don't know whether he's alive or dead.'

'Time really is against us.' Lorraine looked worried. 'We're getting closer to Spitzbergen by the hour – should we ask the Captain once again not to let any passengers off when we dock?'

'He's made his decision but we've two full days left to persuade him to change his mind, or to find our killer, so let's get cracking. But first, I must update him.'

Erika now said her piece. 'First, I promised I'd check whether any telephone calls had been made to or from F150 overnight. The answer is no. No internal ones and no external.'

'Thanks, Erika. So no one was summoned to the cabin by telephone. That means the invitation to F150 was given verbally, probably sometime in advance, or else the visitor was admitted simply by knocking on the door on spec.'

'Shall I call the Captain now? He is expecting you,' Erika reminded him.

'Please.'

She rang Captain Hansteen who said he would come along to the incident room. When he arrived, Pemberton updated him, stressing that they had narrowed down Mansell's movements until a few hours before his death – and reminding the Captain that, in Pemberton's view, Mansell was definitely not the same person as Lionel Cooper. Pemberton reiterated his reasons, providing details of the signatures on the cruise card chits. The Captain looked at them but said the difference in handwriting might be due to the roll of the ship or some other factor like a sore finger!

'No way!' said Pemberton. 'It wouldn't alter to that extent.'

'If there has been a switch of passengers in the way you suggest, then our security measures need to be tightened. I have great faith in our systems and remain unconvinced – those two men are like identical twins. Just look at those photos! It is one man, surely? Using two names and two passports.'

'I'm going to see if I can obtain fingerprints from the homes of both Cooper and Mansell, then I can compare them with the body. That should be proof enough for us that he is one or other of them. We can have them sent here by computer. We really could do with help from the Norwegian immigration authorities – I need to know whether Cooper has jumped ship and is still alive.'

178

'You will have to work hard to convince me, Mr Pemberton.'

'Has Cooper been in touch with you?'

'No, not at all. Why do you ask?'

'If he was forcibly or accidentally prevented from returning to the ship, he might now have recovered from whatever happened to him. That being so, I would have expected him, or perhaps the local police, to contact the ship to explain his absence and to warn you that there's an interloper on board.'

'Well, he hasn't – which supports my belief that there is only one man.'

'Or that Cooper is also dead. Or that the pair of them were together engaged in some kind of deception.'

Pemberton moved on to today's plans and enquiries. 'It's really a case of asking more and more people more and more questions, and trying to narrow down Mansell's movements through sightings by witnesses. Or cameras. Really, though, I need to be asking more questions on shore . . . maybe this enquiry will continue until we return?'

'But if the cruise is completed without the killer being identified, he – or she – will disembark and be lost ashore among nearly 2000 passengers who are rushing home! That's the danger we're facing,' admitted the Captain. 'I cannot detain everyone on board either at the end of the cruise or at any of our scheduled port visits.'

'And I can't arrest the entire passenger list and crew on suspicion! I can't hold everyone until we've checked for fingerprints and DNA evidence. And I can't impound the entire ship as evidence! We have to resolve this before we reach Spitzbergen – and certainly before we return to Southampton.'

'I sympathize with your problem, Mr Pemberton. I wish there was something more I could do to help.'

'How about the passengers not going ashore at Spitzbergen? That would prevent the killer leaving the ship.'

'You know I'm reluctant to do that. The passengers have paid good money for this trip and a shore visit to

Ny-Alesund on Spitzbergen is one of the highlights, the main reason for this cruise. It's not every day an ordinary person can have access to a site used for Arctic environmental research – or to the world's most northerly human settlement and its most northerly post office! And there may be polar bears, reindeer and Arctic foxes to see. For my passengers, this is the cruise of a lifetime. I must let them go ashore.'

'But suppose the weather was against it?'

'That can happen but the forces of nature are something the passengers can understand and we can delay arrival for several hours if necessary. Remember, the ship's newspaper was published this morning and everyone should know about the death. It would be wrong if I decide against that important shore trip simply in case a killer escapes – he is on board now and some will know that. Others might not realize the death was murder, not the way our newspaper reports it. Besides, where can a killer go on Spitzbergen? Without an aircraft, there is no escape. I am sure a clever killer will have considered that.'

'Perhaps those who realize the killer is still on board might be persuaded to help us catch him? In any case, I shall pray for bad weather,' said Pemberton.

He then explained how his table companions had volunteered, reassuring the Captain that they were suitable and would be useful in keeping an ear open for casual conversations around the ship. The Captain thanked him for his work to date and left.

Today, therefore, he and Lorraine would be concentrating even more heavily on passengers occupying cabins on F Deck, if necessary reinterviewing them. If they could not identify potential witnesses with assistance from the portfolio of official photographs, they would call them by name over the tannoy for brief interviews in Odin's Garden. Pemberton remained aware, however, that the times of sightings of Mansell had not been confirmed – there remained doubt about the time he actually returned to his cabin. There was also the continuing question of where he had been between 2.45 and the time of his death. And with whom. And why. What was certain was that someone had visited him in his cabin, someone who was surely known to him. Or known to Cooper? Or to Brother Luke?

Chapter Eleven

Working independently, albeit both using Odin's Garden, Pemberton dealt with the remaining passengers occupying port side cabins on F Deck while Lorraine interviewed those on the starboard side, each calling in their interviewees over the tannoy. By summoning the occupants of five cabins simultaneously, and with couples arriving together, the operation was speeded up; four or five people would usually turn up at the same time and were happy to await their turn, each interview taking but a few minutes. Among them were the occupants of F148, which adjoined the victim's cabin, and F146 close by, none of whom had heard any suspicious noises or witnessed any untoward activity in or around Mansell's cabin. Likewise those next door to Brother Luke and nearby, three invalids in wheelchairs, had heard or seen nothing. Geraldine Norris and her husband, the occupants of F138, had already been interviewed and were not called. They also managed to interview Simon Rogers, the friend of the steward, John Osbourne, who had been accompanying Brother Luke.

If no useful evidence came to light, it would be necessary to expand this activity to include the occupants of all other decks, passengers and crew alike. With many already interviewed, they decided to have a break, not by ordering coffee in Odin's Garden but preferring Vingolf's Hall where Brian, Russell and the others should be waiting. And so they were. Over coffee and biscuits, Pemberton updated them with particular emphasis on the amended time of death along with Mansell's lone wanderings around the public areas of the ship in the early hours.

He then asked for their reports, realizing his helpers were taking this very seriously. In spite of their efforts, little of evidential value emerged – what did become clear, however, was that the death was now being discussed by many of the passengers. From what Brian, Russell and their wives had learned, no one had mentioned any kind of fracas or behaviour which had attracted undue attention. They estimated they had spoken to around fifty people, none of whom had been interviewed previously. But none could help – not even people who had been moving around the ship in the early hours. None had made any comment about the substitution of the monk's companion; that suggested it had not concerned the other passengers or that none had noticed. They had not obtained names of those they had spoken to, but Pemberton did not mind – all he wanted was for people to start gossiping and there was little harm in interviewing someone twice.

As they discussed the case, Pemberton noticed Brother Luke heading in their direction, his chair propelled by a steward. As they halted nearby, the steward said, 'Mr Pemberton, Brother Luke.'

'Ah, good, my eyesight isn't as sharp as it was, Mr Pemberton. Forgive my intrusion but may I have a word?'

'Of course. You can speak in front of these people – they're helping me.'

'Well, when we talked about the trip to the mountain lodge, you asked if anyone had spoken to me. I said yes. You wanted me to remember who it was.'

'That's right.'

'I noticed one of them at breakfast this morning and managed to attract his attention. After I explained what it was about, he is very keen to talk to you. His name is Fisher, he and his wife are on B Deck. I can't remember his cabin number but am sure you will find him.'

Pemberton thanked him, then added, 'I think you should know we've narrowed the time of death of your companion, Brother Luke. We know he was alive at 2.45 yesterday, so the period which now interests me is between then and 8.30. Can I ask you once again to cast your mind back to that time? Did you hear any noises from the cabin next door? Was your sleep disturbed? Did anything out of the ordinary occur?'

'Since we spoke, I've been racking my brains to try and help, but I slept like a log that night. The sea air, you know. I never heard a thing and never left my cabin until I went to breakfast.'

'Those cabins are very soundproof, it seems.'

'They are, but I'm hard of hearing and not well sighted either. Even so, I found it so difficult to believe a man could be killed in the adjoining cabin without me being aware of it. Had I known, I might have been able to save him but I didn't. It is a hard cross to bear, Mr Pemberton.'

Pemberton explained that no further progress had been made but assured the monk he would keep him informed; in return, Brother Luke said he would reciprocate and he was wheeled away to Forseti's Hall to enjoy a string quartet.

'We're going up to the golf nets on Sun Deck, then we'll be on the Lido Deck, both busy places,' announced Brian. 'We'll keep our ears and eyes open up there and ask around to get people talking. We'll visit the most popular areas and the bars. Will you be here for lunch?'

'Yes, around one, see you then,' nodded Pemberton, and so the little party of amateur detectives dispersed.

'What now?' asked Lorraine.

'Let's get back to Odin's Garden to finish F Deck,' he suggested. 'First, though, we'll call in Mr Fisher to see what he can tell us and then I need to examine what we've achieved so far, which isn't much! That means a visit to the incident room, so I wonder if Erika's got the time chart done? I'm coming to the conclusion I'll have to start all over again, Lorraine, just as you suggested. Go back to the beginning, you said. I'm convinced I've missed something which is staring me in the face but I have to say an idea is coming to me . . . slowly though, so I must work on it.'

They approached the receptionist and asked that Mr Fisher be summoned for a chat with Detective Superintendent Pemberton in Odin's Garden and as they waited, both Pemberton and Lorraine sat in silence, each with their own thoughts. She knew better than to interrupt him especially if he had produced the germ of an idea, a breakthrough perhaps. During any difficult investigation he required quiet times to think, and think deeply, and so she settled back to await their newest interviewee. After twenty minutes, a small thin man in his mid-fifties who was sporting a ginger goatee beard appeared. He wore long green shorts, a white T-shirt and heavy trainers. Lorraine nudged Pemberton who glanced towards the newcomer, saying, 'I'm not surprised Brother Luke recognized this chap.' Fisher reported to the receptionist and was shown to their table.

'Mr Fisher?' Pemberton stood up to greet him. When the man confirmed his name, Pemberton introduced Lorraine and invited him to be seated. 'It's good of you to join us. I think you know what this is about?'

'Yes, Brother Luke told me about the murder but said you were interested in what happened at Trollstigheimen Mountain Lodge. He went there, with his companion – we were on the same trip, my wife and I, same coach as them too.'

'We were on that trip as well, but not the same coach,' said Pemberton. 'I must admit I never noticed you at the lodge, but there were lots of visitors, not only from our ship. Other ships had berthed in the fjord. However, when I was there I noticed Brother Luke on his own for a while, after lunch. He was outside in the sunshine near the cafeteria, in his wheelchair and clearly enjoying the atmosphere.'

'Yes, that's when I noticed him, all alone.'

'I was wondering what had happened to his companion but all he could say was that Lionel had gone for a walk.

185

My reason for talking to you is to ask whether you saw anyone speaking to Brother Luke or his companion . . . We need anything really, any small snippet of information which might be relevant to the disappearance of his companion.'

'Disappearance? But he did not disappear, Mr Pemberton, he went there with Brother Luke and returned with him. He wasn't away for long, not many minutes I'd say. I would hardly call that a disappearance.'

'But Luke was alone for a while, I saw him.'

'Me too, that's why I went across for a chat, chiefly to see if he was all right. He looked rather isolated but was happy enough, saying Lionel had gone for a walk to look at the views. Most of the people were doing that but it involved some tricky footpaths on the very high and steep mountainsides, dangerous for a wheelchair.'

'He called him Lionel?'

'Yes, as you did just now.'

'Were you alone, chatting to him after Lionel had gone?'

'Yes, my wife was in the shop, trying to find a souvenir or two to take home, but it was so crowded I left her to it and had a chat with Brother Luke.'

'Was there a reason for your chat? Something personal?'

'No, just a friendly natter, being sociable as you do on cruises. You make friends by chatting to people. I was just being friendly because he seemed so alone.'

'I understand. Did you see Lionel leave?'

'Yes, as a matter of fact I did. As I left the shop, I could see him and Brother Luke chatting, then someone, a man, came up to Lionel, spoke to him and pointed. They both disappeared behind the complex, in the direction he had pointed. I lost sight of them but all around the lodge there are walks, climbs, viewpoints, waterfalls, shops and even a ski club and lift busy with club members not far away. It was very busy with plenty to see. I thought the man was explaining something special to Lionel, suggesting a viewpoint or something to look at.'

'Lionel went away with someone? This is news – so who was it? Can you describe him, or her?'

'It was definitely a man. He walked like a man although he wore a cagoule, dark blue with a yellow hood. The hood was up so I couldn't see his face but he was about the same build as Luke's companion. Most of us had taken clothing suitable for bad weather. I'm afraid I didn't take much notice of him, I thought he was just another of our cruise party wanting to show Lionel the best of the scenery.'

'Did you speak to him?'

He shook his head. 'No, as they disappeared behind the shopping complex and cafeteria, I went to speak to Brother Luke. I remained with him for about five minutes and then went off to find that viewpoint that overlooks Stigfoss Waterfall. I never saw that man again.'

'But you saw Lionel again?'

'Yes, he got back in time to return Brother Luke to the coach.'

'How long had he been away?'

'I don't know, probably twenty minutes or so.'

'I need to know more about that newcomer, Mr Fisher. The weather was not bad, was it? Not enough to justify putting up his hood?'

'No, it was fine and dry, as you know. I thought it odd on such a dry day but sometimes people protect their heads and ears against cold winds.'

'So the newcomer did not return. Are you sure the man who took Luke back to the bus was actually Lionel?'

'Well, yes, who else could it be?' Fisher was now frowning. 'He wasn't wearing the anorak or hood.'

'Was he carrying anything?'

'I'm sure he had a holdall of some sort, most of us had bags or backpacks.'

'Mr Fisher, I have reason to believe that Brother Luke's companion, Lionel, was replaced, and that the swap occurred at Trollstigheimen Mountain Lodge. The replacement gentleman is the murder victim not Lionel. We have no idea where Lionel has gone or what has happened to him. You can see how important your sighting is. So, the man you saw, the man in the cagoule – is he a member of our cruise trip?'

'Oh, I couldn't say. I didn't see him again, either around the lodge or on our bus. To be truthful, I wouldn't have recognized him without his cagoule, it was rather distinctive, having that yellow hood.'

'He could have removed it? Folded it up?'

'Yes, they fold up into a very small space, you can carry them in a pocket but I didn't see him without it. He might have been on one of our buses.'

'Can you describe the man? Thin? Fat? Tall? Thin? Rough age? Any obvious features?'

'Not really. He was about the same build and height as Lionel, certainly taller than me, but I can't say much more.'

'So the man you thought was Brother Luke's companion returned and escorted him back to the bus, and then on board *Ringhorn*?'

'Yes, that's exactly what I thought. I had no reason to think otherwise although I didn't watch them closely. I just noticed Brother Luke being wheeled along by his helper in the normal way and assumed it was Lionel. They returned on our bus with the wheelchair in the boot.'

'Sitting together?'

'Yes, they sat together, as they had on the outward journey. Well, I mean Lionel sat with him on that trip.'

'Did you speak to Lionel on the return trip?'

'No and not to Brother Luke either. They sat together, chatting and then went back on board *Ringhorn*. Just as you'd expect.'

As Pemberton was chatting, Lorraine was taking down the key points of the interview. He paused to allow her to catch up with her notes, wondering whether there was anything else he could ask, then said, 'Thanks, Mr Fisher. This is valuable new information and I must investigate it thoroughly. As you may realize, the killer is still on board and so my advice is not to mention this to anyone. You might like to discuss it with your wife, though, perhaps she noticed something even if she was occupied by her shopping. If you do need to contact me further, you can do so through reception, and I'm sure you appreciate I might want to speak to you again.'

'Thanks for the warning. I'll chat to my wife about this, in the security of our cabin, just in case she noticed anything I missed, and if so, I'll contact you.'

And so the helpful witness departed.

'What do you make of that?' asked Lorraine.

'I believe him, if that's what you mean, but if you're asking whether Lionel was persuaded to leave Luke, however temporarily, then I would also agree with that. That must be when Lionel was replaced, during those few minutes. It must have been pre-planned with a high degree of skill and local knowledge. And how relevant is the cagoule with the yellow hood?'

'There was one in the luggage in Cooper's cabin.'

'Yes, but who did it belong to? Mansell at a guess, but Cooper might have had one. Does it confirm the identity of the mystery man seen at the mountain lodge?'

'No, it doesn't, does it? But the cagoule supports Mr Fisher's account although it merely adds to the puzzle.'

'Right, so how does all this affect our murder, and where is Lionel now? Dead somewhere on that mountain? What on earth is going on, Lorraine?'

'There were hundreds of people milling around the lodge while we were there, not just off our ship, but from other ships as well as bus trips, not forgetting skiers. They'll have dispersed long ago. We'll never trace them so we can't ask them questions.'

'I could get the Norwegian police to interview the shopkeeper and café owner and their staff, but I doubt if they'll have noticed anything among all those people. They'd be far too busy. However, there are things we can do. We can start by finding out exactly who went ashore from *Ringhorn* to Andalsnes, then ask if they saw Brother Luke near the lodge and if so, whether anyone was with him. Those shore trips are usually booked by the passengers before boarding although you can join at the last minute if there's room but in all cases names will be recorded because the trips have to be paid for – with the cruise cards. And we were all zapped off the ship and back again. So that's our next task, Lorraine. Come along, let's have words with Erika.'

When they returned to the incident room, Erika had been busy. She had secured extra pinboards which now bore large copies of all the deck plans, clearly showing each cabin. All bore their numbers and it was easy to see which were inside and which were outside, i.e. those located internally with no window or those having a window or port hole overlooking the ocean, those with balconies, those which were twins or singles along with staterooms, suites and mini-suites. The plans also showed the location of key areas and attractions, and she had added the crew's quarters and office and storage space.

She was now going through the statements and lists of people interviewed, highlighting their respective cabins with a bright orange fluorescent marker pen. On an adjoining board were the lists of passengers, in alphabetical order along with their cabin numbers, and a similar list of crew members.

'It makes me realize just what a mammoth task it is, to interview everyone,' commented Pemberton. 'We've only ticked off a fraction of the entire complement of passengers and precious few crew but this is very useful, thanks, Erika.'

'I've had a crack at making the time chart,' she told him, leading him and Lorraine to her desk. 'Is this what you wanted?'

'Looks good!' He studied it awhile and then said, 'Yes, that's just what we need.'

'You'll see I've placed red stickers on the times Mansell was seen and I've matched those on the deck plans. I've written the times he was seen on those stickers on the deck plans, so we can plot his progress around the ship.'

'Good stuff ... you're a natural detective! So has anything struck you about his movements? Does anything
raise a question in your mind?'

'Sorry, no.'

'Me neither. Everything seems utterly normal, except we
have a man murdered in his cabin without anyone knowing a thing about it. Let's keep this system rolling, it's
bound to throw up something soon. Now, more tasks for
you. I'd like to know details of all phone calls from this
ship to shore since we left Southampton and I'd also like a
photo of Brother Luke when he first used *Ringhorn*.'

'That was some time ago!'

'When he was much younger, yes. That's what I need.
Luke as a younger man. Then I need a list of all those who
went ashore on the recent Andalsnes trip, and up to the
mountain lodge.'

He told her of the sighting of the man who persuaded
Lionel to leave the monk sitting alone. 'That man must
have been Mansell, so I need to know if all our passengers
were booked back on board again.'

'I'm sure we've done that already, but I'll get the Purser's
department to run off a list for a double-check. It's all on
computer so it'll only take a minute or two. Shall I do it
now while you wait?'

'Yes, thanks.' While she went to make the call, he and
Lorraine studied the wealth of plans and lists before them.
Already, this was looking like a genuine incident room,
even if it had much fewer staff, and he scanned the lists,
marvelling at the administrative skills needed to maintain
the smooth operation of such a huge undertaking. Then he
spotted something of interest.

'See this, Lorraine?'

'What?'

'F152, I thought Brother Luke was in that cabin.
According to this, it's somebody called Lionel Chadwin.'

'Lionel?' she frowned. 'Another Lionel?'

'Well yes, there's that, it's not such a common name, but
why doesn't it show Brother Luke as occupant? So where

191

is he? He hasn't asked to be moved, has he? Or is this just an administrative error?' He checked the neighbouring cabins which accommodated wheelchairs. 'Nope, he's not shown in any of the others.'

'You'll have to ask Erika.'

'Lorraine, that's it! The very thing we've missed right from the beginning. Brother Luke. We've been so busy checking the backgrounds and movements of Lionel Cooper and Mansell that we've neglected a really close look at the monk and his background. We don't know a lot about him, do we? After all, everything's revolved around him . . . and he was in the adjoining cabin when Mansell was killed, he has done a tour of the galley and he was there when Mansell replaced Lionel . . .'

'He's an old man, Mark, he's not a killer!'

'We haven't searched his cabin, have we? For blood-stained clothing, a knife?'

'No, we haven't. But you're not placing him in the frame, are you? As a suspect?'

'He's got to be, hasn't he?'

'Even though he's a very old man and says he was asleep!'

'He can't prove he was asleep at the material time in his own cabin, can he? And he is mobile to a degree. But I will leave all those stones unturned until I have more evidence, or more reason to think he's the killer. If I am going to accuse him of murder, I need more positive evidence, not mere speculation. In the meantime we've got to find out who Lionel Chadwin is, and there's something else I want to ask Erika.'

Erika returned and said the list of Andalsnes visitors would arrive in a few minutes, so he took the opportunity to air his questions.

'First,' he said, 'I see Brother Luke isn't shown as occupying his cabin.'

'Well, Brother Luke's not his real name,' she smiled. 'Monks often adopt other names, his real name is Lionel Chadwin, that's on his passport. That's the name I sent to your office in Rainesbury, Lionel Chadwin, also known as Brother Luke.'

'I didn't see those lists, did I? I missed that . . .'

'No, you didn't see them. We sent them direct by email, from our own records. It's like a famous actor or author who uses a professional name – they're so well known by those names that they use them all the time, but we have to use their official name, the one on their passport. We get the same thing happening with some of our entertainers and travelling guest speakers. For official reasons, we record the cabin occupant as the name on the passport and booking form.'

'So Brother Luke's passport and booking form show him as Lionel Chadwin?'

'Yes, but all the regular crew know him as Brother Luke.'

'And although he's a monk, he's never been ordained a priest.'

'Right. I understand he was in a monastery before going into a rest home but he has private means. He's been coming here for years, always as a paying passenger. He always uses that same table in the restaurant – there aren't many tables for two in there – and since he became an invalid, he's always used the same cabin. F152. Three years, I think.'

'And has Lionel Cooper always accompanied him?'

'No, this was the first time. He had other helpers before.'

'So what did he do before he became a monk?'

'I'm not sure, he's always seemed to have plenty of spare time and the money to go on cruises, not just to the Arctic which is his favourite, but to other places around the world. I haven't been here all that long but I know he's one of our most regular passengers. Now he's getting older, he's not joining us so frequently but he still gets special attention from those who've looked after him on previous occasions. One of our crew members has known him for nearly twenty years.'

So was this the vital information Pemberton had overlooked? His mind was now working overtime. So Brother

Luke was not merely an old man, he was a wealthy old man. And a monk no less. Who would inherit his wealth? Was it in cash, shares, property? Had someone tried to kill him in order to inherit? And got into the wrong cabin? Those were always good questions for a detective to ask – and answer. He sensed the beginnings of enlightenment now – a plot to gain the old man's estate. One of the oldest motives in the world. Greed. Avarice.

'So who is the crew member who has known him all this time?'

'She's the chief accountant in the Purser's office, Maria Saville.'

'I'd better speak to her immediately. Can you call her in? We can talk in here, and I'd like you present to take notes. And there is another question I need to ask about the shore trips. Can crew members go ashore on trips which are organized for the passengers?'

'Oh yes, it's one of the perks of the job, it gives us a chance to see the world.'

'So how is that arranged?'

'We have to go in our off-duty time but we don't have to pay. If a trip is heavily subscribed, there might not be room so we'd have to wait for another trip. I've never known that happen, though. Most of the time, crew members just tag on.'

'But they'll be booked off the ship, and back on again? Just like the passengers?'

'Oh, yes, we keep very strict records.'

'Good, now before I chat to Maria Saville, do you have Lionel Chadwin's home address? At the moment, he's in a diocesan rest home.'

'Yes, I can soon find it in our old records.'

'Good, then I can get Paul Larkin to make more enquiries, he didn't get much from the rest home but it's possible the staff know very little about Brother Luke. Now let's see what Maria Saville can tell us about Brother Luke.'

Maria Saville was an elegant fifty-year-old with a trim figure in a smart uniform, a pleasant unlined face, blue eyes and a fine head of fair hair which was swept back from her face. Pemberton realized it was the woman he'd seen chatting to Brother Luke during that first night in the restaurant; he invited her to be seated at a table in the office. He sat opposite with Lorraine and Erika at either side.

'Thanks for coming. Can I call you Maria?'

She smiled her consent. 'Yes, everyone does.'

'I am Detective Superintendent Pemberton and this is Detective Constable Cashmore. I believe you are aware that we are investigating a murder on board?'

'Yes, we have been told.'

'I need your help, Maria, I need you to be open and frank. The victim was the companion of Brother Luke and although we are investigating the background of the deceased, we have not explored that of Brother Luke. I must add he is not under suspicion of being the killer, but I have a feeling he might be central to the enquiry for reasons I have not established – and for reasons he might not be aware of. In short, I need to know more about him, possibly for his future safety. I appreciate there might be an issue of confidentiality, but this is a murder investigation.'

'I understand.'

'I'm told you have known him since he started using your cruise liners?'

'Yes, we go back a long time. He wasn't a monk then, that was something that followed the death of his wife. He wasn't even a Catholic.'

'Can you tell me about it? With as much detail as possible? I would add that this discussion is in complete confidence which is why we are using this room.'

She began by saying that, as a young girl, she was always good at mathematics and had a flair for understanding finance and business accounts; her first job was in an accountant's office but because she wanted to see the world, she later obtained employment with the cruise line, at first being a steward working in the bars and restaurants.

195

'That's where I met Lionel,' she said. 'It would be just over twenty years ago, he had lost his wife and thought a cruise would help him get over the loss, while meeting others. He was a very quiet man, shy too, and although we placed him on a table with four others, he never really warmed to them. He spent a lot of time on his own, he seemed to prefer that.'

'And you chatted to him?'

'He would often sit on a stool in one of the bars if I was behind the counter and chat to me. As crew members, we had to be careful if passengers tried to form a relationship but he never made a pass at me, he just wanted to chat. And so, in time and thanks to him coming on other cruises on this ship, I got to know him quite well. The other crew members liked him too, and eventually they recognized him each time he came with us. He's grown older, of course, he now looks his age.'

'Has he any family? Children?'

'He has no children, he told me that. His wife couldn't conceive but I believe there are relations. He said they seldom came to see him, never sent Christmas cards or birthday cards, never knew him. I think that upset him, especially when he lost his wife. He was very much alone, Mr Pemberton, I felt sorry for him.'

'So he was always alone, was he? On those earlier cruises?'

'Yes, always, but at first, of course, he wasn't in a wheel-chair. He developed some illness whose name I forget, but it takes away the use of the legs. That happened about the time I was moved from being a steward and offered a post in the Purser's office. Having accountancy experience helped. It meant regular hours, a more settled routine, but I lost touch with the passengers. I missed that, there's something pleasing in getting to know our passengers. Mind you, whenever I knew Lionel was coming on board – I got copies of each incoming passenger manifest and would look out for his name – I always made a point of having a nice long chat and a drink together. There was never any hint of a romance, I should add!'

'I saw you chatting to him that first evening, in the restaurant.'

'Yes, I checked he was using his usual table and went along to greet him, saying we'd meet up later. I've seen him several times around the ship in the evenings and we've had a quiet chat and drink, sometimes without his companion.'

'Clearly, you'd class yourself as a friend?'

'Yes, very much so. I think he needed someone. He took a long time to get over the loss of his wife, in fact he might not be over it yet.'

'You're not married, are you?' He noticed she did not wear a ring.

'No, this kind of work, not having a settled lifestyle, doesn't lend itself to being married. I've no regrets, I've seen too many unhappy unions.'

'So what can you tell me about Lionel? I'm particularly interested in the years before he became a monk – and that he seems to be wealthy.'

'I don't know what he's worth. I didn't like to pry and he never really talked about it. From what he's told me, though, I know he's from an aristocratic background and inherited money and property. Then he became a property developer in quite a big way. He would buy derelict country houses and farmhouses, modernize them and sell some, but keep others to provide a rental income. He once told me he loved old rectories and faded country houses, wanting to restore them to their former glory, as he put it, and see them put back into use.'

'Is that the sort of house in which he lived?'

'Yes, he was brought up to that kind of life, but when he turned seventy he thought it was time to retire. He bought a run-down old mansion and restored it – it needed a new roof, damp course, central heating, floors, the lot. He did tell me he had enough money to do what was necessary – and sufficient left untouched by that work to provide him with an income. When the house was finished, though, he moved in, he said it was such a lovely place he couldn't bear to sell it or rent it to anyone else! He said it was the sort of place his wife would have liked.'

'Do you know where it is?'

'I don't have the exact address, but it's somewhere in North Yorkshire, near Northallerton. It's between the dales and the moors, an ideal location and very accessible to the main railway lines and trunk roads.'

'But I thought he lived in some kind of rest home?'

'He does now, but that's a fairly recent move. Even with the big house, he used to go into the rest home for a break. He likes solitude but conversely likes being cared for. He gave the home some big donations. Now he's an invalid, he spends more time there, but he also stays in a monastery, Bulford Abbey. He still owns the mansion and rents the land to local farmers. That income funds his time in the monastery and rest home. I understand the big house is not occupied by anyone else because he likes to go back occasionally – a housekeeper lives in a cottage in the grounds and keeps it aired and clean. He hates being a burden, you see. He hates the idea of getting things for nothing! He's always wanted to pay his way. When he became wheelchair-bound, it was difficult getting around the monastery so he told me he intended going into a home, to be cared for. His health was getting worse, I believe he is now being treated for a heart condition, and he is well into his eighties. He declared his health problems to us when booking this trip. To be honest, he can't cope with that big house any more and I think he realizes that. He's lucky, though, to have enough money to do anything he wants.'

'So what's he going to do with the mansion?'

'He never said, Mr Pemberton. From what he told me, it had quite a lot of land and is worth a few million pounds – he's got a lot of share investments too – but he has no children. No one to leave it all to. I don't think he's decided what to do with it. Last year, when we talked, he hadn't made a will. Being an accountant, I told him he should do so as soon as possible, otherwise his wishes – if he had any – would never be carried out.'

'So somebody – or some organization – is going to inherit a very desirable property. Hotel groups are always on the lookout for suitable premises to convert,' remarked Pemberton. 'Brother Luke seems to be sitting on a gold mine. Surely, from that kind of background, there must be other relations?'

'He said none of his family ever kept in touch, so it seems there are some out there, but he wouldn't talk about them. I don't know who they are.'

'Clearly, he liked talking to you, if he told you all this.'

'It came out gradually. I think he wanted to tell someone, perhaps to get their suggestions about what to do with his wealth. I never asked questions and only suggested he made a will. We enjoyed each other's company – and still do.'

Pemberton turned to Erika who had now returned. 'Any luck with those earlier photos of Lionel Chadwin?'

'The gallery is working on them right now, Mr Pemberton.'

'Good. Then we'll know what he looked like as a young man too! Now, Lorraine, is there anything you'd like to ask Maria?'

'I was intrigued by Brother Luke's reaction to the loss of his wife,' said Lorraine. 'I'm wondering why he should turn to religion after her death? Not only to adopt a new religion, but to become a monk no less. It's quite a drastic change.'

'She was a devout Catholic, Miss Cashmore. He attended Mass with her and was deeply impressed by her devotion, especially when she failed to conceive, and then became ill. It was cancer of some kind. She accepted both as the will of God, without complaint. He was deeply impressed by that; he took her to Lourdes and Fatima, in the hope God might grant them a family or a cure for her cancer, but it never happened. She never lost her faith, though, and that impressed him. It was why he decided to convert to

Catholicism – I think part of his decision was because it was something his wife would have understood.'

'And by becoming a monk, he would renounce his worldly goods?'

'Not necessarily, not all monks have to renounce their wealth. I know it bothers him, though, especially having the big house and money in the bank, but he had no wish to dispose of it without a good deal of very considered thought. And that is why he hasn't yet made a will, although he does give a lot to charities and his church. He is still thinking about it, he wants to do the right thing, he wants his acquired wealth to be beneficial to others, not just to a business concern or an individual.'

'Now, we know his personal assistant on this trip was also called Lionel – Lionel Cooper – and the dead man is his look-alike, Richard Mansell. Did Luke ever talk about these people? Or people of that name?'

'No, never.'

'Did he ever strike up a friendship with other crew members?'

'No, he was very shy really. For some reason, he took to me even though I never tried to force a relationship or friendship.'

'Maybe he recognized a genuine friend. Thanks for all this help,' said Pemberton when Lorraine had no further questions. 'I think you have shed a great light on this matter. Thank you – you will be available if we need to ask you more questions?'

'Yes, of course, just contact the Purser's office.'

When she had gone, Pemberton said, 'I think I'm beginning to see a glimmer of light among all this.'

'Not the midnight sun?' smiled Lorraine.

'No, a chink of real daylight!'

Chapter Twelve

From the information supplied by Erika, Pemberton saw that trips ashore were meticulously organized and comprised several hundred passengers divided into groups and sub-divided into further units. Each complete unit was sufficient to fill a coach – fifty people or so – but sometimes one load was smaller, accommodating any overflow from elsewhere. Those who had booked a place were told to assemble in the theatre at a given time and, as they entered, coloured stickers were issued to define each party, e.g. red Group 1, A1; or red Group 1, A2; or green Group 2, A1. Passengers were shepherded on board one of the many tenders which would carry them ashore, and once off the ship, they were advised to seek a coach bearing their coloured sticker and relevant number. It was a simple but well-tried system which had been developed through experience.

Pemberton scanned the list with his usual speed, noting that most of the Andalsnes visitors were passengers rather than crew. His wish was to ascertain whether any crew members had gone ashore to Andalsnes because they, as well as the passengers, would have to be eliminated from his enquiries. On the printout were two crew members, William Rogerson and Rebecca Turrell.

'Do you know either of these?' he asked Erika.

'Sorry, no. We've over 700 crew, and some are newcomers with only a few working in the offices. I don't know them all.'

'In addition to interviewing passengers who went ashore, I'll need to talk to those two. I'll call them in together, unless they're working nights and are in bed. Maybe they are friends? Can you fix that? I'll talk to them in Odin's Garden, as soon as they can get there. Say twenty minutes if they are available?'

'I'll get in touch with them.'

'Thanks. And there's something else I need to know. I've already established that no phone calls were made from F150 between 12.32 and 8.30 – our initial time of death – but because we know that Mansell did not return there until 2.45 or thereabouts, that now becomes the relevant time. Mansell was roaming the ship until 2.45. If a telephone invitation was made to someone, it could have been done from one of the public phones on the decks. If that happened, who did Mansell ring from such a phone to issue his invitation? Can we find out?'

'It's possible to determine which public phones have been used but calls within the ship's confines are free, such as cabin to cabin, and so records are not readily available. A call to a shore line, of course, will be charged to the cruise card and so that kind of record can be found fairly easily. We're working on that.'

'Good, and I'd be interested in any calls made during the night but especially between 12.32 and 8.30, from call boxes to on-board numbers.'

'I'll do my best,' promised Erika.

'And I've been thinking,' Pemberton continued. 'There's a couple on board who I haven't noticed since we assembled in the boarding lounge. A tall blond man with a statuesque blonde woman, Nordic-looking and very handsome. They must have been using a different restaurant from us and occupying themselves in different ways, they're not the sort you could overlook. I need to talk to that man.'

'Sorry, unless I have more information I can't give you a name,' said Erika.

'I'll get my other teams to keep their eyes open,' he smiled.

'Why are you especially interested in them?' asked Lorraine.

'I noticed the man taking video pictures of us all waiting in the boarding lounge. There was a steward standing at the back, available if we needed help. He was called Lionel. How about that, eh? Another Lionel? I'd like to see if he was captured on those pictures.'

'I can get a list of stewards' duties for you,' Erika said. 'That will show who was on duty in the boarding lounge at that time.'

'His duty wouldn't be restricted to our boarding party, would it?'

'No, he'd be available to everyone arriving that day; as your group would leave the lounge another group would replace you and wait there until called.'

'Yes, I noticed that. Right, I'd be pleased if you could find out who he was – and I'd still like to see that man's film of us all. And there was another man taking photos in the departure lounge but I doubt if I could identify him.'

'So we'll all seek tall handsome blond people. What's next?' asked Lorraine.

'A chat with those crew members,' said Pemberton. 'Then we need to issue our latest orders to our troops, we can do that over lunch. And we need to speak to everyone who went ashore to Andalsnes although Mr Fisher's evidence will keep me happy for the time being. But before all that, I need a chat with Paul Larkin back on shore. I'll do it now. Erika, have we Lionel Chadwin's previous address yet?'

'Yes, it was Starthorpe Hall near Thirsk,' and she provided the post code.

'Thanks, this is a big help.'

While Erika began her various other new tasks, Pemberton rang his office in Rainesbury and was quickly connected with DI Larkin.

'Morning, Paul, Pemberton here, speaking from some-where on the ocean wave. How's things back at the ranch?'

Paul updated him, assuring him everything was fine and adding that he had not yet discovered any more about Mansell, Cooper or Brother Luke. He was awaiting responses from police forces who inevitably placed such requests at a lower priority than their own work. He would demand more urgent co-operation. There was no report either from the Norwegian police about Cooper's fate – they had made a preliminary helicopter search of the region around the mountain lodge but nothing had been found. They said a full-scale manual search had not yet been arranged due to the lack of positive information – such a search would require climbing experts, helicopters, police dogs and high-power cameras.

Then Pemberton added, 'I've a new task for you, Paul, this time within our own force area. For urgent treatment, I might stress! Very urgent in fact.'

'Fire away, boss, I'll give it priority.'

'It's about the monk I mentioned earlier. I know you've done some research but I think he might be the unwitting catalyst to our murder. I don't consider him a prime sus-pect, he's too old and frail, but I want some enquiries into his background. He's quite a character, he hasn't always been a monk; his real name is Lionel Chadwin. He's from a posh background and is a former property developer, a widower with no children, whose last known home address was Starthorpe Hall near Thirsk, between there and Northallerton, I believe. He still owns it but it's un-occupied, except for a housekeeper who lives in the grounds. He's got money too, lots of it. Can you make enquiries into his background, family, business – every-thing? I think the death of his companion might somehow be linked to the disposal of that mansion – it seems the old man hasn't made a will. I smell a plot here, Paul; the sharks are gathering. Who's after his worldly goods, I ask myself? The answer may have caused one murder already, and possibly two. Can you do a bit of urgent digging?'

'With that purpose in mind?'

'I want to know who might be hovering in the background, waiting to pounce when the old man dies. If he dies intestate, the laws of inheritance will prevail – somebody could find themselves with a nice ancestral pile and money to run it. We need to look into his family. Are there some nasty cousins lurking in the undergrowth?'

'In cases like that, there's always nasty cousins lurking in the undergrowth, sometimes getting rid of the opposition! Do we need to target anyone in particular?'

'R. W. Mansell for starters – it's vital we get to know more about him. And then Lionel Cooper – we need more on him as well.'

'Are they related to the monk then?'

'I don't know, but I reckon it's a distinct possibility.'

'I'll do it myself, boss. I'll start immediately!'

Happy that Larkin was personally involved in such an important part of the investigation, Pemberton turned to Lorraine. 'Right, so far so good. Let's see if those crew members have arrived in Odin's Garden.'

When they entered the reception area, two stewards in uniform, a man and a woman, were sitting at the table Pemberton always used, clearly having been directed there by the receptionist. They stood up smartly as the detectives approached. Pemberton checked their identities and cabin numbers – they were William Rogerson and Rebecca Turrell. He introduced himself and Lorraine, and settled down. Rogerson was not the steward he had noticed hovering in the background during their boarding routine.

'Thanks for coming,' he addressed both and explained his reason for calling them. They understood; all crew members were aware of the enquiries.

'I believe you went on the outing to Andalsnes, and up to Trollstigheimen Mountain Lodge?'

'Yes, we did,' said William Rogerson.

'Together?'

'Yes.'

'Now, I'm interested in the movements of one of our passengers, a monk in a wheelchair called Brother Luke. He also went on that trip, with his companion, a man called Lionel Cooper. Did you see them?'

Rebecca responded. 'Yes, we were on the same coach, we saw them near the café and gift shop, they're easily noticed.'

'Ah, this is good. Were they alone?'

'Yes, and as we were deciding whether to go for a coffee and cake, or walk over to the viewpoint over Stigfoss Waterfall, we suddenly realized the monk was all by himself.'

'Did you see where his companion went?'

'No,' said William. 'I thought he must have gone off to find a toilet, I think there are some at the back of the complex.'

'Did you see anyone with the monk just before his friend left?'

'Sorry, no. He was all alone.'

'Did either of you speak to him at that time? Or his companion?'

'No, we decided to go into the café and gift shop first, before heading for the waterfalls; most of the others had gone to the waterfalls first, so we thought the shop and café would not be so crowded. As we went inside, the monk was still outside in his wheelchair. Alone. That's right, isn't it, Rebecca?'

She nodded in support of her friend.

'Did you see a man in a cagoule approach the priest? The cagoule was dark blue with a yellow hood, and the hood was up even though it was a dry day.'

They shook their heads. 'Sorry, no.'

'We have a witness who said the man in a cagoule went and spoke to the monk's companion, pointed in some direction after which the two of them went off together.'

'No, we never saw that. Sorry.'

'So you saw Brother Luke all alone in his wheelchair as you entered the buildings. Where was he when you came out?'

'He'd gone. I don't know where he went but we later saw him as we boarded our coach for the return trip. He was already on board and his chair was folded and packed in the trunk compartment.'

'Was he with his companion?'

'Yes, the man who has been with him all during the trip. They were in the same seats.'

'Did you notice anything different about his companion?'

'No, nothing, we just saw them as we went on board, but we sat in front of them during the journey, so we couldn't see them, or hear them talking. To be honest, neither of us took much notice of them.'

'Thanks. And so when you returned to the ship, they went on board without any fuss or problems?'

'Yes, just like the rest of us. Searched by the security crew, electronically and manually, bags and bodies, and then checked back on board. Nothing out of the ordinary happened.'

'Did you notice any other crew members on the trip?'

'No, I think we were the only ones. We don't know them all but I think we'd have known which were crew and which were passengers.'

When it was clear the young couple could provide no further details, Pemberton thanked them and allowed them to leave. He was satisified with their answers, which would probably reflect the responses he'd get from any passengers on that trip, but it was two more names to cross off the list. They returned to the incident room where Erika told them that the Purser's office had checked their records of telephone calls.

'There weren't any.' She showed them the computer printout. 'No calls were made from the public phones on any deck on the day in question between midnight and 9.30 next morning. I might say, Mr Pemberton, that that is quite normal. Almost the only time those phones are used at night is when there's an emergency of some kind – someone slipping and breaking a leg, being taken ill, assaulted perhaps, that sort of thing. If passengers want any other help during the night hours, urgent or not, they use the phones in their cabins.'

'Thanks, I had to check.'

'And I've got some early photographs of Brother Luke, hot from the photo gallery.' She picked a plastic folder from her desk. 'Several go back to the time he first sailed with this ship, when he was known as Lionel Chadwin. He didn't have a beard then either. Each was taken just before he boarded, as you know.'

He accepted the folder, opened it and studied the contents for a few moments, then walked over to the notice-board with its array of lists and other information. Pinned to it were photographs of Lionel Cooper, taken when he was boarding for this trip, and the death mask of R. W. Mansell. Pemberton abstracted a photograph of Brother Luke taken on his first cruise; he was then more than twenty years younger and looked quite different from his present appearance. The caption called him Lionel Chadwin.

'Notice anything?' he asked both Lorraine and Erika.

'Good grief!' Lorraine gasped. 'Aren't they all alike?'

'As peas in the proverbial pod! I'd call it a definite family likeness, it's obvious to anyone, except maybe themselves,' said Pemberton. 'I hope Paul Larkin can find out more – this has strengthened my belief there might be some family element to all this. So my next question is whether Lionel Cooper is a relation of Brother Luke, and whether R. W. Mansell is – was – too, and indeed whether Cooper and Mansell are related. As more than one person has noticed, those two are like identical twins.'

'They have different names, supported by passports,' pointed out Erika.

'But the same date and place of birth! Remember people can change their name by deed poll or be adopted as children, and there are other ways of acquiring new identities and different names. Now, if I was on shore, I'd be asking for DNA samples from Brother Luke, Lionel Cooper and R. W. Mansell – and perhaps others, in an effort to establish a blood link. But without that, we must keep plodding on.'

'Are you going to question Brother Luke about all this?'

'I'd like to hear what Paul discovers first,' he said, adding, 'but yes, we'll have to confront him at some stage but I still need a little more substance to support my ideas before I talk to him.'

'Ideas? You have other ideas?'

'Yes, another is festering in my mind . . . I'll talk to you later about that because I need to do a little more research. Brother Luke is my immediate target, the focus of all this, even if he's not in the frame.'

'Do you think he could be aware of this going on around him?'

'It's difficult to say, he's never suggested Lionel Cooper had a family resemblance but we must remember his eyesight isn't all that good. When I asked him how well he knew Lionel, he said he'd accompanied him on this cruise but that was all. People can have relations they've never met or seen, it happens in lots of families and some never spot a likeness. So far as Brother Luke is concerned, Lionel Cooper is just another volunteer who does good works. I don't know whether they could even be considered friends.'

'But is he telling the truth?'

'Would a monk tell lies?'

'It has been known!' she responded.

'Then it's our job to sort the truth from the lies. Now, though, I think we've earned ourselves a nice early lunch and maybe a glass of wine. Care to join us, Erika?'

'Yes, that would be nice.'

'Good. Our friends – our team in fact – will be in Vingolf's Hall and I regard you as a member of the team.'

Brian, Russell and their wives had already arrived and had had the foresight to secure a table tucked into a corner. When Pemberton's party arrived, he noticed that Ron and Ellen had also joined them. The only snag was that Ellen always seemed to object to talk of murders over lunch, but on this occasion, Pemberton would suggest she might care to leave them if Rob wished to be involved. Pemberton wanted more of his forensic expertise, particularly regarding the interesting position of the murdered body on the cabin bed.

The lunch was a buffet with a wide selection of hot and cold meals and an appetising array of soft drinks, wines and beers. They made their choice and eventually settled at the large oval table. At first lunch proceeded with no talk of the enquiry. It was only at coffee stage that the subject was introduced by Pemberton.

'Sorry to talk shop, Ellen,' he said. 'But this is one of our business meetings – you're welcome to stay because we need all the brains we can muster. If you want to leave us, we won't be offended!'

She waved a glass of white wine at him in the gesture of a toast, saying, 'I'm as intrigued as anyone so long as you don't talk about post-mortems and bodies!'

Seeing she had no desire to leave, he called for their reports. Russell acted as spokesman.

'We split up and visited several public areas this morning,' he told them. 'We concentrated on the top two decks – Lido and Sun Decks, both of which were busy with outdoor types such as swimmers, sunbathers, sports people or merely those wanting to sit quietly and read in the sunshine. It's nice and sheltered from the wind up there, thanks to those high glass sides – and there's plenty of sunshine even at this latitude. One thing we all found was that most of the passengers we talked to are now aware of the enquiry and there is a big desire to help – clearly, they want the killer traced as soon as possible. I'm sure some fancy themselves as detectives.'

'That's a welcome development,' said Pemberton. 'So did anyone notice anything of interest to us?'

'That's the strange thing, Mark. No one noticed anything out of the ordinary, except that a lot of people stayed up late to watch the midnight sun, from various vantage points. From what we learned, it seems most were happy to see it at midnight, watch it for up to an hour, and then head for bed. Very few stayed up later, except those in the casino and nightclub where no sunshine reaches! On the various routes back to their cabins, none reported anything odd and few, if any, were on their own. Most had friends or family with them who could back up the stories. We paid special attention to whether any had noticed Brother Luke's companion wandering around in the early hours, but none had. I think most were safely back in their cabins when he was moving about the ship.'

'Just like a town or village going to bed, and no one seeing what happened during the night.'

Pemberton told them about his checking of the telephone calls, his interview with the two stewards and the ongoing puzzle about what happened to Lionel Cooper at Trollstigheimen Mountain Lodge; he said no reports of his whereabouts, dead or alive, had been received from the Norwegian police but they were awaiting more positive information before launching a more intensive search in that remote mountainous region. Enquiries were also continuing in England in an attempt to discover more about the backgrounds of Cooper, Mansell and Brother Luke. At this stage, he decided not to acquaint these helpers with his reasons for delving into the background of Brother Luke.

He concluded, 'What I need next is to talk to a blond man, Nordic appearance, and his wife who is also blonde and beautiful – they were taking a video film just prior to our departure. I'd like to see their film, or any other films of the departure, not just of our group but others. If you spot him, find out who he is. I'd like a word with him. You might notice him taking more films.'

'Right, we'll keep our eyes open.'

'Explain that his film might help me trace more witnesses. I might recognize people I want to talk to, in particular a steward who was standing at the back of the boarding lounge. I've not seen him around the ship since that time except once when he was on duty in Hraevelg's

Hall as we watched the midnight sun. It goes without saying, of course, that I need to speak to anyone wandering about the ship in the early hours; I have yet to confront any night duty crew members, or indeed others who might have been off duty and enjoying the ship's facilities at night. However, I am going to speak to that crew member very soon, the one who was on duty as we were boarding. Erika is trying to find his name for me.'

'I've got it,' she said. 'It came through just before we left for lunch. I think it will surprise you.'

'Surprise me?'

'I decided to wait until after lunch!' She smiled mysteriously. 'I didn't want to spoil your enjoyment. I'll tell you later!'

'Fair enough, but he's next on my list for interview. So thanks again – and good hunting. Shall we meet here again today, say 4.30 for tea?'

And so it was agreed.

Russell said he and his team would continue to concentrate on the upper outdoor decks but later in the day and this evening they would visit the indoor public places, in particular the lounges, bars, casino and nightclub, hopefully to mingle with a different set of passengers.

'And it's the crew for me and Lorraine,' said Pemberton. 'Thanks, all of you.'

'Do you need me?' asked Rob as Pemberton was leaving. 'I don't seem to be making much contribution to this.'

'As I said before, I want you to have another look at the murder scene, but not just yet,' said Pemberton. 'But there are still certain things I need to clarify first. I want to have a chat about the way the body was lying when it was found. I'll see you at tea, but if I miss you, then we'll meet over dinner as usual.'

As they walked back to the incident room after lunch, Pemberton explained to Erika why he had not told the others about his concerns that Brother Luke's family might be involved.

'That's the kind of information we prefer to retain until we have more evidence to support it,' he told her. 'Besides, I wouldn't want the others talking about that to members of the crew or passengers. At this stage, it is for our ears only.'

And so they returned to the incident room to consider which crew members to start interviewing – but first, he wanted to speak to the one he'd noticed in the departure lounge.

'So why all the mystery about his name?' he asked Erika.

'It's Lionel Chadwin. I hadn't noticed earlier as I've never had reason to check the entire list.'

'Chadwin? Good grief! So how long has he been working on the ship?'

'I don't know, I haven't had a chance to check yet.'

'Lionel Chadwin?' Lorraine couldn't believe it. 'Same name as Brother Luke! Is that a coincidence, or does it mean something to us?'

'It's not uncommon for people to have the same name,' Pemberton said. 'But in this case, I think it's important. There is a likeness between him and Brother Luke's younger photographs – that's why I want to see that video. I spotted the lad in our departure lounge wearing a name badge with Lionel on it, but haven't noticed him around the ship since then except once when he was on night duty. The similarities struck me forcibly when I saw the photo of the young Brother Luke. And he is so like both Cooper and Mansell. So who is this young man? And what is he doing on the ship? And the name Lionel – with three key characters called Lionel, could it be a family name? He was in Hraevelg's Hall watching the midnight sun when we were there. I saw him standing close to Brother Luke but, so far as I know, he didn't make any approach. What do we know about him, Erika? Will his personal details be in your files?'

'Yes, we carry the personal files of all crew members. It will record the date of his appointment, his previous work, his CV and so on.' She used the intercom to talk to the Purser's office and said, 'It's on its way.'

Chapter Thirteen

Lionel Chadwin's personal file, like those of his colleagues in the crew, had not been computerized. It contained original personal papers such as references, staff assessments, his CV and job application form. It also showed his full name was Lionel Richard Chadwin. His details, along with a recent photograph, were on a large blue card lodged at the front of the file. Erika said that if he transferred to another cruise liner within the group, whether temporarily or permanently, the file would be handed over to that ship although a copy would be kept for reference. Pemberton took the record card across to the photographs on the noticeboard and held it up so that Lorraine and Erika could see Lionel's photo.

'See the likeness to Cooper and Mansell? And young Brother Luke? It's amazing. I'm beginning to think this lad is part of a very large family. He reminds me of a former boss called Halford. He was injured on duty and spent three months recuperating. To fill the time, he started to compile his family tree and discovered a branch he knew nothing about. Their home was a village over 150 miles away. They'd lived there for generations. Halford had never been but off he went to the churchyard to search for their graves. When he arrived, an old man was cutting the grass. He stopped his mower when he saw Mr Halford and said, "You'll be one of those Halfords, are you?" He'd spotted the likeness – and I think this family is the same. The men look like peas from the proverbial pod!'

From Lionel's record card, Pemberton saw that he was twenty-eight years old, and had been born at Westonkirk, a village near Barnard Castle in Co. Durham. He had attended the local primary school and then Barnard Castle's renowned school, leaving with eight GCSEs. He had not tried to gain entry to a university because he wanted to earn money and fancied work in a large hotel. He secured employment as a porter and then as a waiter before graduating to a trainee management position. As he grew older, and having a wish to see more of the world, he had left the hotel to find work on cruise liners where his experience would be very useful. *Ringhorn* was the first and only ship upon which he had been employed, and he had joined it two years ago. Reports from his supervisors said he was a good, diligent and honest crew member, able to use his initiative and to work unsupervised. Like all stewards, he had to be adaptable and he had performed a range of duties including luggage handling, bar and restaurant work, deck games supervisor, children's entertainer, theatre assistant backstage, croupier, cabin care and security. He was described as having a pleasant personality.

'They get their pound of flesh out of these crew members!' commented Pemberton. 'All right, Erika, let's call him in if he's available.'

'I called him earlier,' she smiled. 'He's off duty at the moment, I caught him in the gym, he's a fitness freak! He's waiting in reception.'

'Well done. Right, I'll interview him in here.'

Dressed casually in a green T-shirt, blue jeans and trainers, Lionel was a gangly young man with the unmistakable facial features of the young Brother Luke. With neat dark brown hair, brown eyes and a clean-shaven face he looked nervous as Erika shepherded him into the incident room and settled him at the table. He shuffled the chair closer and sat with his hands clasped before him. Pemberton and Lorraine went to meet him.

'Hello, Lionel, I'm Detective Superintendent Pemberton and this is Detective Constable Cashmore. Thank you for coming.'

He made no reply, his nervousness showing as he clasped and unclasped his hands. Watching him for a second or two without speaking, Pemberton could visualize the monk looking just like this many decades ago.

'You know about the murder of a male passenger in Cabin F150?' he began. 'We'd like to talk to you about it.'

'I don't know anything about it, except what I was told. I never did it, if that's what you're thinking.' He was surprisingly well spoken, and he followed his denial with a nervous laugh.

'We're not thinking anything at the moment, we're just trying to establish what happened and whether anyone, such as you, during your duties as a crew member, noticed anything unusual on the night in question. However, before I continue, there is a strange coincidence which affects you. Have you any idea what it is?'

'No, should I?'

'Probably not. Let me explain. You will have seen a monk in a wheelchair, he joined us at Southampton. He's Brother Luke.'

'Yes, he's a regular passenger. They said it was his friend who was murdered.'

'Right. Now the monk's name is Lionel Chadwin.'

There was a long pause during which the young man frowned, looking puzzled and uncomfortable, then he replied, 'I thought it was Luke something-or-other. Everybody calls him Brother Luke.'

'He's a monk, they often take a saint's forename – rather like actors and authors have professional names. But officially he's Lionel Chadwin. That's the name on his passport, and on the official passenger manifest.'

'I don't know what you're trying to say. I know loads of John Smiths and Alan Browns, we meet them all in this job. I once had two Sebastian Johnsons on board, they'd never met each other till then.'

'I don't think Lionel Chadwin is a very common name, and I find it interesting that we have two of you on this ship, two of you who look very much alike.'

'What, with that beard? And I'm not that old either!'

'You're like he was in his younger days, Lionel, minus the beard. So I must ask this – are you related to Brother Luke?'

'Not to my knowledge, no. How can I be related to him? I've never met him before, I had no idea another Lionel Chadwin existed.'

'You've been on this ship for two years, I believe?'

'Yes, about that.'

'Brother Luke's been cruising on board too, during that time. He's a regular.'

'Maybe so but I've never known his real name. I've always known him as Brother Luke.'

'Can you recall meeting him on an earlier cruise?'

'I'd seen him, yes, moving about the ship. You can't really miss him but I've never got to know him. You can't get to know all the passengers.'

'Do you ever see a full list of passengers, or a full list of crew?'

'No, never. They like to keep things confidential.'

'So if a Lionel Chadwin came on board, you would be unlikely to know about it, unless something drew your attention to the coincidence?'

'Right, and nobody's told me we had another Lionel Chadwin on board.'

'That may be so, but I'm very intrigued by your likeness to Brother Luke, and indeed to his companion.'

'His companion as well? The chap who was killed, you mean? Was he related to the monk?'

'I don't know but the similarities are astonishing. Can I ask who your parents are?'

'No problem. Dad was Cliff – Clifford – Chadwin and Mum's Olivia, she was a Batsfield, both old Durham families. Dad was a lot older than Mum, he'd be in his eighties now if he'd lived, but he died a few years ago. Mum's fiftyish – I'm never really sure how old she is.'

'And did your father have brothers or sisters?'

'No, he's an only child, Mum is too. There's just them and me and Suzanne in our family. She's my twin sister, she works in the offices at Durham University. Not married, not yet anyway. I can't think why we look like Brother Luke or why I have the same name. You've got me there, Mr Pemberton. You'll have to let me know if you learn anything.'

'And you must do the same for me! So have you ever asked your parents about another branch of the family?'

'No, I've never had reason to. Dad never mentioned it. I think he would have told us if there had been some distant relations, or if he'd had brothers and sisters. He never told us about his background but I think he'd travelled a lot. I can't think why he got married so late and then produced a pair of twins, there must have been life in the old dog, eh?'

'Would you describe your family as wealthy?'

'No, not at all. Far from it. Dad worked for ICI on Teesside, on the chemical side, managing one of the labs, but he retired a long time ago. He gave me and Suzanne a good education, but there was never money to spare. Mum worked as well, in a library, to make ends meet. Good parents.'

'Do you know if your parents have ever tried to construct a family tree? It's a very popular pastime now that computers are such a help.'

'No, I don't see much of my mum or sister now I'm working, I'm at sea most of the time, even for my leisure time, weekends and short breaks.'

'You don't get home much?'

'Not really. When I get a longer holiday I tend to go off with my mates, somewhere sunny, not back to cold and rainy Durham.'

'Would you object if I tried to find out whether there is

a link between you and Brother Luke? Or a link between you and his companion?'

'Mind? No, why should I?'

'All right, I'll start a little digging into the family history of the Chadwins and if I turn up anything, I'll contact you. Now, I must ask these questions – everyone is being asked them, so they're not especially directed at you. We'll be starting to interview all the crew very soon, and more passengers, asking everyone on board where they were between, say, midnight and half past nine yesterday morning.'

'I was working, Mr Pemberton, night shift. Started at eleven that evening and finished at seven in the morning, then I crashed out in my cabin. I came round about three in the afternoon. I wasn't on last night, it was my night off, like tonight.'

'And your cabin is where?'

'G Deck, 105. A single.'

'So what were your duties that night?'

'We call it deck patrol. There were five of us, working under a senior steward. Our job is to patrol all the decks at night, when most passengers are in their cabins, just check-ing things are all right. Dealing with anything that crops up. Most times, the first couple of hours are spent showing ourselves in the public areas – bars, lounges, Prom Deck, casino and so on – being on hand if passengers want any-thing out of hours. It might be anything from a sticking plaster for a blister on their foot to somebody getting locked out of their cabin.'

'I saw you in Hraevelg's, when we were watching the midnight sun.'

'Yes, I was there, we show ourselves where the people gather. Then after one o'clock, when it gets quieter, we do a round of all the decks, just checking things are all right.'

'All of them?'

'Yes, the lot. Passengers can get anywhere if they really want, especially if they've had too many drinks and start being adventurous, so we do all the public decks as you'd expect, but also those with nothing else but cabins, and even downstairs in reception, the medical centre and the crew's private quarters.'

'It sounds rather like police officers patrolling their beats at night!'

'Well, yes, I suppose so. Most of the time nothing happens but we split up to cover all the decks and meet up every hour in the forecourt of the cinema to compare notes.'

'The cinema? Why the cinema?'

'It's the most central point in the ship, Mr Pemberton, and private at that time of night.'

'I understand. So did anything unusual occur during yesterday's patrol?'

'Not a thing. There were people about after one o'clock, a lot had been watching the midnight sun so I suppose it was busier than it usually is at that time of day but it didn't take long for them all to return to their cabins. I'd say it was all quiet after three o'clock, that's when the casino and nightclub close. But only a handful stay late in there. They're never any bother.'

'Did you visit F Deck?'

'I did a complete circuit of F Deck cabins about two o'clock and another at five, checking reception at the same time, and the Purser's offices, but there was nothing out of the ordinary.'

'Would other stewards also check F Deck?'

'Yes, we work as a team and change our routes all the time, alternating between the decks. With five of us patrolling we have a rotation system so each of us checks all the decks at least twice. It keeps us fresh and alert!'

'So how do the security cameras fit into the scheme of things?'

'They're partly to check on us! At least, that's what we always say even if it's not true. Officially, they are to pro- tect us and the passengers. But obviously with only five patrols and one supervisor, we can't be everywhere at the same time, and so the cameras are little more than an aid to our work. We stewards don't check them, by the way, there are special security officers to do that.'

'I've already spoken to them and seen some film,' said Pemberton. 'We know that Mr Mansell, that's the deceased, returned to F150 with Brother Luke after watching the midnight sun, but didn't go into his own cabin. He left at 12.32 and didn't return until 2.45 or thereabouts. It meant he was somewhere else for two hours or more. Did you notice him during that time? Did you or your colleagues see him wandering about and ask if he needed help or advice?'

'Sorry, no. But even if I had seen him, it's not our practice to stop and question a passenger, they're free to visit any public part of the ship at any time. The only time we might question them would be if we think they are ill or lost or in need of help. We might greet them with "Good evening" as a means of getting them to speak; would you believe some are afraid to ask even if they are walking around the decks alone at night, probably lost.'

'Did you hear any unusual noises near the wheelchair cabins? See any unusual activity?'

'Sorry, no. I've been thinking about it since I learned about the death but I never heard or saw anything. Certainly I never saw anyone wandering about down there, or knocking on doors, or shouting or whatever.'

'And did anyone ask you to do anything special during your patrol?'

'Special?'

'Well, I thought it was possible to obtain food throughout twenty-four hours but from what I've seen, most places are not staffed after midnight or one o'clock. So if I wanted a sandwich or a drink at three in the morning, how would I get it?'

'Oh, I see, yes. Most people ring from their cabins and have stuff delivered there but if they're out and about on the decks, they can ask a steward. We'll make sure they get what they want. Nobody asked for anything.'

'So is the galley open all the time?'

'Not to passengers, no.'

'I was thinking of the night duty crew. Can they gain access during the night?'

'Oh yes, they have to, to place passengers' orders and collect them for delivery. There are always four night duty chefs there, either doing prep work for early next day or coping with night-time orders.'

'So how do you get into the galley?'

'There are locks on all the doors, coded numbers. There's a different number for each day, changing at midnight. We just code in the daily number and push the door open, it closes automatically. You can open it from the inside without a code, it closes when you've got out.'

'And how are you told what the number will be?'

'Like I said, we meet every hour to compare notes, the senior steward is given the daily code by the duty chef, and he tells us.'

'Is there any likelihood of a passenger getting to know that code?'

'I wouldn't think so, Mr Pemberton. We're given it in secrecy, it's more than our job's worth to reveal it to a passenger or an unauthorized crew member. We're very security conscious, we have to be, for all our sakes.'

'But stewards don't use that system for entering cabins to service them?'

'No, they're issued with a cabin master key. Each deck has its own master key, they're checked out and in again, there's hell to pay if one goes missing.'

'Do you know the names of all the stewards and the supervisor who were on night duty at the same time as you?'

'I can get them, or you could get them from the Purser's office.'

'I think it might be a good idea if I spoke to you all together, to go through that morning's activities – with such a fine, observant and helpful body of crew members on duty, someone must have noticed something of interest to our enquiries.'

'Well, yes, that would be a good idea. Do you want me to do that?'

'No, it's kind of you but I'll do it through official channels, I have to make sure the Captain is always involved in what I'm doing. Well, I think that's all for now, Lionel, thank you for your time. I might want to talk again, especially if I gather up all your colleagues who were on duty that night.'

'All right, no problem. Now, you mentioned a family history. Shall I ring my mother to ask if she knows anything? Dad might have told her.'

'That might help us a lot, it might shorten the enquiry! Or I could call her if you give me a contact number.'

'She might be alarmed if she gets a call from a detective, Mr Pemberton. Maybe I should break the ice? Tell her you'll be ringing?'

'Good idea. I might add I have a team of officers checking the background of Brother Luke, Mr Mansell – and Lionel Cooper.'

'Cooper? Who's he?'

'He was Brother Luke's original companion, the one who boarded with him. It's my belief he was replaced by the man called Mansell.'

'Replaced? How do you mean?'

'I have reason to believe that when Brother Luke and his companion, Mr Cooper, went ashore to the Trollstigheimen Mountain Lodge, Cooper was replaced by Mansell – unofficially, I might say, and contrary to all the rules.'

'I don't understand. How could anyone be replaced?'

'That is what I need to ascertain, but I'm convinced it happened, even if the two men looked remarkably alike. It is my belief that when Mr Mansell came on board, he was in possession of Mr Cooper's cruise card, and forged his signature when making purchases.'

'Oh my God . . . this is dreadful . . . So who, really, is the dead man?'

'That's Mansell, we're trying to find out more about him. He's not an official passenger.'

'So he wasn't really Brother Luke's companion? I saw them around the ship, but I never noticed any difference.'

'Neither did anyone else. Because Lionel Cooper came on board with Brother Luke, his name is in the ship's records. There has been no official replacement of Brother Luke's companion. Mansell was not known to anyone on this ship.'

'So where is Lionel Cooper now?'

'We don't know. The Norwegian police are conducting a search on shore. Now did you go ashore to Andalsnes and the Trollstigheimen Mountain Lodge?'

'No, you can check. I'd been on night duty and was in bed. Look, Mr Pemberton, this is all very difficult and confusing, you've thrown a lot at me . . .'

'I have. I suggest you go to your cabin for a while, think it all over, and then you can come back to me if you have any more information for us, particularly after the talk with your mother. Meanwhile, I will gather up your colleagues who were on duty that night.'

'Yes, all right.' Lionel's voice was now hoarse and he looked very shaken. 'Am I allowed to discuss this with Brother Luke? Our identical names? That we might be related?'

'I'll break the ice with Brother Luke, on your behalf. I'll tell him what I suspect, then I'm sure he'll want to talk to you.'

'All right, I'll wait.'

Pemberton allowed him to leave. 'So what do you make of him?' he asked Lorraine when the steward had gone.

'I'm not sure,' she admitted. 'He sounds innocent but I'm experienced enough to realize he could be a suspect.'

'Why do you say that?'

'He was roaming the ship at the material time, legitimately because he was on night duty. He knows the security systems and how the cameras operate, he could have made sure he wasn't caught on film. And he could get legitimate access to the cabin and the galley; he could even get his team mates to cover up for him, I'm sure they do that now and again if one of them wants to skive. He might even

224

have had a master key to get him into F150 – he might have got in without being invited. And we must remember this ship is a huge place – the combined area of its decks is like a small town. There are plenty of places to lose yourself if you want to be unseen while you're doing something you shouldn't.'

'And his motive?'

'I don't know. We can't rule out a homosexual approach in the cabin, can we? Could Mansell have persuaded him to enter his cabin, using some pretext?'

'It's possible. But remember he didn't know it was Mansell in the cabin. According to the records, the occupant was Cooper. We don't know whether he knew who occupied that cabin, and he says he didn't notice that Cooper had been replaced by Mansell.'

'Does that matter, if it was a homosexual attempt at seduction? Passengers do attempt to seduce crew members, male and female. It happens all the time.'

'I think it does matter, Lorraine. Think of the possible family connections. Just suppose this murder had not been committed on this ship. Suppose it had occurred in a village or small town community, with most of the key players being from a single family. What kind of approach would we be making in that situation?'

'We'd be looking for a family motive. Money, property, jealousy, secrets, revenge . . .'

'Exactly. Apart from money and property, most families have secrets and jealousies, revenge too. I think that's what we should be looking for here. Remember we could have the murder of one twin by another.'

'But Lionel, the crew member, didn't know or even suspect Mansell was a relative, did he? Or Cooper.'

'Didn't he?'

'Are you saying he knew all along?' she asked.

'I'm not saying he knew. I'm not saying he knew that Brother Luke might be a relative either, or that Cooper might be a long-lost cousin or even Mansell. What I am asking myself is that if he *did* know, or even suspect, that one or all of those men could be a relation, how would that change the situation? Is that where we need to start looking for a motive? And would that change my approach to this enquiry?'

'Do you think he knows about the secretive family background, but is not admitting it?'

'That wouldn't surprise me,' said Pemberton. 'I have to work on that possibility and this is where the enquiry becomes difficult – had this been on shore, I would have gone immediately to interview his mother, I would have wanted to see her and gauge her reaction when I confronted her, but I can't do that. I have to rely on other police forces to make the necessary enquiries, and that's always less than satisfactory.'

'But that young man will surely contact his family about all this, won't he? If there is any kind of motive buried in the family history, they'll be alerted very soon.'

'I'm not sure whether his family knows its real history. Remember his father's dead, so his mother – and sister – might not be aware of all the family secrets.'

'We'll know whether he contacts them by telephone, all calls ashore are recorded so that payment can be collected, and if he uses the cyber-study facility to send an email, we can trace that. And he might already have done so, to tell them of the murder.'

'He'd only do that if he knew the victim was a family member, surely?'

'Maybe not, maybe he makes regular calls home, and with a murder on board, the chances are he would tell his folks, as exciting news rather than something involving them. A lot hinges on whether he knew about those family connections.'

'Well, as you reminded me earlier, Lorraine, this is where I need to go right back to the beginning. We'll talk to the stewards who were on duty with Lionel on the night of the murder, just to see if any of them noticed anything, and then we'll conduct our next major interview – back where we started. With Brother Luke being the key to all this.'

Chapter Fourteen

In Odin's Garden, Pemberton and Lorraine shared the task of interviewing the four remaining night patrol stewards and afterwards, when the two detectives pooled their knowledge, it was evident that Lionel Chadwin's account of that evening was realistic. His colleagues could confirm there had been no unusual incidents, the evening being memorable only because the midnight sun had provided such a brilliant display. None of the four stewards had been summoned to a passenger cabin for any reason and none had delivered a late-night meal or drink. However, all admitted there were many occasions, some lengthy, when one or other of them was out of view and out of personal contact with the others. Nonetheless, they could keep in touch because they carried mobile radios which could provide swift assistance if it was urgently required. It was not as if their lives were at risk or they were expected to cope alone with a life-threatening incident – after all, they were not police officers on patrol and much of their work was of a domestic nature.

'Right, let's see what their supervisor, the senior steward, has to say,' said Pemberton. Lorraine rang Erika and asked her to summon him; both she and Pemberton would conduct the interview. His name was Jan Winkleman, pronounced Vinkleman.

A Dutchman, he proved to be tall, blond and athletic in appearance with striking blue eyes and an easy manner. Like Lionel and the others, he was off duty and dressed in casual but smart clothes. After establishing his name and cabin number, Pemberton began with his usual preamble at which Winkleman said he understood the nature of the enquiries.

'It was a perfectly normal night's duty,' Winkleman assured them. 'Nothing out of the ordinary came to my notice, except many passengers were later than usual in returning to their cabins, but certainly we had no trouble or problems with any of them, or with crew members, and no reportable incidents.'

'Reportable?' questioned Pemberton.

'We have to report and record certain things like passengers or crew being injured, say in a fall, or cutting themselves on broken glass, or being attacked, or if we think they are in need of professional help, say a doctor. It is not unknown for potential suicides to wander about, so we keep an eye on them in case they try to jump overboard . . . and we report that kind of thing so that all deck patrols are aware of them. We have to be careful though, some people just like walking around the ship alone at night, so we mustn't think they are all at risk or misbehaving. We must not upset them by suggesting they are up to no good or contemplating suicide!'

'But not all your tasks are reportable?'

'Not by any means. If we are asked to order a late snack or drink for delivery to a cabin, that would not be reportable. There is no charge for food although if the passenger required alcohol, it would be signed for to provide a record.'

'So how does the ordering of food or drink work? I thought a passenger would simply ring from the cabin and place an order with the duty receptionist or direct with the galley?'

'Right, and one of the stewards on duty in the galley would deliver it to the cabin.'

'So how would a deck patrol steward become involved in that?'

'A good example would be someone heading for their cabin after a late session in the casino or nightclub. They

228

might hail a steward who happened to be nearby and request food or drink, either where they were sitting, or in their cabin – and so we would comply.'

'How? By making the delivery yourself?'

'Sometimes, yes. We always carry a pad of cruise-card chits and so we would go to the galley, let ourselves in and ask the duty chef to make up the order. If there was a duty steward in the galley, he or she would deliver the tray to wherever it was wanted, but if they were all busy, we would do it ourselves. The important thing is to make sure the customer's order is executed as quickly and efficiently as possible.'

'But there would be no record of that transaction unless there was something to pay for?'

'Right,' said Jan. 'All the food is included in the cost of the cruise, along with tea, coffee and some soft drinks. As I said, alcoholic drinks must be paid for, so the passenger would be asked to sign the necessary chit.'

'So you, as supervisor, would not be told by your crew about an ordinary event like a passenger ordering a sandwich and cup of tea for their cabin or elsewhere in the early hours of the morning?'

'No, it's unnecessary.'

'And no passenger can gain access to the galley except as part of an organized party, or perhaps as a special guest?'

'That's true. Certainly, they'd never gain access during the night hours.'

'But what about other times? Surely a passenger could find a way of getting in? I must say I got inside during these enquiries, although I have to admit I was quickly pulled up by an alert young lady. I got little further than the doorway which happened to be open because the galley was busy.'

'That's how things work, we need to keep passengers out for both security and hygienic reasons. In theory no unauthorized person can gain access but when meals are being served the doors are not locked; to have to unlock them on each trip would be intolerable to waiters serving meals and clearing tables. I must say it has been known for passengers to gain entry, invariably from one of the restaurants when things are frantically busy and usually to make a complaint about something trivial like a dirty spoon or a piece of over-boiled broccoli. Some are too impatient to wait for a waiter to deal with it, but it's unlikely they would ever get completely inside.'

'Most if not all would be stopped near the entrance, as I was?'

'Yes.'

'I would imagine, though, that if some unauthorized person did get inside at night, they might not be noticed, or could even hide – after all, the galley is a huge place with tall shelving and high units forming islands, and with a skeleton staff on duty, they couldn't be everywhere at once.'

'We like to think it is a safe and secure place, Mr Pemberton, but of course you know, and I know, it is always possible to breach any security system with a little careful planning and thorough research – and some luck.'

From what they heard from Jan, the night had been remarkably uneventful, and he had not noticed Mansell on his perambulations, nor could he recall seeing the monk in his wheelchair. So Pemberton allowed the senior steward to leave, thanking him profusely.

'It's time to talk to Brother Luke again,' he told Lorraine. 'I wonder where can we find him. I doubt if he'll be in his cabin at this time of day, especially as it's teatime.'

They returned to the incident room to update Erika on their interviews and told her they were now going to find Brother Luke for another chat. Erika rang his cabin but there was no reply.

'There's no concert this afternoon, so let's try Vingolf's Hall, it's the most popular place for tea. We'll probably find our colleagues there too – which reminds me. After chatting to Brother Luke, I need to look again at F150 with Rob Easton. I need his expertise.'

'You've obviously got some ideas about all this?' smiled Lorraine.

'I'd like to put them to the test before I make a fool of myself by announcing I've found a possible solution. After all, I could be wrong. So come along, Lorraine. Time for tea!'

When they arrived, Vingolf Hall's was as busy as ever with people enjoying a traditional afternoon tea with small sandwiches, cakes and biscuits while a pianist played softly in the background. Russell, Brian and the girls had commandeered a large table just inside the starboard entrance; it was away from the rather chill wind blowing off the grey and choppy sea. The outside temperature had dropped considerably as they headed to the extreme north although a few stalwarts, warmly clad, were taking tea at outdoor tables. Russell, Brian and the girls, who had enthusiastically joined their husbands in this enquiry, updated Pemberton on their activities. From what they said, it was evident that the suspicious death had become one of the main talking points among the passengers, undoubtedly causing them to compare notes about that evening.

What emerged was that very few passengers had ventured down to F Deck simply because there was no reason to do so, particularly during the late hours. Likewise, with Mansell known to have been moving around the upper decks between 12.32 and 2.45 or thereabouts, it seemed that the people who were around during those times had no memories of him. So had he deliberately kept out of their sight? Or had people been too intent on regaining their cabins after the splendour of the midnight sun? Everyone who had been spoken to could account for their movements during those key times. Brian presented Pemberton with a handwritten list of cabin numbers. 'These are the people we've spoken to. They're in no particular order but I thought you'd like a note of them.'

'Thanks, you've done well. Clearly there were passengers and crew around on most of the decks into the early hours but none noticed Mansell or any unusual occurrences. I can get Erika to cross these people off our lists. Now, so far as our enquiries are concerned, I've spoken to the stewards who were on deck patrol during the material times, but I've gained nothing from them either. It seems the killer was either very lucky or very clever in avoiding both the cameras and patrols during his visit to F150. We can't dismiss the possibility that Mansell invited the killer back to his cabin, for reasons we don't know. Was it done during his late-night trek around the ship? So when or how was the invitation issued, and to whom? That person is still on board, remember, and might still be armed and therefore dangerous. We might already have spoken to him or her – if we have, or if the passengers are now discussing it, then he or she will be fully aware of our enquiries.'

He paused to allow them a few minutes to digest the full import of that, but did not tell them of his intention to conduct more enquiries into the family of Brother Luke, neither did he mention that one of the stewards had the same name as the priest. That was for later. At this stage, he was content to let this helpful group do what was the equivalent of house-to-house enquiries – essential but time-consuming and often not very productive. As they compared notes, Rob and Ellen joined them and so Pemberton provided an update, not referring to his own special knowledge in front of Russell, Brian and the girls, but telling Rob he now intended having another chat with Brother Luke in the hope he might elicit more information about both Mansell and Cooper. It was a white lie, of course – he wanted more information about the monk's own family.

'And Rob,' he added, 'I haven't forgotten about our further look at F150.'

'I'm ready when you are. Has something cropped up?'

'I have a theory, let's just say that for the moment.'

'All very intriguing. Call me when you're ready.'

Having exhausted the little information he wished to impart at this stage, Pemberton bade farewell to his friends, saying he would see them at dinner.

'Come along, Lorraine, let's look for Brother Luke and find a quiet corner for a chat. I'm not going to enjoy this, but it has to be done. After all, he is now a suspect.'

They found Luke in Honir's Hall, a small room adjoining the library on the port side of D Deck. While the library was a place for selecting and borrowing books, Honir's was a quiet place for reading them along with newspapers and magazines, or for writing letters and diaries. Brother Luke was alone, having released his steward for a break while he read, and he was currently the sole occupant of this small, dark panelled room. With his thick-rimmed spectacles perched on the end of his nose, he was concentrating on his reading but alert enough to realize someone had entered the room. Even so, Pemberton called out 'Brother Luke' to announce their arrival.

'Ah, the constabulary again!' He smiled and put aside his book. 'Are you looking for me? Mr Pemberton and Miss Cashmore, I believe.'

'Yes, we are looking for you.' Pemberton was pleased the old man both recognized and remembered them. It meant he was not senile and that his brain was functioning well. 'We'd like another chat with you, in confidence.'

'Well, we are alone in here but I don't know for how long. Anyone might come in but I've given my helper time off, he'll come back for me at 5.30.'

'Then we can talk until someone else enters,' said Pemberton, noting the monk was hearing them without difficulty – he was sporting a hearing aid, something he did not wear all the time. The potentially difficult interview would now be much easier.

'Have you found the person who killed Lionel?' was the priest's first question.

'Not yet,' said Pemberton, not wishing to confuse things by reminding him the victim was not Lionel Cooper. 'That's why we need to talk to you again.'

'Well, as I said before, there's nothing I can tell you. I saw nothing and heard nothing, even though I was next door. Dreadful, really dreadful, someone taking another's life within feet of me. I've worried and prayed a lot since then. Someone must have heard or seen something, surely?'

'We've not found anyone yet,' admitted Pemberton. 'But there is more I wish to discuss with you. It is a very delicate matter but it is important. I need to know about your family.'

'My family? I have no family, Mr Pemberton. My wife died more than twenty years ago and we never had children, not because we didn't want them, it just never happened.'

'It's not that aspect of your family that interests me. It's your relations – do you have brothers? Sisters? Cousins? Nieces? Nephews?'

'I can't see what that can have to do with a murder on board this ship out here in the far northern seas.'

'It might be relevant, I have to explore the matter. Let me start by telling you this: one of the stewards on board this ship right now is called Lionel Chadwin.'

'Lionel Chadwin? Good grief! The same name as me?'

'Yes, it is rather odd. Has he made contact with you?'

'No, he hasn't, but that's not surprising. It's typical of my relations, if indeed he is a relation. They never make contact with me, never have done and never will. They ignore me completely.'

'Never make contact?'

'I know people will say that, as a man of God, I should forgive them their trespasses and so I will, when they contact me. But the longer they refuse, the more difficult it becomes. I have tried to find them and welcome them to my home – I used to send them Christmas cards, years ago, but received none in return. Now I've no idea where they are living, how many of them there are, what they do for a living . . . nothing. I know nothing at all about them, Mr Pemberton. They might as well not exist. So what makes you think this steward might be a relation?'

'His name for one thing, but also because he looks like you. Or looks like you did when you were younger.'

'Well, I must admit the male members of our family have always had a reputation for looking like one another, it's a family trait, you can see it in old portraits and photographs, and in the past, Lionel was a regular name for the first-born male. So if this man is a relation, why has he not contacted me?'

'I don't think he realized you were called Chadwin, he knows you as Brother Luke. He has no access to passenger lists and had no idea there was a Chadwin on board. Those lists are confidential. Besides, there are more than 1600 names, a lot to remember.'

'Well, I think he should be told who I am, then perhaps he will contact me. You might suggest that if you are in touch with him?'

'I will be talking to him again, so yes, I'll do that. So how might he be related to you?'

'I have a twin brother. Had a twin brother, to be correct. He died some years ago. He was younger than me by a mere two hours or so. Twins are a feature of our family, they seemed to turn up all over the place until I got married and then nothing. Not from me, anyway. But my brother was, well, what my father called a wrong 'un. Always in bother, both at home and with the police, always doing some dodgy deal or other, travelling around the world to avoid his debts, you name it and Clifford did it. He was the proverbial black sheep. My parents had no other children and were very patient with him; he was always welcome to come home like the prodigal son but when he did he always wanted more money to pay off his debts. Having supported him for years, and with no improvement from Clifford, my father eventually got fed up and said, "No more." It seemed Clifford would never change and so, with Dad putting his foot down, he went off to South Africa, saying he was going to farm and make his fortune, then we lost contact with him. We had no idea where he went. Before leaving, though, he'd got a woman pregnant here in England. She went to South Africa with him. She was a nice girl called Marion Edwards and Clifford reckoned they'd got married on a remote beach overseas in some obscure religious ceremony. We never found a record of his wedding and he had no certificate to prove it. Later she gave birth to twins, illegitimate of course, because there was no proof of a wedding. And she died in childbirth. In South Africa. A lot of stigma surrounded illegitimacy in those days, and so Clifford had the twins adopted but insisted they retain their family forenames – Lionel and Richard. They had different surnames, of course, taking those of their adoptive parents – different parents too – and so I lost touch with them. Clifford and his sons vanished from my family circle. Vanished completely. I never saw them again.'

'Did the twins ever try to trace their real parents?'

'I have no idea, Mr Pemberton. No one has approached me about it. I know it's common practice nowadays to try and trace one's biological parents, often with the help of computers and genealogy experts, but it didn't happen in those days. Lots of adopted children grew up never knowing their real background.'

'Did you ever hear from Clifford again?'

'Yes, just once, after my father died. Mother died before him, so when Father died, all his money and property came down to me. There was no one else. It was quite a substantial inheritance – a large house, shares, money, antiques and so forth – and it enabled me to further my business as a property developer, in a big way. Clifford got nothing, no one had any idea where he was anyway, or even whether he was alive. He'd not been seen for years, twenty years or more. He'd cut himself off. Completely. So far as the family was concerned, he didn't exist.'

'So his death was presumed, under the seven-year rule?'

'Yes, it was.'

'But if he had been known to be alive, he would have benefited?'

'Yes, he would have received a half share in Father's estate. He'd have got a lot of money. With Mother being dead, there were just the two of us, Clifford and me. But, as I said, we thought Clifford was dead so I got the lot.'

'Your father willed everything to you?'

'No, there was no will, Mr Pemberton. That is the point I am making. Our family never made wills. Whatever the value of the estate, it automatically went to the surviving children, divided between them but not equally. There was some kind of sliding scale. The Chadwins have always done it like that.'

'And have you continued that practice? Of not making a will?'

'Until now, Mr Pemberton. But my position is different from my ancestors in that I have no children. For a long time, I have been contemplating the disposal of my wealth and property. I have been telling myself that I must break with family tradition and make a will, I don't want the Government to gets its filthy hands on our inheritance. To be honest, I am thinking about leaving everything to the Church but I know I must make a will for that to happen – and make one very soon! It is something that has been troubling me for some time. I feel I still need more time to consider the matter in depth, but time is not on my side now.'

'But it seems you might have relatives, Brother Luke. Lionel Chadwin might be one of them.'

'But they have never shown any interest in me, not even a Christmas card or birthday card.'

'Maybe they didn't know of your existence? Did your brother tell them? So what happened to your brother?'

'He wasn't dead, Mr Pemberton. About a year after my father's death, I got a phone call from him, saying he was back in England. It was a great shock, I must say, and he asked after Mum and Dad. I told him they were dead and after a long conversation, he asked about disposal of the estate. I told him he'd got nothing because he'd been presumed dead, so he said he would make a claim for his share of the estate. But I never heard from him again.'

'And was Clifford then living in England?'

'Yes, and it seems he was very much a reformed character. He'd returned permanently and was living in County Durham. I heard the same thing from a mutual friend although Clifford never came to visit me. It seems he'd got himself out of debt and settled down to a normal life. I believe he had done quite well in South Africa, and had come back to this country where he bought a property in County Durham, married a local girl who was much younger than him, and produced twins. More Chadwin twins!'

'Twins?'

'Lionel and Suzanne. Although he's my age, Clifford managed to produce a second family by a young wife. I heard that from the same mutual friend. He died not long afterwards, but left his widow and twins comfortably off.'

'So we know there is a young Lionel Chadwin. If you saw him, that's the steward Lionel Chadwin, you might think he was your brother's son, your nephew in fact.'

'The likeness is there, you think?'

'I do.'

'Family likeness among the males is a feature of the Chadwins, even if I don't notice it! So if he is Chadwin flesh-and-blood, why has he not approached me? I can't understand it, I've done nothing to antagonize any of my brother's family but they've always kept their distance. I wonder if he poisoned them against me?'

'According to young Lionel, he had no idea there was another branch of the family, his father had never told him. He had no idea you were really called Lionel Chadwin either, but he thinks the coincidence of his name and yours is just that – a coincidence.'

'And is it a coincidence he happens to be on this cruise?'

'I don't know. I wish I could answer that.'

'I'm a regular on this route, it's one of my favourites. And one often comes across people with identical names,

238

even unusual ones, so it could be nothing more than a coincidence.'

'I don't think you'd say that if you got a good look at him.'

'Maybe I have seen him around the ship, but my eyesight is far from good. I'm not too bad with close-up work, reading or recognizing people across a table, but anything further than that is little more than a blur. Even if that steward came to serve me a drink, I doubt I would see the resemblance, and I can't read their name badges.'

'You recognized me and Lorraine.'

'Your voice, Mr Pemberton. As I said earlier, I have a good ear and memory for voices. Remember, I told you Lionel's had changed.'

'There is another vital factor, one you should know about. I have interviewed Lionel Chadwin, the steward. He tells me his family are from a village called Westonkirk in Co. Durham. His father was called Clifford but is now dead being much older than his mother who is Olivia. And the young Lionel has a twin sister, Suzanne.'

'Good grief . . . this is uncanny. But why have they kept themselves away from me all this time? Clifford must have hated me to make them behave like that. What on earth could he have said about me?'

'As you say, you did inherit all the family money and property. He got nothing. That is often enough to set brother against brother, family against family.'

'Clifford brought it upon himself by his behaviour. He wasn't thrown out by his family – he rejected them and left the country voluntarily, never to contact us again. No wonder we thought he was dead, we did search but found nothing to say he was either alive or dead. He'd just vanished.'

'It's not my duty to get involved in family matters, Brother Luke, but I want to ring Lionel's mother in Durham to see how much she knew about her late husband. I'll let you know what she tells me.'

239

'I'd appreciate that, and then I must make an effort to speak to him. It is my Christian duty. Can you ask him to make himself known to me?'

'Yes, I will, and thank you for being so open, what you've said is most useful. So now, can I ask another very personal question? It might be relevant to my enquiries.'

'You could have brought about a family reunion, Mr Pemberton. I find that quite moving, having been so alone all these years. I cannot blame the children for the behaviour of their father.'

'That's generous of you.'

'Not really, family is family, and it would be quite something to discover that I am really an uncle! So what is it you want to ask?'

'This is also very delicate and you don't have to respond immediately. You may need time to consider what I am going to say, but I must remind you that it is my duty to carry out an investigation into a murder. Having heard your story, however, I believe the victim could also be a relation.'

'Lionel Cooper? You're not serious, Mr Pemberton? How can this be true?'

'The victim is not Lionel Cooper. I have reason to believe that he was replaced by a man called Richard Mansell; we do not know what has happened to Lionel Cooper, he has vanished from the ship.'

'How can this be? You asked me about Mansell earlier but the name meant nothing, and now you say Lionel has vanished? I don't understand.'

'The Norwegian police are searching for him in the region of the mountain lodge you visited.'

'I don't think I can cope with all this . . . You mean in the midst of a murder enquiry, I am surrounded by nephews all of a sudden . . . all here, on this ship . . . but why? Why in the name of God?'

'I don't know. Now, Mansell could be Clifford's son, Richard, the one who was adopted. Now known as Richard Mansell. And Lionel Cooper, the man who accompanied you, might be his twin brother. From what I have learned, there does appear to be a strong case for thinking Lionel and Richard may have been your brother's twin sons. Their names are correct and so is the family likeness; furthermore, both were born in South Africa on the same day. And Richard was left-handed with Lionel using his right. I might add that this is pure speculation on my part, I need to make positive identifications, probably through fingerprints, but I must consider the possibility as part of my investigation.'

'I have no idea what to say about the murder, Mr Pemberton, but so far as the family business is concerned, there could be a ring of truth in what you suggest. Whenever we've had twins in the family, one has been right-handed and the other left-handed. A family trait! My brother, Clifford, was the left-handed one. But Lionel? The man who was my companion until he vanished? Was he really my nephew? He never gave any hint of that! Mind, I did sometimes spot a family resemblance, the way his eyes moved, his lips and so on, and his carriage. I wish my eyesight was better but there was definitely a sign of the Chadwin gait ... but my beard would conceal my features. Isn't it odd, though, they should be here with me? And the younger Lionel ... and the dead man ... but no Suzanne ... What on earth is happening? Am I responsible for all this?'

'I don't think you can blame yourself. Maybe Lionel Cooper wanted to get to know you better before he broke the news of a relationship? He seems to have been a very decent man. Perhaps he was protecting you? Worrying about your growing old and alone. Now, of course, we don't know where he is, or what has happened to him, so we can't ask him.'

'Oh, this is dreadful ... so what were they all doing on this cruise?'

'I'm not sure, that is something I must determine – and, of course, I have to find a motive for Mansell's death.'

'So what is your question?'

'You haven't made a will but can I be rude and ask the approximate value of your estate? I need to find a motive, you see, and a dispute over a large inheritance can often provide the necessary trigger for violence, even among brothers.'

'Wealth is a problem, especially at my age. As I told you, I have money, but no direct family. So far as money is concerned, all I need is enough to live on, and that is not much. I am well looked after. And yes, I own a mansion, lots of land, other houses, and I have substantial savings and shares with a good income as well as antiques, original oil paintings and so forth. Value? It's hard to say but I'd estimate around eight to ten million. Income from my investments allows me to take nice holidays. Unlike some orders of monks, I have not taken a vow of poverty! After all, I am not an ordained priest, merely a monk who helps out with monastic work. I make sure my wealth benefits the Church, I pay for my keep and make regular gifts to the monastery, local churches and charities. I have the trappings of a successful businessman but like to think I use my wealth with charity and wisdom. I have a trusted housekeeper living in a cottage in the grounds, looking after the main house. The others are rented. She's on a modest salary and I allow her to employ a gardener and any other tradesmen as necessary, at my expense. And I allow the Church to use the house for seminars, retreats and that sort of thing. All at my expense.'

'And you gave up all that to be a monk?'

'At my age, I find it easier to get others to look after things for me. But with no family, what was I to do with it, Mr Pemberton? It is truly a dilemma, believe me – and it might be even more difficult now there are relations! I have been contemplating making a will.'

'It would solve a lot of problems.'

'I think you are right, but now I have others to think about. After all my time of being alone, I may have a family – I must try again to get to know them. Do you

242

think they will want to know me? As a person, I mean, forgetting the money.'

'I'm sure they will. So Brother Luke, have you been aware of anyone researching your family history? Asking you personal questions? Determining their relationship to you? It's very easy now, tracing one's relatives, thanks to the internet.'

'I can't say I have been aware of any interest in me. Why do you ask?'

'Under current law, if you don't make a will, then upon your death your estate would go to your nearest relative, your brother, if he was alive. If he is not alive, then it will go to his descendants. Your nephew and nieces, even if they were illegitimate – which it seems they are not. The question of whether Lionel Cooper and Richard Mansell were legitimate and might have inherited may require a lot of legal research.'

'Are you saying someone has been digging into my private life, behind the scenes, with the intention of getting their hands on my estate?'

'It's very odd that we have on this ship, at the same time as you, three men who are highly likely to be close relations, the sons of your brother. One is dead, another could be. They never told you who they were or tried to make any family contact. So why are they here?'

'You tell me, Mr Pemberton. I am rather naïve about these things.'

'Who knew you were coming on this cruise?'

'Who didn't know? Friends, neighbours, people in the rest home, church members . . . I've been coming for years, anyone who knows me knows I take a summer cruise, and it's not always on this ship and not always to the Arctic but usually with this cruise operator. Most of the crew know me. I have come to the Arctic in recent years, I love the midnight sun.'

'As Brother Luke and not Lionel Chadwin?'

'Yes, in more recent times. This is not a very monkish kind of holiday perhaps, but it enables me to keep in touch with the outside world and to find quiet times to consider my future.'

'Have you discussed disposal of your estate with anyone? Or mentioned making a will?'

'Not really. It is widely known that my family never made wills. People in the monastery and the rest home knew, they're my family now – were my family – even if this dreadful event has changed things so dramatically.'

'You said you were thinking of leaving everything to the Church. Have you mentioned that to anyone?'

'Maybe I have let it slip while thinking aloud, but it has never been a firm decision, just an idea floating around in my ancient head. I must give the whole thing much more thought now. I mustn't dither any longer. For a businessman, I am very indecisive, aren't I?'

'I can't help you make that kind of personal decision, Brother Luke. No one can, except to say you don't have to leave everything to just one person or organization. You can share it out, with that kind of sum you can make a lot of people happy! But it's entirely up to you. Now, so far as my enquiries are concerned, that's all for the time being, though I might wish to talk to you again.'

'Of course, I shall be here. And you will tell that young man to make himself known to me?'

'Yes, of course.'

They left the monk alone in Honir's Hall, and as they walked along the deck towards the staircase, Pemberton said, 'You didn't ask any questions?'

'No, I think you covered everything. The old man was responding to you all the time. Personally, I mean. He respects you. I think any interruption by me might have destroyed his concentration. You've given him a lot to think about. So what now? You didn't question him as if he might be a suspect. You didn't say you might want to search his room.'

'No, I need to do more work on my theory but right now it's time we updated the Captain,' said Pemberton.

Chapter Fifteen

In the incident room, Captain Hansteen with Erika at his side listened to Pemberton's account although it did not include his theory. Theories were seldom viable without supportive evidence and currently all that concerned Pemberton was the gathering of facts to identify a suspect or prove the case. Hansteen explained that his security team had thoroughly searched the ship for a stowaway – either the killer or the missing Lionel Cooper – but had found no one. They had also scrutinized the night cameras yet again but had come up with no new leads or information. The Captain had spoken personally to his crew members with an emphasis on events and movements in and around F Deck at the material time. That had drawn a blank. No one had noticed anything of significance.

'So what's your next plan, Mr Pemberton? Your enquiry has made little progress and we are rapidly approaching Spitzbergen.'

'There's still a little time left, and my officers in Rainesbury are conducting urgent enquiries into the background of Brother Luke, Lionel Cooper and R. W. Mansell. The Norwegian police are still seeking Lionel Cooper dead or alive, so a lot of important work is being done away from the ship. I might add that an enquiry of this nature on shore could take weeks.'

'We don't have weeks. In fact, after leaving Spitzbergen we have just one week before returning to Southampton, with several more shore visits on the way back.'

'Yes, I have seen the itinerary.'

'The point is that every shore visit gives the killer yet another opportunity to vanish. I know I'm repeating myself but if we don't trace the killer by the end of the cruise, he will disembark at Southampton and disappear. You can imagine how that will damage the reputation of both this ship and its owners.'

'When we return to Southampton, Captain, I will require the murder cabin to be thoroughly examined by forensic experts, irrespective of what happens between now and then. I am sure that, given time, the killer would be identified and found even if I don't unmask him or her – DNA and fingerprint evidence are good friends of the police. If it did become necessary, we could trace every passenger even after they have left, and every member of crew, and obtain their DNA. Comparison with what we find in the cabin would be simple.'

'And how long will it take for all that to be done? The cabin examination, I mean.'

'How long is a piece of string?'

'The ship will arrive in dock at 8 a.m. on the final day, and depart at six on another cruise. We cannot delay departure, it is far too costly.'

'If we alert the shore police in advance, they can come on board fully briefed the moment she docks. A full working day should suffice. And don't forget, there is also the dead body of a murder victim to take ashore and matters like formal identification and an inquest to arrange. The shore police will attend to all that.'

'You'll make the necessary arrangements?'

'I will but all that is some way off, Captain. I am confident I can identify the killer before we reach Spitzbergen.'

'I sincerely hope so. All I can say now, Mr Pemberton, is good luck! If you need any more assistance from me or my staff, please ask. So what is your next task?'

'I need to identify all cruise liners which docked at Andalsnes shortly before us, and to determine whether anyone is missing from any of them. I am especially interested in *Velia*. In particular, I need to know whether R. W. Mansell was a passenger and whether he left that ship and failed to return. It would be helpful to know whether its itinerary was similar to ours too.'

'Your reason?'

'It could explain how Mansell arrived in Andalsnes around the same time as Lionel Cooper.'

'After hearing your account, I must admit, with some reluctance, I am coming to accept that a passenger replacement did occur. That possibility would have escaped me, I am afraid, had I been the investigating officer. I thought our systems were foolproof, and I must congratulate you on coming to that conclusion. Clearly, we shall tighten our security procedures, but I can understand how other cruise ships might have aided our interloper.'

'And look at it like this, if the body of a man is found on those Norwegian mountains, it could well be identified as the man missing from another cruise ship. It could be wrongfully identified as Mansell in other words – all it needs is a piece of paper bearing his name. It's a neat way for him to create a new identity!'

'I follow your reasoning.'

'If Mansell has been reported missing from a ship, the Norwegian authorities would be alerted by the ship in question, wouldn't they? And with Cooper and Mansell looking so much alike, the authorities could be misled.'

'You do think Mansell wanted to completely replace Cooper, don't you? Assume his identity, in other words, after leaving *Ringhorn*?'

'Yes, I'm sure that was his plan. He still had some of his own papers on him when we found him, perhaps he needed them for his final plans. All this is still just conjecture, I need proof – and positive proof can only come through formal identification of the victim. We might have to await our return to Southampton for that, probably with fingerprints taken from his known haunts or home.'

'It can wait, I am sure.'

'Other cruise ships do follow the route we have taken as I'm sure you know – I've noticed them in ports at which we have called,' said Pemberton. 'More than one may arrive at the same destination within a short time. We know Mansell obtained cash in Bergen, another popular stopping place. I think he used a cruise ship to reach Bergen too, presumably then continuing to Andalsnes. After joining our ship at Andalsnes and achieving his purpose – getting rid of Cooper – he might have intended rejoining his original cruise liner at some point on its return journey. I would imagine he could claim he'd got lost, mistaken his timing and missed the ship, either that or he'd return home on this one. A phone call to the ship could establish his story. For that reason, I'd like to know if any ships are due at Spitzbergen at the same time as us. Perhaps he intended returning via that route? Or did he want to become Lionel Cooper and return to England with his new identity? He'd have to pay Cooper's credit card bills, of course. We found his card in the cabin – Mansell had managed to get hold of that. Robbery perhaps?'

'It's rather complicated but your argument makes sense. We do have contact with other cruise lines and do our best to co-ordinate our visits and timetables. It is true that several ships can be in the same port at the same time. Leave that with me, I'll make the necessary enquiries. Is there anything else I can do?'

'Not at the moment. In view of what Brother Luke has told me, I must speak to my colleagues on shore and make another call, I'll do that next. The information about his family will help them greatly. Then I need to find a quiet corner, somewhere to think things through. The answer to our riddle is here, Captain, it's just a case of identifying it. In fact I may have the answer, but before making up my mind I must speak to Dr Easton. That's my next task.'

'I'll get reception to page him for you. When would be convenient?'

'I'll meet him in F150. Say an hour and a half from now? He knows what I wish to discuss. I want another look at the murder scene with him, I need his expert opinion. Meanwhile, I'll find a quiet corner and if I am wanted you can contact me through Lorraine. She has some things to do in the incident room and will take any messages from my colleagues on shore.'

'Of course. I wish you well. Now I must return to the more mundane task of steering this ship through the Norwegian Sea.'

Using the contact telephone number on Lionel Chadwin's record card, Pemberton rang Mrs Chadwin in Durham with Lorraine listening on an extension. Her son had already spoken to her and explained events on board *Ringhorn*, consequently Pemberton's enquiry was made much simpler.

'All I need to know, Mrs Chadwin, is whether you, Lionel or Suzanne knew about the family history?'

'Not until very recently, Mr Pemberton. My husband never spoke about his background before he met me, other than to say he had spent most of his earlier life in South Africa. He did tell me he had been married before, in South Africa, and that his first wife had died, but he never mentioned children. He had no papers about his family either; when he died, I cleared out his belongings and there was nothing, not even a birth certificate, so you can see how difficult it was, dealing with his death. You can imagine how much of a surprise and shock this has all been.'

'Has anyone made an approach to you and your children about the family history?'

'A man called a couple of months ago and said he might be a relation. He asked about my husband and suggested Clifford was his father. His name was Mansell, he said he had been adopted at birth. I told him I knew nothing about that, and my husband was dead so he couldn't shed any light on it and I had no family tree or records. He told me about the Lionel Chadwin at Star-thorpe Hall between Thirsk and Northallerton, and said he had a twin brother. I mentioned my own children but didn't give him any details. I didn't like him, a stranger, talking to them and upsetting them. He seemed very interested in Clifford and then said he would go away and do some more research, promising to come back and tell me what he'd learned.'

'So he knows you have children?'

'Yes, but that's all, he has none of their details.'

'And did he come back?'

'No, never.'

'Did you mention this to Suzanne and Lionel?'

'No, I kept it to myself until I was sure of the situation, Suzanne and Lionel knew nothing of this visit, nor of the family background.'

'Did you try to do your own research?'

'Once, I went to Starthorpe Hall, but that Lionel Chadwin was away on business, according to his housekeeper. He was often away, she said. I didn't stay and didn't explain the reason for my visit. He's clearly a very rich man. I've not been back there. I don't know what to make of all this, it's all so sudden . . . Lionel mentioned a murder, on the ship. He thought it might be a relation . . .'

'I think it's Mr Mansell, but that is just a theory I'm working on, Mrs Chadwin. I have no proof of his identity and there is a lot more work to be done.'

'Oh, that's dreadful . . . you don't think . . . I mean . . . my Lionel is not involved, is he?'

'All I can say at this stage is that I have no suspects in mind, Mrs Chadwin.'

'Oh, I see. I don't know what to say or do . . .'

'If you could ask your daughter whether anyone has been trying to find out the family history from her, it would help. Lionel can't recall anyone approaching him.'

'I'll speak to her about it.'

'Thank you. I'll be in touch again.' And he rang off.

After leaving a message updating Paul Larkin on Brother Luke's family history, Pemberton collected the necessary photographs of the body at the murder scene. Leaving Lorraine to her chores in the incident room, he returned to his cabin for an hour's reflection upon what he had learned to date.

He made himself a coffee and settled in the armchair, mug in hand, as the grey Norwegian Sea provided a continuous moving picture with its swell and a myriad of birds. A whale passed by, its tail showing as it dived deep into the ocean, and an albatross soared past on huge wings. Sitting there alone and in total silence, his mind went through everything that had happened since he had been asked to investigate this murder, and things that had happened before that. Steadily, his mind isolated incidents, actions and observations which might be relevant and as he worked through the assembled evidence, he knew his theory was strong. But he also wanted the benefit of further advice – and that's why Dr Rob Easton was so vital.

Soon it was time to meet him. Pemberton was first to arrive at F150; clutching the file of photographs, he entered with his master key and stood in the centre of the floor, alone for a few minutes to reappraise the scene. Then Rob Easton arrived.

'So, Mark, what can I do for you?' was his first question.

He closed the door then joined Pemberton in again studying the cabin while standing completely still.

'In the light of what I have discovered, Rob, I think my original interpretation of what happened here was flawed.'

'Flawed? If it was, I didn't notice. Everything seemed very straightforward, apart from the curious replacement of the cabin occupant. Everything indicated the victim had enticed or invited his killer into the cabin in the early hours of the morning for reasons we don't know. A homosexual approach perhaps? Whatever the reason, something happened and the killer stabbed him in the chest. Blood on the clothing and wall followed that. The killer fled, made sure

251

no one else would enter the cabin for some time, and got rid of the knife. Then he resumed his normal role among crew and passengers until he could leave the ship. The alarm was raised by a fluke, the overheating of the water heater. That's where we enter the story.'

'I find it very puzzling.'

'Really? I thought it was all very clear cut, so how do you read the situation?'

'You've had another look at the photographs of the scene?'

'Yes, thanks to Erika.'

'Let's take yet another look together.' Pemberton opened the file but retained it in his hand, not wishing to contaminate any surface at the crime scene. 'This shows the victim on his bed – his back is partially supported by the wall,' and he indicated the wall which abutted the right side of the bed. 'His head is high on the pillow, his torso partially on the bed and pillow, and his feet touching the floor.'

'As we saw him.'

'Yes, with arms and legs awry.'

'So?'

'Could he have been sitting on the bed with his feet on the floor and his back resting against the wall? And stabbed while in that position? As he was stabbed, could he have fallen or slid sideways into that position, after momentarily flailing around with his arms to protect himself?'

'I'm sure his back was supported in some way when the knife struck, otherwise the stab might not have been fatal, he could have moved backwards away from the blade to reduce its effect. So yes, the wall could have provided that support, with his body falling or sliding into that position as he died. Why do you ask?'

'Suppose he was sitting on the bed with his feet on the floor and his back against the wall, talking to someone? That someone was also sitting on the bed at his side. A perfectly natural thing to do in a cabin like this.'

'With the body in this position, anyone else sitting on this bed must have been on his right. The post-mortem showed the stab wound was delivered from the victim's left, with the wound sloping towards the right. I agree that if the victim *was* lying on the bed at the time of the attack, head on the pillow as we can see, with the knife sloping from left to right upon entry, the stab could have been effected from the floor of the cabin, probably by the assailant standing, kneeling or crouching beside the bed.'

'A left-handed or right-handed assailant?'

'I'd opt for right-handed. It's possible a left-handed person could have delivered that blow but to gain the necessary physical power, I think a left-hander would have to have been squatting near the feet.'

'I follow. The killer could not have delivered that blow if he had been seated on the victim's left? Besides, there's no space to sit on his left – the pillow's there and there's also the partition which separates it from the dressing table.'

'Which means the killer must have been somewhere on the floor, not on the bed,' smiled Rob.

'Not necessarily.'

'Go on, Mark,' and now Rob was frowning as he tried to fathom Pemberton's reasoning.

'Suppose the visitor *was* sitting on the bed to the right of the victim, and at the invitation of the victim. For a cosy chat even if it was in the middle of the night. And suppose Mansell had already killed Cooper and was now going to dispose of another victim. He draws a knife hidden under his pillow or elsewhere and attempts to stab his visitor, but the visitor is quick enough, alert enough and strong enough to divert the blow – it goes into Mansell's own chest.'

Rob ran the scenario through his mind and then nodded, 'It's feasible. A murderous blow inevitably has a lot of force behind it, and a diversion of the blow, with that force still behind it – and some added force – could continue the strike even to a slightly different destination. It could prove fatal ... yes, but Mansell would have to have been left-handed for that to have happened.'

'He was,' said Pemberton.

'So where did he get the knife from?'

'He ordered a steak the night before his death, and a bottle of red wine to accompany it. He would be given a steak knife by the waiter – and that's easy to conceal up his sleeve.'

'So you are suggesting that Mansell, the interloper, was really a would-be killer, and if so, does it turn this incident into an accident? Misadventure perhaps?'

'There'd have to be a trial for manslaughter at least, but a lot would depend upon the coroner and, of course, any statement made by the person responsible.'

'And who was responsible?'

'I have some more work to do on that, Rob.'

'Can I ask why you think Mansell was the villain of the piece?'

Pemberton explained that, when searching Mansell's belongings, he learned he had drawn money from a cash machine in Bergen, the same day *Ringhorn* had called at the port. Later, Mansell, in his cagoule with the yellow hood, appeared at Andalsnes where Lionel Cooper disappeared. He got rid of Cooper so he could take his place, using Cooper's cruise card to board the *Ringhorn* and gain access to his cabin. And effectively taking his place on board after stealing his wallet and signing chits in Cooper's name while acting as Brother Luke's companion. The likeness between the two men was such that no one noticed the substitution – Mansell would take full advantage of that. Not even the monk noticed even if he did experience one or two reservations. If he had commented on it, Mansell would have had a plausible explanation.

Pemberton then referred to Mansell's left-handedness and his liking for alcohol, and explained about Brother Luke's business background, his wealth and the family he never saw, referring to the twins which appeared in every generation, one being left-handed and the other

254

right-handed. He told of the background of Brother Luke's twin brother, Clifford Chadwin, and how he had lost his inheritance as everyone had thought he was dead. He explained how Clifford's first two twin sons, Richard and Lionel, from a marriage supposedly consecrated overseas, had been adopted, never to benefit from the family wealth. Luke got everything.

He told Rob that enquiries were currently being urgently conducted on shore to trace the background of the people concerned, but it was Pemberton's view that Richard Mansell and Lionel Cooper, with their adopted parents' surnames, were the natural twin sons of Clifford, the man who had been disinherited. The entire family fortune had gone to Lionel Chadwin who had no children and whose wife had died early – and now Lionel Chadwin was Brother Luke, a monk who did not want all that wealth.

But there was also another Lionel Chadwin on board, a steward, who apparently knew nothing of this background to his family. Until now. But did Mansell know about this newcomer? Another relation, a half-brother, another person to claim any future family inheritance? And a legitimate child.

'So, Mark, the top and bottom of all this is that some unscrupulous person wants to get his hands on Brother Luke's fortune?'

'Wanted to get his hands on it, he can't, he's dead now and I think he killed the other possible inheritor – or the inheritor as he saw it. His twin brother, Lionel. In any case his birth was never legitimized, neither was Lionel Cooper's. It's doubtful whether he could have established a valid legal claim, so Mansell chose the illegal route. He wanted to make himself the sole heir, as he saw it.'

'Ah! So who will inherit now?'

'That's a matter for Brother Luke, if he can be persuaded to make a will. The Chadwins never did, rightly or wrongly, they had their own system of dealing with the family wealth.'

'So who do you think is the killer?' asked Rob.

And there was a knock on the cabin door. It was Lorraine.

'Mark,' she said, 'there's a telephone call for you in the incident room, it's Paul Larkin. He says it's urgent, he's holding the line.'

Chapter Sixteen

He picked up the handset. 'Hi, Paul, Pemberton here.'

'Hello, boss, I'm ringing on my mobile from North-umberland, thought you'd need this stuff straight away. I've been in Mansell's house, got the key from a neighbour because of what's happened. He lived alone, no wife or family, so the neighbour's looking after his indoor plants and garden, watering them and so on.'

'Great. So what can you tell me?'

'The neighbour was helpful. Mansell's a bit odd, he's been in hospital with mental problems for which he blamed the Falklands war in 1982; he was discharged from his unit with a sick pension. He's undergoing regular ther-apy even now – he's thought to be prone to violence, he insists on carrying a knife. For self-protection, he says, from his enemies.'

'He'd never smuggle one on board this ship nor any other, but he managed to get one into his cabin. Or some-one did.'

'Where there's a will ... anyway, boss, his army pen-sion's enough to live on but he earns extra by gardening, painting and decorating, general handyman stuff. According to his neighbour who reckons she knows him better than anyone, he's an obsessive with a big chip on his shoulder about his birth. He thinks he was wrongfully done out of his rightful inheritance and lately he's been try-ing to unravel his background; he discovered he was adopted and has been trying to trace his real family. It's become his latest obsession, so she told me.'

'Is there anything to say he'd discovered his link with the Chadwins?'

'He's obviously got most of his research on his computer which I haven't attempted to access, but from papers lying around his study, I'd say he's definitely discovered the link. There are papers with the name "Chadwin" on them, in what could be his handwriting, and there are notes about cruises with the times and ports of call for Cooper's trip. It seems he discovered Cooper was his long-lost twin brother.'

'Any note of Lionel Chadwin? His young half-brother?'

'Not that I can see among all his stuff, no. Just lots of notes about Cooper, he seemed to know a lot about him, where he lived, worked, spent his leisure time, the help he gave to others and his work with a parish in Middlesbrough. There's nothing to say they ever made contact though.'

'How about Brother Luke?'

'Yes, there are notes with Lionel Chadwin's name on them, the old man that is. And his home address, but it doesn't seem he realized Lionel senior had become a monk. From stuff lying about here, it's all to do with Chadwin's business and his wealth. I haven't found any references to Brother Luke, the monastery or the rest home – it seems Mansell was totally absorbed in tracing Cooper once he knew he was his brother and it smacks of an obsession when he became determined to make contact even though he booked a different cruise ship.'

'It's there, is it? Reference to another cruise ship? What's it say?'

'It's the *Velia*. The *Ringhorn*'s a different line but there are brochures, timetables and schedules for both. No doubt he could have obtained a cabin on *Ringhorn* if he'd really wanted to, there are always last-minute cancellations, so why go to the trouble of using another ship? Let's face it, if he really wanted to make legitimate contact with Cooper, all he had to do was knock on his door.'

'Exactly. I think he went to all that trouble to cover his tracks, Paul. He saw Cooper as a rival to the wealth he thought he should have and wanted him dead so he could inherit the lot. And he wanted an alibi, so what better than assume the dead man's identity? Kill the elder brother . . .'

'He killed his own brother, you mean?'

'I can't be sure yet, but it looks that way. The body's not been found, alive or dead. Brotherly love, eh? In the meantime, we need to preserve everything in the house, Paul. But well done, this is great news. Just what I wanted. And we'll need to have the house fingerprinted – we need samples of Mansell's prints to compare with the body we've got here. I think I've got enough background information to be going on with; you know what to do with the house and contents.'

'Sure, I'll have words with the local police as well, to make sure it's secure for one thing, and to get them to do all the Scenes of Crime stuff.'

'Good. And did you have time to call at Brother Luke's mansion?'

'I did, on the way up here. A wonderful place, boss. I had words with the housekeeper, she lives in a cottage in the grounds but she had no idea her boss was a monk! He's never told her that. Whenever he turns up at the house, which is about once every three months, he doesn't wear a dog collar. She has always been under the impression he's been away on business and had another home somewhere. In her mind he was simply a man with pots of money who spent his life travelling around the world, in spite of his age. She did say, by the way, that in recent weeks and months, a man called at the house, trying to trace Lionel Chadwin. She told him he was away on one of his business trips or one of his cruises on *Ringhorn*; that's what she told the caller.'

'She said he might be on *Ringhorn*?'

'So she says.'

'I must admit I've often wondered whether Chadwin really is a monk, or whether his style of dress is worn to mislead the rest of us!'

259

'What she told me confirms he is very wealthy with no family, and she says he is a wonderful old man. Wouldn't harm a fly, according to her, and very generous to others. But she says a lot of people have been trying to wheedle their way into his affections. He's acutely aware of that.'

'Maybe that's why he wants to look like a monk? Pretending to have nothing?'

'Possibly.'

'Did she say who these people were? The man who called at the house, or those trying to wheedle their way into his affections?'

'No, they never said but she didn't recognize any of them. Two of them were men, though, and one a woman. All said they would come back, hoping to catch him at home. I couldn't get a description out of her either, except the men were middle-aged and looked similar.'

'And the woman?'

'Not much of a description. Fiftyish, she said, reddish hair worn long, nicely spoken with a north-east accent.'

'And did these people all come at the same time, or separately?'

'Oh, all separately. But within a few weeks of each other, and all within the last three months or so. With this sudden interest in Mr Chadwin, she wondered if there was something going on in the background of his life, something she didn't know about.'

'Like someone ferreting into his family history? So back to the monk, Paul. Any more on him?'

'Not a lot, but from what I've learned, he does appear to be genuine. I've asked at the diocesan rest home in Middlesbrough and he's well known there, paying for his keep and giving them extra cash. His contributions help to keep the place running. They love him but don't know much about his background. He turned up one day asking if they would accept him, saying he would pay and adding he had no family, and so they took him in. He was in a wheelchair at that time. They were pleased to take him, as

I said, his money helps to keep the place going. They don't ask too many personal questions.'

'Most modern monasteries can care for their own elderly residents in house,' commented Pemberton. 'But perhaps this old chap, even if he was a monk, was allowed to indulge himself, especially if money is not a problem. OK, Paul, do what you can at Mansell's house, go back tomorrow if you think it's necessary. Remember we might need evidence to prove he killed Lionel Cooper, enough to convince a coroner – that's if Cooper is dead! You've confirmed some of my suspicions. If we need someone to positively identify Mansell when we get back to Southampton, would that neighbour do it?'

'I'll ask her,' promised Paul.

When Pemberton replaced the handset, Captain Hansteen was waiting to speak to him.

'I heard that,' he smiled. 'More ammunition for your theories, Mr Pemberton?'

'Yes. It seems Mr Mansell was a devious character to say the least, and of doubtful sanity. He came on board *Ringhorn* after killing and disposing of his twin brother, Lionel Cooper, deliberately to assume his identity and possibly become acquainted with the man he knew as Lionel Chadwin. He had no idea it was really Brother Luke. He could leave the ship bearing Lionel Cooper's identity and the dead Cooper, if found, would be identified as R. W. Mansell. Mission accomplished! A perfect murder.'

'My enquiries from *Velia* support that,' said Hansteen. 'Mansell joined the ship at Southampton as a solo passenger, went ashore at Bergen and again at Andalsnes on organized trips but he didn't return to the ship at Andalsnes. In accordance with procedures, the Norwegian immigration authorities and police were alerted, but he has not returned. Sometimes people do miss the boat, and rejoin later, usually contacting the ship to explain their absence. But Mr Mansell has not been seen by that ship's crew since leaving *Velia* about an hour before our ship arrived in Andalsnes, neither has he been in touch by telephone. And he did book a tour which went up to the Trollstigheimen Mountain Lodge, around the same time as our tour.'

'And Spitzbergen? Is *Velia* due to call there?'

'Yes, two hours after we're due. I think we now know he will not be rejoining that ship but he wouldn't want to rejoin *Velia*, would he? He couldn't, not if he wanted Mansell to be declared dead.'

Pemberton said, 'I disagree. I think he could have rejoined *Velia* – he'd kept his cruise card for that ship but I think that would have been as a last resort – that's if things had gone drastically wrong on *Ringhorn*. I think he could have convinced the authorities he really was Mansell even if his victim's body had been discovered by that time. After all, a piece of paper with a name on it is hardly positive identification!'

'He was backing it both ways, you mean?'

'Yes, he could be Mansell on *Velia* until disembarking, then Cooper!'

'Have you any word of Mr Cooper being found? I understand the Norwegian police have intensified their search, probably due to representations from *Velia*.'

'Good, but I've not received any reports of him,' admitted Pemberton.

'I've not heard either.'

'But if a body is found in Norway, the police will think it's the man missing from *Velia*,' pointed out Pemberton. 'I'm sure any of that ship's crew would identify him as Mansell, especially if there's something in his clothing to that impression.'

'A neat way of disappearing from the face of the earth! So what happens next?' asked Captain Hansteen.

'We need to have a chat, Captain. You, Lorraine and me, with Erika taking notes. I don't think I need include Rob Easton, I can update him later. It's a summary of events, for the ship's log. It will take the best part of an hour, I guess.'

'There's no time like the present,' said Hansteen. 'My colleagues know where I am if required in an emergency and we can conclude before dinner, can we? I am expected at the Captain's table!'

'That's fine,' said Pemberton. 'I suppose we should all meet in the library, but that's not very private in this case, so let's find a table and some comfortable chairs here in the incident room.'

'With a pot of tea and cakes perhaps?'

'Why not?'

When they were settled, Pemberton, speaking without notes, said, 'I don't feel there is any need to reiterate the events in Cabin F150 – we are all very familiar with them. What has emerged during our enquiries is that Brother Luke is the focal point; what you may not know, Captain, is that Luke is a very wealthy man in his own right, an estate owner whose real name is Lionel Chadwin. He was once married but the union did not produce any children and his wife died some years ago; thus he is the sole owner of inherited and accumulated wealth which, according to him, is valued at several millions. I have no official figures, but at the moment such detail is not important. The fact is he is very wealthy, so we must ask what is going to happen to his estate when he dies.

'He is now over eighty without any children and he is an invalid. Throughout their history, the Chadwins have not been ones for making wills. They have relied on their own system for disposing of the estate. Quite simply, it passed down the generations, being divided between any siblings. We know that is not the ideal method but in that way, Brother Luke – Lionel Chadwin – inherited the family wealth and estate. He inherited the lot even though he had a twin brother – the twin brother was presumed dead. Now into the drama step more Chadwins. Brother Luke's twin brother, Clifford, was a ne'er-do-well who was the proverbial black sheep, always in debt, always in trouble. Eventually his father refused to bail him out any more, so he fled the country and went to live in South

263

Africa. He went through a local form of marriage out there, of which no record exists, and produced twin sons, Lionel and Richard. Lack of a formal marriage, according to English law, means they were illegitimate, but that can be challenged. I think Mansell believed his father's marriage was legal, and that he should have inherited. However, Clifford's wife died and he had his twin sons adopted by two different sets of parents, hence the different surnames. Clifford then disappeared and because nothing had been seen or heard of him for more than seven years, when the time came to dispose of the family fortune, he was presumed dead. He got nothing. It all went to his brother Lionel, or Brother Luke.

'I might add that none of Clifford's family have ever tried to make contact with Luke, and although he tried to keep in touch with them, he got no response. It seems he was frozen out. However, Clifford was not dead and returned to England where he married again, rather late in life. He produced another set of twins, Lionel and Suzanne, clearly legitimate. He has since died but before returning to this country it seems he had become a reformed character and also comfortable financially, due to his own efforts. What is very strange, Captain Hansteen, is that the young Lionel Chadwin is a steward on this ship.'

'I find that most odd, uncanny in fact.'

'The steward Lionel had no idea Brother Luke's real name was Lionel Chadwin, he had no idea that the old monk in the wheelchair was his uncle, his father's brother. He has been interviewed and knows now, I might add.'

'Brother Luke has been coming on cruises with us for several years, Mr Pemberton, he joined us long before he became wheelchair-bound, but always alone. Everyone calls him Brother Luke even if his passport shows otherwise.'

'His real name is in the official files, Captain,' pointed out Erika.

'Which I do not have time to inspect in detail! But go on, Mr Pemberton.'

'We now turn our attention to Clifford's first set of twins, Lionel and Richard. Lionel is a family name. As I said, they were adopted upon the death of their mother, a request being that they retain their Christian names even while assuming the surnames of their new parents. I am convinced – but have no proof – that Lionel was Lionel Cooper, the man who accompanied Brother Luke on board this trip. Whether Lionel knew that Brother Luke was his uncle is something I may never know – I suspect he did, otherwise the coincidence is just too great. I think he may have been very caring towards the old man, probably knowing of the relationship but not revealing it until a suitable moment. That moment never arrived.

'We detectives tend to be suspicious of coincidences! I am equally convinced that Richard became Richard Mansell. If you examine photographs of the younger Brother Luke, taken by this ship's photographer some time ago, and photos of both Mansell (in death) and Cooper when boarding, the family likeness is astonishing. Knowing what we do about Mansell's character and background, along with his current obsessive nature and wartime mental illness, it is feasible he developed a fatal desire to regain what he felt he had lost and had been entitled to all those years ago. And it seems he wanted it all for himself. Sadly, I cannot interview Richard Mansell to find out how his mind worked. Clearly, he knew his uncle had not made a will – the Chadwins never did – and so I think he became obsessively determined to right that former wrong by eliminating the one man who might stand in his way, his twin brother, Lionel. He could kill Lionel, the elder of the two, and assume his identity – that way, the murder would be concealed. Then he could lodge a claim for the share of estate which should have gone to his father, then down to him. It is possible that he intended to kill Brother Luke too, but perhaps not on *Ringhorn*. That could have happened later back on shore – to expedite his inheritance. I think he merely wanted to find his uncle on board to talk to him, to establish the present situation so far as any inheritance might be involved. Remember he was a determined obsessive, he was not thinking rationally.'

'So he concocted this elaborate scheme?' asked Hansteen.

'Yes, but then, rather belatedly, he discovered there was another contender for the prize, a legitimate half-brother called Lionel. And his twin sister. So far as I know, he had no idea that this Lionel was on board *Ringhorn*.'

'How did that come to light?' asked Lorraine.

'I think Mansell was prowling the ship late at night, visiting the sort of places where you'd expect to find a wealthy man enjoying a cruise – the casino, nightclub, late bars and so on. I think he would be asking the stewards which was Lionel Chadwin – after all, we're all anonymous on board! We don't carry name tags so we don't have to give our names to anyone unless we wish to. So if he did ask a steward to get a message to Lionel Chadwin, it would have gone to young Lionel.'

At that point, there was a knock on the door and a young woman entered, saying, 'I'm sorry to interrupt, Captain, but I have received an urgent message from the *Velia*. The Norwegian police have been in touch with the Captain to say the body of the man missing from that ship has been found. A Mr Mansell. It seems he fell down Stigfoss Waterfall, nearly 600 feet. He had papers on him which give his name. And there is a steak knife not far from the body, thrown down perhaps . . . it's identical to those used on *Velia*.'

'Thank you, Ruth. Tell them I shall call them shortly to discuss the matter.'

And she departed.

'One more piece to fit our jigsaw!' said Pemberton in the few moments of silence which followed.

'Of course,' said Hansteen. 'But we know that the body is not that of Mansell, but almost surely Lionel Cooper. And killed with a steak knife, Mr Pemberton?'

'Or robbed of his wallet at the point of the knife before being pushed over . . . we shall have to find out.'

'Cautious as ever!'

'Exactly,' said Pemberton. 'But whoever he is, the Norwegian police will have to decide this question: did he fall or was he pushed? But I think it explains why Mansell was on board this ship. Having disposed of his rival, he could have returned to Southampton and walked off *Ringhorn* as Lionel Cooper, complete with Brother Luke in his wheelchair, a cabinful of luggage and no known links with the deceased found in Norway. And he could have used Lionel's credit card, which had already been approved, to pay his bills. A nice plan, if it had worked. But it didn't.'

'So what really happened in F150?' asked Captain Hansteed. 'Do you know?'

'I'll come to the death in F150 in just a moment. I think Brother Luke survived simply because he was Brother Luke, although I doubt if Mansell intended to kill Lionel Chadwin senior, particularly as he knew there were two possible inheritors still alive in Durham, as he understood things. Mansell had been asking questions at Starthorpe Hall where even the housekeeper thought Lionel was away on business or possibly on *Ringhorn*, with never a hint he was really a monk. It seems Lionel Chadwin had two secret lives which he concealed from almost everyone. That he is on board at this time is what brought Lionel Cooper on to this ship. He became the monk's trusted companion – and perhaps he knew the truth? We shall never know whether or not he realized the old man was his uncle but it seems Cooper never tried to take advantage of the situation. He was far too decent!'

'So was the monk at risk during all this?'

'If his real identity had become known to Mansell, then yes, I believe he would have been at risk, but only later when all other contenders for the prize had been eliminated. By those I mean Lionel Chadwin and his sister. Mansell knew about them but I don't think he realized young Lionel was a steward here. At the time Mansell boarded this ship, having killed his brother; his entire

267

mission, fuelled by hate and revenge, was to assume his identity, which he did, and hopefully to become acquainted with old Lionel Chadwin – which he didn't. Or not to his knowledge! At the beginning, that was the extent of his plan. He intended walking off this ship having committed the perfect murder. By an odd quirk of circumstance, one of his rivals happened to be on board. But when young Lionel made himself known, you can see how Mansell's new, urgent and desperate plan began to form. He had no time to lose – such a chance might never happen again. So Mansell invited him to his cabin. Ostensibly for a chat about possible family links.'

'An unexpected shock for Mansell! But would Lionel agree to that, if he was supposed to be working? Go to someone's cabin?

'He might have promised to pop in for a brief exploratory chat, even dodging the security cameras in case he got into trouble from his own boss for skiving. But it is quite normal for stewards to visit cabins upon request, with food and drink and so on. Now, if this young steward was a relation – remember Lionel's mother had mentioned her family – then Mansell would have to get rid of him. If necessary, he could get rid of Suzanne later. He was obsessed, remember. He had armed himself with a knife at dinner that evening. A steak knife. It wasn't to kill Cooper, he'd already done that, but it seems he liked to have a knife with him at all times – probably a relic of his days in the front line. Frightened of enemies or something. And he had a lot to drink beforehand, probably to drown his guilt at killing his twin brother.'

'So he never invited Brother Luke to his cabin?'

'No, why should he? He had no idea the priest was his uncle. He'd only been on *Ringhorn* for a few hours and so when he asked a steward to point out Lionel Chadwin, he must have received a huge shock. So he invited young Lionel in with the sole intention of killing him, a sudden and unforeseen twist to his plans, one which might have compelled him to leave *Ringhorn* and take his chance back on *Velia*.'

They were all silent as the truth began to dawn and then Pemberton said, 'But it didn't work out. Young Lionel, fitness fanatic, was too strong and too quick – as the blow was being struck with considerable force, Lionel deflected it and the knife went into Mansell's own chest. Lionel didn't panic – he tried to stem the bleeding as best he could, then realized he might be culpable and simply left the cabin, taking the knife and putting a "Do Not Disturb" sign on the cabin door.

'He didn't notice the water heater in the mug, it would be concealed behind the panel abutting the bed, and there'd be no need for lights, thanks to the midnight sun. I think his hands would have been bloodstained, and even his shirt cuffs, but he could dodge the cameras until he got changed or got rid of the stained clothing. Probably any stained clothes, and the knife, would go overboard. He would know where and how to achieve that, out of sight of the cameras. And a uniformed steward walking around the ship in the early hours was not unusual, certainly not suspicious. If he was seen by the cameras or by any witnesses, his presence would be considered absolutely normal.'

Pemberton then outlined his reasons for coming to this conclusion, stressing the location of the body on the bed, the angle of the wound and Mansell's left-handedness.

'But when we interviewed him, he never gave a hint he might be responsible,' said Lorraine. 'I never spotted any signs of his guilt.'

'He was lying,' said Pemberton. 'Which is why we need to have him here for further questioning. If what I believe is true, then he might be guilty of manslaughter, although I think self-defence would be an apt plea. He's not a murderer, Captain, he was simply defending himself when things went horribly wrong, but we need to get his version of events and then compare his story with what the evidence supports.'

'Will you call him or shall I?' asked Captain Hansteen.

'I think you should,' Pemberton smiled at the Captain. 'After all, the case is your responsibility.'

Under close questioning from Pemberton, Lionel Chadwin admitted the tragic death, which was clearly accidental, and that he had been panicked into trying to cover it up. Pemberton was satisfied with his story, for it was supported by the evidence. Young Lionel had been too terrified to admit it earlier, in case he was charged with murder. He was placed in a secure cabin until *Ringhorn* returned to Southampton where he would be handed over to Hampshire police for the necessary formalities to be completed. With more help from Erika, Pemberton would prepare a report for that force, and for the coroner.

'Who's going to tell Brother Luke?' asked Lorraine eventually.

'I think that is my duty,' said Hansteen. 'But thank you, Mr Pemberton and Miss Cashmore, I can only state my heartfelt thanks. I will report to my superiors that the case has reached a most satisfactory conclusion and I am sure they will get in touch with you.'

'And before we return to England, I might just pop ashore on Spitzbergen!' laughed Pemberton. 'It sounds a nice quiet place.'

'And don't you dare get involved in anything up there,' said Lorraine. 'Those polar bears can be quite vicious!'

'But not as bad as a Chadwin spurned! And I wonder where those big blond photographers got to?'

'Don't you even think about trying to find them!' she said.